RED FOX WOMAN

judy ann davis

Black Rose Writing

www.blackrosewriting.com

ISBN: 978-1-935605-62-1

PUBLISHED BY BLACK ROSE WRITING

www.blackrosewriting.com

Printed in the United States of America

Red Fox Woman is printed in Times New Roman

*Dedicated to my husband and best friend, Scott,
for all your patience and encouragement*

*Special Thanks. . .
To Reagan Rothe and Black Rose Writing for their assistance
and to Stephen Sprinkle of Sprinkle Pottery of Texas
where ring flasks still exist.*

One

Colorado Territory, 1868

Flint Ashmore expected a warmer welcome than a shotgun poked through a crack in the tool shed when he rode into the ranch along Cherry Creek.

Especially since he now owned the place.

The old man who sold it to him was dead, and anyone stopping to rest a spell should have asked his permission.

Even from where he sat atop his bay, he could see a flash of red hair and pair of luminous eyes staring at him from the other end of the barrel. He motioned for his two brothers riding beside him to ease their mounts away. He had great respect for the power of a shotgun, and there was little sense in getting all three of them killed with one pull of the trigger.

"What do you want?" a voice called out.

Flint thumbed back his hat and folded his hands calmly over the pommel of his saddle, taking care not to make any quick motions. The voice was obviously feminine, and women and guns were like matches and kerosene. It was better to keep them separated if possible.

Overhead, the sun drilled burning hot rays into the already parched earth, and Flint felt a trickle of sweat slide down his back. It had been two months without rain and every water hole in a hundred mile radius of Golden was turning into a giant bowl of cracked mud.

"We're the Ashmores from the ranch just west of here. I'd like to talk to the man of the house, your husband perhaps?"

Warily, the woman stepped out into the dusty yard, shotgun still in her hands. She was tall and willowy thin, but Flint surmised most men would be prone to miss that detail. Flaming red hair, brighter than a summer sunset, would draw their attention first. It tumbled almost clear to her waist in a thick mass of riotous curls and tangles. And the good Lord had blessed her with eyes so brilliant green they'd shame a meadow in springtime.

"I have no husband," she said. Her revelation was anything but warm.

"My, oh my, oh my," he heard Marcus whisper under his breath from somewhere near the corral. "Can't wait to see how you're going to handle this one."

Flint threw him a murderous glance, but the bear-like man was not one to be intimidated. He winked, and followed it with an unabashed grin. Of all four Ashmore brothers, Marcus was the only one who could find humor in the most horrendous and hellish moments.

The woman lowered the shotgun, but made no move to speak further.

"Mind if we light for a spell?" Flint asked. He tried hard not to display any irritation, even though the heat was stifling, and there was something that was nagging him about her icy stare and lack of hospitality.

Behind her, another young woman stepped into the glaring sunlight and squinted at them. Smaller in build, she had taffy-colored hair and ruddy cheeks which looked like they had been scrubbed clean with burlap. She seemed to be assessing the situation for a moment, then turned and spoke quickly, almost sharply to the red-haired one in a sing-song language Flint recognized as Scandinavian. Danish, perhaps.

"Julia, please, we must mind our manners," she said. "These men have ridden in the hot sun and are surely in need of a drink."

"Anna is right," the red-haired woman agreed reluctantly, "this is no way to greet strangers." She juggled the shotgun to the crook of her right arm and pushed a tendril of damp hair from her eyes with the other as she corrected herself, "Neighbors, I mean."

Anna stepped forward and gestured toward the house, speaking in almost flawless English. "I will fix you something cold to drink, ja? Something good to eat. The heat is horrible and it's only morning. Come, please come and get some refreshments. It will only take a minute." She walked away in a brisk, no-nonsense gait toward the farmhouse, her chunky clogs sending puffs of dust billowing around the hem of her worn blue gingham dress.

The red-haired woman watched her leave before she turned and spoke to them again. "Please, gentlemen, step down and come into the shed where it's at least tolerable."

She flung open one side of the weather-beaten, double doors and propped the gun against it. It was then Flint noticed her hands. They were covered with red mud that snaked up her arms and onto her elbows, and her apron was streaked and smudged as well.

Wondering what and where she had been digging, he dismounted and followed her into the interior where the dirt-packed floor offered a cool refuge from the scorching heat. The pungent smell of earth and hay filled his nostrils. It took him but a moment to realize the reason for her appearance. Under the window at the far end of the shed, a potter's wheel stood in the slanting rays of the sun and glowed pink from the dye in the red clays.

"You're a potter?" he asked, not trying to hide his surprise. His eyes scanned the shed again. The last time he had been inside the tool shed, it had been piled high with rotting wood, rusting junk, and broken furniture and tools. Now, the entire shed was open, airy and clean. Evenly spaced rows of drying shelves covered the walls and a thick layer of clean-smelling straw was strewn beneath them to cushion the fall of a mishandled piece.

"Yes. . .yes, I am." She glided silently through the cool shadows to a table along the wall where buckets of raw clay stood beside a wooden tub for washing and began to splash water over her hands and arms, turning the clear liquid to a brownish pink.

"I was hoping I'd have some time to ride over and meet you." She reached for a cloth, dried her hands and moved toward him. "Sorry about the remaining clay on my fingers. You've caught me in one of my creative moments."

"Flint Ashmore," he said, taking the still-damp hand she extended. "Do you have a father or brother I might speak with, Miss---?"

"Neither." She cut him off brusquely. "My father is dead, and I have no brothers, nor sisters for that matter. I am quite alone, except for Anna and Sven who agreed to accompany me here from back East."

"I see." Scowling, Flint tried quickly to collect his thoughts. Behind him, he heard Marcus chuckle and his younger brother beside him swear softly under his breath.

This was not going as planned. He had come to toss her off his land. Now the last thing he ever dreamed of was to come face-to-face with an unmarried woman who might decide to dig in her heels and decide she was staying. And a potter to boot. No matter what, he was not giving in to any feminine begging or pleading, and certainly not any tears.

After all, he and his brothers had purchased the ranch and its spring-fed creek so he'd never have to depend on another man again. Only

Rusty Gast's generosity had sustained Ashmore cattle through the dry spells when the water holes on their property had dried up and turned to ugly brown mud. The old man had been a neighbor and close friend, and his death had left a hollow spot in everyone's life.

When he made no move to introduce the others, she stepped boldly around him and extended her hand.

"Hello," she said and smiled brightly. "I'm Julia Gast."

"Gast?" The word flew out from all three Ashmore brothers' mouths in perfect unison as they stared at her in disbelief. Uncomfortable silence filled the shed as they traded furtive glances among themselves, caught off-guard by her revelation.

Finally, Flint cleared his throat and asked, "Just how are you related to Rusty Gast?"

Apprehension began to slowly gnaw at his very confidence. The only thought that popped into his head was the word, absurd. What was happening was truly absurd. It had to be a mistake. Rusty Gast had never mentioned any children. He had married late in life, and his wife, also deceased, had been barren.

"My uncle."

He studied her for a moment, then berated himself for not seeing the resemblance sooner. There was no doubt she was a Gast from head to toe. The startling red hair, her sharply defined Irish chin and those ridiculously small feet, much too small for someone her height.

Heaving a weary sigh, Flint removed his sweaty hat and rubbed his temple. A pain began to throb inside his head and beat like an Indian war drum. The trickle of sweat was now a river of sweat pouring down his back. This was definitely not turning out as he had planned. What was Julia Gast, Rusty's niece, doing here in the Colorado Territory? And on Ashmore land? Land he legally bought and owned? Land he was so certain he owned, so proud that he owned, that he carried the bill of sale with him everywhere, safely tucked away in the breast pocket of his shirt.

"Is the heat troubling you, Mr. Ashmore? Is everything all right?" he heard Julia Gast ask. She stepped forward, peering at him with obvious concern.

"I guess that depends upon your definition of all right, Miss Gast," he replied.

Two

Julia Gast watched the three men with a mixture of suspicion and bewilderment. If these men were her neighbors, come to welcome her, she had never witnessed such strange behavior in her entire life. The big burly man was grinning from ear-to-ear, like a person who was anything but sane and sound. The youngest one stared at her in stony silence. And Flint Ashmore looked like he was about to pass out right on the mud-packed floor.

It was the burly one who came to his senses first, his big paw-like hand automatically reaching for hers.

"I'm so sorry, forgive our manners. I'm Marcus Ashmore. Pleased to meet you." He gripped her hand and vigorously worked it like a pump handle. "I didn't know Rusty had any near relatives," he admitted and gestured to the swarthy-faced man beside him, wearing buckskins and knee-high moccasins. "This is Tye, our youngest brother."

"Brothers?" Her eyes circled the group, trying to find similarities. She noticed all of them wore guns.

Marcus's square face smiled. "Yes, and all bachelors. There are four of us total, if you don't count Betsy--five if you do. Flint here is the oldest, just turned twenty-seven this Sunday, then me, then Luke, who's roaming the countryside somewhere up North, then Tye here, who's twenty-one like Betsy."

"Oh my goodness, twins!"

"No, ma'am," Marcus said. "Not exactly, you see, Betsy is adopted."

Julia watched Flint Ashmore's eyes, the color of wet sand darken as Marcus's babbled the last revealing statement.

"Confound it, Marcus," he said, interrupting, "we don't have to bore the lady with a complete family history. The day is not getting any longer, and we still have chores awaiting us that need some daylight." Of all the brothers, she realized, Flint seemed to be the one in authority, the serious one, who gave the orders and made the decisions.

But the burly man merely grinned, like a bear with a slab of bacon, brushing his brother's testy behavior aside like he was accustomed to it.

"Well, ma'am, I suppose Flint is right. No sense in burning your ears off with needless details. You'll meet my sister, Betsy, soon enough. She's the little mite who helps to run the General Store in town. Everyone eventually gets to know her right well. If you need anything, she's the person you can count on. She knows everyone and everything happening in Golden."

He chuckled, a long and low chuckle that rose from his chest, and Julia quickly decided she liked the giant, congenial man. Unfortunately, she wasn't so certain about his oldest brother. The man could actually be handsome, she decided, if only he would wipe that surly look off his face. His hair, darker than polished onyx fell over his forehead to touch a scar above his brow, and his face was a symmetrical collection of planes and sharp angles anyone with an eye for art would appreciate.

To cover her edginess, she turned her attention to Tye, who appeared to be the quiet, taciturn one among them.

Julia smiled. "I must say, your name is unusual."

"Real name is Tydall, ma'am. It's my mother's family name, but most folks call me Tye."

"It's certainly a nice way to keep your lineage alive."

"Guess maybe you could say that," he admitted shyly, blushing. "To be honest, Ma was running out of names after Luke and wanted to be sure Pa didn't name me after one of his mules."

"Mules?" Julia laughed.

"Yeah, Pa really took a shine to his mules. Even named my sister after his favorite." He chuckled and shook his head. "My pa had an odd sense of humor."

"I suspect so," Julia agreed. She watched his gaze stray to the collection of fired pottery she had brought from Pennsylvania. It had been a feat to get them all carefully and secretly wrapped, then crated in straw and shipped. It had cost her plenty for the freight alone, not counting the money she had used to grease the right palms and avoid a paper trail that would lead to Colorado. But she was pleased she had not left the pieces behind.

"Go ahead," she urged. "Take a look."

Tye carefully picked out one of her most prized pieces--a ring flask and studied it appraisingly, almost reverently, stroking the smooth, reddish brown circle with callused fingertips. "Haven't seen one of these since we left Virginia, ma'am," he said in a wistful voice. "My pa used to carry spring water in it. His flask kept it cool and sweet, unlike the tin canteens."

"It's not a favorite with a lot of potters," she admitted. "It requires more time and patience than most pieces. Take it if you like. It'll be my gift to you as your new neighbor."

She watched Flint Ashmore straighten his spine and shoot a look at his youngest brother that was colder than the clay she had been working.

Quickly, but gently, the young man replaced the flask to the shelf. "Maybe once you've made more, I'll buy one," he offered.

Anna appeared at the door. "Do you want Sven to take the gentlemen's horses to the well, Julia?"

Julia tucked a strand of hair behind her ear and smiled at the Dane. "In a minute, Anna, but first you and Sven must meet our neighbors."

She made the introductions quickly, ushering both Danes inside, and finishing with, "Anna and Sven Holberg are two of the best potters Lancaster, Pennsylvania, has ever seen. I'm fortunate they decided to come West with me."

Again, it was Marcus who reached for Anna's outstretched hand first. "Pleased to meet you, Mr. and Mrs. Holberg," he said with a smile. "I hope you're not disappointed in Colorado."

"Yust Anna and Sven," the Danish women replied. "We are brother and sister."

"Well, then, we should start over." There was a mischievous twinkle in Marcus's eyes. "*Very* pleased to meet you, ma'am."

"Ja, I am pleased, too," Anna said, her cheeks blushing between the coils of hair at her ears. "We do not get company this far out. Come, you must have something to eat and drink, I insist. I have made lemonade, and there is some cinnamon bread cooling in the kitchen."

"We'll use the porch," Julia suggested. "Maybe you can share your thoughts on raising stock, Mr. Ashmore."

The words had barely left her mouth when all the brothers visibly stiffened and a chilly silence descended around them again. Tension, like lightening, leapt from one to the other as they again stared at Flint. Outside the drone of a disgruntled bee intensified the stillness.

To her relief, it was Marcus who again came to her rescue.

"I think it might be best if we leave Julia and Flint to discuss some business without us," he announced, then turned and smiled good-naturedly at Anna, "but I could sure use a glass of cold lemonade. It's so dang hot, the sun could wilt a fence post."

"A fence post, you say? That is a phrase I have not yet heard." Anna smiled and swept her hand toward the house, herding the men through the open doorway. "Well, come, come. The food is ready. The drink is cool."

As they filed out, Julia's eyes fastened onto the shotgun. Quickly, she looked away, frowning. Her father would have been appalled she had pointed a weapon at anyone. But then, if her father hadn't died, she wouldn't have had to run away like a thief in the night, leaving without even telling her friends of her intentions or whereabouts.

"Marcus can wipe that shotgun off and take it to the house for you," Flint offered. "If it sits in the sun much longer, you'll scorch the skin off your fingers."

His hand slid to his gun, which hung naturally from his side like a third hand. Julia noticed it was old, but well-oiled, without a speck of dirt on the grips. Even his holster, though dusty from traveling, was well-tended. She winced at the sticky clay now splattered on her shotgun. The last thing she wanted was for one of the men to touch it. It wasn't loaded, and she wasn't about to admit she didn't have any idea how to use it. She had found it in her uncle's bedroom with some of his personal belongings.

"Just leave it be," she found herself saying, "I like to keep it close by."

When the shed was vacated, Flint nervously removed his hat, then reset it on his head again. His eyes scanned the shelves slowly before they traveled back to her and he spoke. "I believe there's been some sort of mistake."

"Mistake?" She squinted up at him. "What kind of mistake, Mr. Ashmore?"

He hesitated a moment again. "This wasn't exactly supposed to be social call, Miss Gast," he admitted. "You see, we own this ranch."

"Own?" Julia felt the color drain from her face. Her heart did a quick flip flop, then froze in her chest. "Why, that's impossible, Mr. Ashmore."

From his chest pocket, he fished out a piece of paper. "I have the bill of sale, signed and dated by your uncle." He shoved it gently toward her.

With trembling hands, Julie carefully unfolded the document and stared at it. She recognized the crude, almost childlike scrawl of her uncle's signature at the bottom of the page. It was authentic, she had no doubt. Rusty Gast's signature was one that could not easily be duplicated. Suddenly she felt sick to her stomach.

"This can't be," she said in a whisper, barely choking out the words.

"I'm sorry to have alarmed you," he said quietly, "but before his death, we paid Rusty for the ranch." He looked at her and saw the pain and fear in her eyes.

"So did I." Her words were still a whisper as she looked up and stared back at him.

She moved to a small tin on the shelf above the wash table and withdrew another piece of paper, an exact replica right down to the date and signature, and handed it to him.

Flint studied the paper thoughtfully. He looked up, frowning. "Your uncle seems to have been a complex, if not dishonest man."

"How dare you?" she sputtered. "My uncle was one of the kindest men I've ever known!"

"He appeared to be the same when he lived here, but his sense of humor seems a mite twisted, don't you think?" He folded the paper and handed it back to her.

"I'm sure there's an explanation."

"I'm sure there is."

"Have you secured the deed?" She fought to keep the sharpness from her voice. Tremors of anger coursed through her veins. She gripped the paper so tightly her fingers ached.

"No, ma'am, I was waiting for Rusty's lawyer to return from Massachusetts. I was told the papers would be in order, and I'd only have to present my bill of sale."

"The same instructions were relayed to me." She turned and tucked the paper into the tin, snapping the lid on. "I have Uncle Rusty's hand-written letter to prove it."

"I suppose you have a bill of sale for the equipment?"

"No, of course not. I assumed the equipment came with the ranch."

Once again, he pulled out another paper, worn thin on its creases, and shoved it toward her. "No, the wagons and tack belong to me. I bought them well over two months ago."

Julia gasped.

"Yeah, nice man, all right."

There was a hint of smugness on his face, and suddenly the anger she had tried so hard to control, rose up and bubbled out. Without the wagons she had no way to bring the raw clay from the creek bed and no way to get her pottery to town or supplies back to the ranch.

"I need those wagons, Mr. Ashmore."

"I need the ranch."

"As do I. A dozen horses are probably in Denver now, waiting to be delivered by two men I recently hired."

"The water, Miss Gast, is crucial to my spread."

"My pottery business, Mr. Ashmore," she spit out, enunciating every word, "is dependent upon that creek!"

Their angry eyes met for what seemed like hours.

His cocksure stance and icy glare only fueled her anger more. When she refused to back down, refused to look away, he finally gave in, glancing away. "I'm sorry," he finally said.

"Sorry? *You're* sorry?" The words came out sharply as a million thoughts hammered her brain.

She had traipsed half-way across God-forsaken country and given up everything she owned, including her father's farm to reach this ranch. She had eaten enough sand and dust to fill every road rut from here to Pennsylvania. She had left friends behind who didn't even know her whereabouts, and never would. Sorry? He was sorry? That's all he could say?

She watched him move to the doorway and stop. He swung his tall frame back around. "I've never been accused of being a patient person, but there are times when I've been known to make exceptions," he said. "I'll give you two weeks..."

He jammed the papers inside his breast pocket. "...in which time we will probably have this misunderstanding resolved. Then I'd like you packed up and off my land. You may use my equipment until then." He jerked at the brim of his hat and turned to leave.

Julia felt her heart slam against her chest. Every nerve in her body vibrated like violin strings strung tight and played out of tune. How could he be so sure she was the one holding a false bill of sale? Her uncle would never do anything to harm her, and certainly nothing so underhanded. If Flint Ashmore thought she was going to just give up, turn tail and hand him what rightfully belonged to her, he was wrong.

Her anger turned to raging fury.

"Your land?" she shouted at his retreating back. "*Your* land? Horsefeathers! You can get off *my* land." She knew she was out of control, purple with riotous rage. But no man was about to take what was hers. She had paid her uncle the entire sum he had asked, right down to

14

the last red cent. She had the bank drafts to prove it.

Heart pounding, she rushed after him, painfully aware his brothers and the Holbergs were curiously watching. He stopped at the water pump, took a ladle and reached for the pump handle.

Julia rushed up beside him. "You may be generous with your equipment, Mr. Ashmore," she hissed, grasping the rusty handle before his hand could touch it, "but I am not as generous with my water."

His head shot up and he gave her a blistering glare capable of scorching the devil himself. Julia's stomach dived, but she held her ground. This man, she realized, could be dangerous when provoked. Very dangerous. She heard the ladle clatter as he tossed it in an empty bucket beside the pump.

"One week, Miss Gast," she heard him say in a firm voice. "My patience just ran out."

He strode to his horse and mounted. The other Ashmore brothers scrambled off the porch like someone had thrown a stick of dynamite at it. Leather creaked, horses snorted and clouds of dust swirled up into the air.

"Shoot-fire, Flint," Marcus Ashmore's deep voice rumbled out, above the clatter of hooves, as they rode into the glare of the sun, "I leave you for ten minutes with a beautiful woman, and what do you do? You start a dang fight!"

Three

"The way I see it, Flint, we're huggin' a two-headed snake," Marcus said. He rubbed his jaw thoughtfully.

All three brothers were seated around a table in the back of the Finley's General Store. Daylight had only begun to color the sky a brilliant red.

"We can't pitch the girl out into the buffalo grass with all those fragile jars and pans, and no place to go, and we can't let her stay. You gonna see that lawyer first thing this morning?"

Flint Ashmore dropped his head into the palms of his hands and squeezed his burning eyes shut. Last night he had tried to think of every possible reason Rusty Gast would have for selling his ranch twice. Then he had pondered every possible solution to obtaining the title free and clear.

To make matters worse, the image of Julia Gast kept haunting his thoughts. Never before had he been attracted to a woman like he was to her. Even covered with that infernal mud, she had an earthy pureness that enthralled him, far beyond just physical needs. He wondered whether Rusty Gast had any idea what kind of mess he had created when he penned his name to two bills of sale.

"Well, are you gonna?" Marcus prodded again.

"Of course," Flint snapped.

Tye studied him a moment, then spoke, "With those circles around your eyes, you could pass as kin to a raccoon. I'd suggest if you plan to wear the floor thin all night, you snuff the light. A child could have picked you off with a poor-sighted rifle."

"I knew you were out there," Flint said wearily. "Anyone poking around our place would be leaving wearing some lead." It was a standing joke that Tye valued his mounts more than a warm bed. His brother's nightly trips to the barn to check the horses were as routine as breathing.

"And if you were pushing up locoweed, what good would that do us?"

"Plenty," Marcus chimed in. "We'd be obliged to pay them for polishing off one mean cuss."

Together they laughed.

"Flint's always got an ugly side when he's tired." Betsy Ashmore yawned and walked through the doorway to stand next to Flint. Unlike him, she was a tiny thing, but every Ashmore brother had learned the hard way she was anything but a china doll. Despite the early morning, she had already washed her face, braided her hair, and donned a white apron over her green cotton dress.

Flint looked up, suddenly realizing their boisterous conversation must have awakened her. Almost single-handedly she managed the General Store, owned by old man Finley. Many days when the store was busy, she stayed in town, sleeping in a room in the back. A small kitchen adjoined it. All the brothers took the liberty of letting themselves in the back door when they came to check on her.

"If you'd marry me, Betsy, I'd be inclined to give up all my bad habits," he said teasingly and yanked on the long blonde braid that fell down her back.

She swatted him playfully on the shoulder, her blue eyes sparkling. "Land sakes, I can't marry you if I'm promised to Luke whenever he decides to give up his wandering ways!"

"You'd take a gunslinger over a rancher?" he asked in mock disappointment.

She laughed. "The only reason I'd marry you, Flint Ashmore, is to have a rabble of good-looking children around my feet!"

"Whoa," Marcus piped up, "watch what you say. Then we'd be surrounded by a slew of onerous little buggers. How many Flint replicas can a person tolerate?"

Suppressing a smile, she wagged a finger at Marcus. "You," she chided, "have no room to poke fun at poor Flint. You're like an ugly badger when you're not fed properly. I'd never want a slew of you either!"

Marcus winked. "Then how about stirrin' me up something before I bite your hand? Flint was so itchy about that Gast ranch that we left before daylight. The bunkhouse cook didn't even have a pot of coffee over the fire."

When Betsy left, Flint stretched out his legs, tipping his chair back. He stared grimly at his brothers as he considered their plight. He wished his father were still alive. The man had a rare ability of looking at any problem from more than one angle. Step back and think it through, he always warned. *Even a pile of sour apples can make a pretty good-tasting pie.* Well, they were certainly up to their ears in sour apples all right. With a potter laying claim to their tree!

The rattle of pots and pans in the kitchen drew Flint's thoughts back to the present.

"How's the water holding out?" He looked over at Tye.

The young man shook his head. "Low, real low. Last time I checked the herds, I even found some of Norwell's cattle in our eastern valley."

"Norwell's?" The name brought Flint upright in his chair. Frank Norwell was the most prosperous rancher in the area and his Flying N spread, the largest around. There was nothing they had in common except their visible dislike for each other, and ten miles of shared border to the northeast.

"Take it easy, Flint, I chased them back over the hill. Cattle are bound to get mixed together. If the drought holds out much longer, they'll all be searching out larger holes along the creek. Problem is, I think we're missing a few more than I'd like."

"You think someone's rustling them?"

Tye shrugged. "Sometimes a hungry renegade grabs a calf or two."

"I'm not talking about Indians."

It was well known that most ranchers in the area turned their heads the other way when a Ute helped himself. They had an unspoken truce. The Indians fed their starving families and during a raid, left the benevolent ranches alone. It wasn't something anyone boasted about for fear of angering the Army, sent there to enforce the treaties that pushed the Ute farther south.

"How many have disappeared?"

"About two dozen, I reckon."

"That's a lot of lost cattle." Their gazes caught for several seconds.

"Yes," Tye admitted, "but before you jump clean out of your skin, let me take a few men out to see if they've pushed farther back into greener areas. This drought is baking the grasslands to a crisp."

Flint eased back in his chair and contemplated their conversation. What his brother was saying was true. Hardly a drop of rain had fallen in over eight weeks. Even the trees were mere bundles of wilted leaves, bowing listlessly, praying for a reprieve from the unbearable heat.

"All right," he finally said. "Let's try to get some kind of tally to give us a bit of comfort. You know we can't afford to lose even a dozen."

If the truth were to be told, he thought to himself, they couldn't afford to lose one. They were barely making ends meet.

Tye nodded, and they sat in silence until Betsy appeared with a pot of steaming coffee, four mugs, and three plates of bacon, eggs and bread. She took a seat at the table, sipping her coffee pensively, as her brothers attacked the food before them.

"Marcus is right, Flint," she said. "You just can't turn that potter out, even if you end up legally owning the ranch."

Already aggravated over the loss of the stock, Flint growled, "We're not taking in every stray that stumbles through here, Betsy. We need that ranch."

"What if she has no place to go?"

He laid down his fork and stared at her. "And I suppose you think it's my problem?"

She stiffened. "Just where would I be, Flint Ashmore, if your mother and father hadn't taken me in?"

"Where would *we* be?" Marcus corrected her. He rubbed his stomach and stuffed another forkful of eggs in his mouth.

"Probably without another Ashmore to offer an opinion," Flint said sourly. The minute the words left his lips, he silently cursed himself a thousand times.

A hurt look fell across Betsy's face. She stared at table top, fighting back tears.

"Ah, Betsy, I didn't mean it that way. It was a joke."

Tye's fork stopped midway to his mouth and he scowled. "Then you'd darned well better tell her you're sorry, big brother."

"Excellent idea," Marcus agreed.

Flint's glanced at his brothers. "You two seem to be getting mighty protective."

Anger flashed briefly in Tye's eyes, but when he spoke, it was in his usual quiet, methodical way. "What do you think, Betsy? It wouldn't take much to put a matching scar above that left eye of his. I could just carve it on ." He slipped his knife from his moccasin and laid it on the table beside his plate.

"No." Marcus said in a deadpan voice. "Let me hack it on with my fork." That brought a smile to her face.

Flint sighed. He knew perfectly well this was no time to get everyone riled. All four brothers worshipped Betsy as much as he did, from the first moment when their father found her in his mule shed, abandoned at a week old. And he knew she loved them undeniably, each with his own set of faults. She was the best thing that ever happened to the family.

Life had been easier seven years ago in Virginia, before the War, before their father packed them all up to go West. Betsy had been only fourteen when a group of men had come to the house, insisting Tom Ashmore enlist his oldest sons in the Confederate cause. A fight had erupted and someone pulled a gun. Rebecca Ashmore stepped in front of her husband and took the bullet meant for him. Stunned, Betsy had watched Luke, barely sixteen years old, take three men down single-handedly through a haze of smoke while Flint and Marcus cut down the remaining two. That very evening, the woman she had come to love as her mother was buried and the wagons loaded. Tom Ashmore vowed none of his sons would fight and die in a war he had no interest in. His plantation had never owned slaves, he had paid every Darkie a meager wage even when times were hard and the crops were blighted.

"I'm sorry, Bets," Flint said and placed a hand gently over hers, "but without water, we just might as well sign the place over to Norwell, pack up and move on."

"I know," she conceded quietly.

His hand slid from hers, and he drummed his fingers absentmindedly on the table. Since their mother's death, Betsy had kept the family ledgers, never letting a penny slip by unaccounted for.

"How much extra cash do we have?" he asked her. If it came down to a stalemate, he figured he might be able to buy Julia Gast outright or pay her off in some type of installments.

She pursed her lips. "Not enough if you plan to keep the herd fed, make repairs to the bunkhouse and still pay the mortgage and men." Then she smiled, dimples appearing on her smooth flawless face. "Oh, yes, and keep Tye in those fancy clothes."

"He doesn't buy his clothes," Marcus said, wolfing down another mouthful of food. "He steals them from renegade Utes prowling the area."

"Trade for them," Tye corrected him and grinned. "Like I keep telling you, those Indians make far better friends than enemies."

Marcus swatted Flint on the front of his shirt. "Now Flint here is a different story. He takes to those fancy duds. Betsy can hardly keep him in clean shirts."

"At least his vests are leather and saves on the washing." Betsy rose from the table and started to collect the plates. "Mother always said a handsome man should not hide his looks in cheap clothes, and an ugly man would do well to pay twice the price to make himself presentable to the ladies."

"What I can't figure," Flint said, "is why Julia Gast *and* the Ashmores here paid twice for a rundown ranch that Rusty could have sold to Frank Norwell and gotten three times the amount." He watched his sister set the plates back on the table and pensively stare into space.

"No, what we need to know," Betsy said, gnawing at her lower lip, "is not why Rusty sold the ranch twice, but what happened to the money including the cash for the equipment."

Flint's chair scraped against the floor as he rose. "Confound it, Betsy, you're beginning to scare me."

"Why?" she asked with a startled look.

"Because you're beginning to think like me."

Flint Ashmore was not surprised to find Julia Gast seated in a plush leather chair in the office of John Greenfeld, Esquire, when he arrived later that morning. And it didn't take an idiot to see that either the ride into town had tired her, or she had spent a sleepless night as well. Her face was pale, and her eyes were swollen and bloodshot like she had been crying. Even so, she was a beautiful woman. He suspected she was twenty-five years old at best. In the dim light of the shed the other day, he had not seen the tiny line of freckles that brushed across the bridge of her nose and cheeks, accenting her green eyes and flaming red hair.

He moved toward a seat beside her in front of Greenfeld's desk. At his approach, her hands tensed around her reticule. Her fingers were long and slim, but they were work-roughened hands, reddened from being immersed in water and wet clay.

"Good morning," he said.

She returned his greeting in a low voice, averting her eyes, and he realized she was more upset that he earlier suspected.

The thought bothered him for some odd reason. He dropped into the chair and removed his hat, hanging it over his knee. "I want you to know," he said, "no matter how this turns out, you still have my admiration."

"Admiration?" Startled, she looked at him.

"Yes, I've never met a woman potter, and certainly no one with talent like yours. I only wish we could have met under better circumstances."

She managed a tentative smile.

"That's not all." Grinning lopsidedly, he added, "And I've never met any woman with such a defensive temper."

Her face turned the same color as her hair. "I'm sorry about that. It was an unkind, thoughtless act to not give you a drink of water on such a sweltering day."

"I don't know what came over me," she admitted, sheepishly. "I've never been prone to throw fits." She smiled and their eyes met, brown against green, raw earth and tender grass.

If they had been anywhere else but in Greenfeld's office, he would have reached out to touch that flaming, red hair. That luscious, brilliant red hair. The color of fire itself.

The sound of a door opening forced him back to reality. John Greenfeld crossed the room, and Flint rose to greet him.

"Hope your trip East was pleasant," he said. Flint couldn't help but admire the old lawyer who now had a thriving business just keeping the miners claims in order and settling local disputes. Greenfeld had been a friend since the first day they moved to Golden, and he had processed the mortgage papers for their ranch.

"Yes, it was, immensely pleasant. Boston is thriving city now." Greenfeld seated himself, shuffling through a pile of papers on his desk. "Now let's see here, the way I understand it, you both have bills of sale for Rusty Gast's ranch, correct?"

Both Flint and Julia extracted their papers.

Greenfeld perched his spectacles on his nose, examined the papers closely and grunted. "Both look official to me."

He withdrew a piece of paper from his top desk drawer. "The deed I was directed to draw up lists two owners." He swallowed and looked uncomfortably, first at Julia and then at Flint. "The deed lists Julia Gast. . .and Betsy Ashmore."

"Betsy?" Flint exploded and shot out of his chair. Beside him, he heard Julia choke out a sigh of relief

Lawyer Greenfeld shrugged. "An Ashmore is an Ashmore, right?"

"My name is on that bill of sale!"

"Are you saying it's not legal and Betsy is holding another?"

"No, no, of course not," he replied quickly, "I arranged it myself." He buckled down into the chair. What was he thinking? If the bill of sale was deemed to be invalid, he'd lose any hope of securing water for the cattle. And where would he stand with the agreement for the equipment he bought? Betsy's name on the deed was far better than none.

Greenfeld leaned back in his chair and tapped the folded deed on the desk's top. "You don't seem pleased, Flint."

Not pleased, Flint thought, that was an astute perception of the entire dilemma that had befallen them. Disgusted and angry were also an accurate description. And puzzled.

"How did this happen?" he asked, scowling. "How can I be certain there isn't fifty other blasted papers, identical to these, floating around the territory?"

"Wouldn't matter, this is all you need now. It's valid, I assure you. I transferred it myself."

"Why only Betsy's name?"

"It's what Rusty instructed me to do, a week before he died."

"You didn't question him?"

"Didn't see a need to. I told you, an Ashmore is an Ashmore, right? You knew Rusty was always partial to Betsy after she nursed him with that broken leg two summers ago. Lord knows he stopped often enough at that General Store, not to buy supplies but to jaw with Finley and your sister. A man does funny things when he gets up there in years."

Flint shook his head to clear it. Never had he expected the nightmare before him. He turned and walked to the window and stood in a slanting ray of light, looking out but not really seeing anything before him as he tried to make sense of something so illogical. Finally, he turned and spoke, "Did the old man have a will?"

The lawyer nodded.

"Would it be asking too much to divulge anything he might have wished?"

"I've only had a chance to scan it briefly. There was no cash mentioned. Primarily it disposes of some personal possessions--a knife for Tye, a saddle for Marcus, a rifle for Luke, and a locket for Betsy. Oh, and a note for you to pay his bills at the General Store and feed mill."

"Pay *his* bills?" Flint whirled on the lawyer. "You must be joking!"

Greenfeld flinched in surprise. "I didn't write the darn thing, Flint, the old man did! Don't take it personal. Anyway, Betsy said she'd take care of his bill at the store."

Flint crossed the room in angry strides and flattened his hands on the lawyer's desk. "I have shelled out money for equipment I'm not using, for supplies I've never seen, and for half a ranch, and you tell me not to take an unpaid bill at the feed mill personal?" He laughed cynically. "Do tell, how do you suppose we handle our joint ranching venture when one owner wants to run cattle over the land and the other fashion mugs and jugs and whatnot from it?"

"Work it together, sell out to each other, or sell it outright and divide the cash."

"No," Julia Gast said, coming swiftly to her feet. Her reticule fell to the floor with a loud muffled thump. "I'm not selling!"

Flint had almost forgotten she was there. He pinned her with a piercing gaze. "For once, Miss Gast, I totally agree."

She let out another breath of relief. When she tried to speak, her voice came out in a choked, halting voice. "This is. . .this is all so sudden. . .so shocking. We need a day to sleep on it. . .to think it through. Could we meet at the General Store, sometime, say around noon… maybe tomorrow. . .to discuss this?"

He nodded. It was the first sound idea he had heard in the last half hour. He needed time to formulate a plan, and he needed time to talk with his brothers and sister. He swept up the reticule and handed it to her. Her eyes were full of confusion, perhaps even fear, but she smiled wanly in appreciation.

Greenfeld cleared his throat nervously. "The deed," he said, waving the paper in the air.

Two hands shot out for it, but Julia was quicker.

"Give it here," Flint ordered.

"You don't trust me?"

"Ma'am, right now I don't trust anyone."

"Fine, Mr. Ashmore," she said stiffly, "neither do I."

Before he could blink, she ripped it in half, straight down the middle, and shoved a piece into his hands. "There, that should temporarily solve our dilemma, don't you think?"

From behind his desk, Greenfeld's eyes popped out like a bullfrog's.

Without a word of farewell, she whirled and glided over the oriental rug toward the door, her reticule dangling like a pendulum on her slim wrist. The room was deadly silent, so silent the click of the door latch sounded like a gunshot when it closed behind her.

"A most striking woman," Greenfeld said in a low voice, still staring at the door with a look of disbelief. "A most unusual one, too."

"Yes," Flint agreed, "that she is."

Yet, it was only much later, after he regained his senses and departed from Greenfeld's office, when the revelation hit Flint full force: Julia Gast's purse held something heavier than just mere trinkets.

Four

With a heavy heart, Julia Gast walked up the street, struggling to understand what had happened. Around her the town was a flurry of activity, but she hardly noticed as she dodged the shopkeepers swatting at the layers of dust on the walk.

For the first time in a long time, desolation took hold of her, and she wanted to cry. How could her uncle have done this to her? Never, in all the letters he had exchanged with her, had he mentioned the fact that he was selling the land to anyone but her. What had made him change his mind?

She wiped away a tear forming in the corner of her eye. She had come out West to start a new life and leave her troubles and disappointments behind. Her mind circled back to Lancaster. There was no way she could ever return.

She remembered the morning she had fled to the rectory of St. Thomas Church and begged Father McMillen to help her escape before she became the wife of Captain Charles Bloomington. Her father had died peacefully, thinking she would be well taken care of, protected and provided for by a man of social standing and sound means. He never had an inkling that Bloomington had his eyes on their farm and best breeding horses instead of her. And he never knew the good Captain and Union war hero had forbidden her to continue with her pottery business once they were married. It wasn't fitting to have hands like a washer woman and fashion things from dirt, as he so eloquently put it.

At first the old priest had been reluctant to help, but once he learned Bloomington suspected she had aided some wounded Confederates during the War, he caved in. Bloomington's bitter hatred for the South, and anyone connected to it, was well-known throughout the area despite the fact the War had been over for three years.

No, Lancaster was definitely out of the question. She could never risk going back.

She sighed and glanced up the street where Anna was waiting with the wagon. Standing by the tailgate, her back straight, she was in a heated argument with a rumpled-looking cowhand.

Julia hurried to where they stood facing each other in a stand-off.

"Is there a problem, Anna?" she asked.

"This man says we are nesters," the Dane replied stiffly.

Julia looked at the surly man. His eyes were bloodshot and he smelled like he had just dropped too much cash in the saloon. Two pearl-handled Colts were strapped to his slim hips and the hatband on his very expensive hat was trimmed with silver conchos.

"It appears to me that everyone is a nester when they first settle here," she said, forcing warmth she hardly felt into her voice.

He sneered, weaving unsteadily on his feet. "Well, ma'am, that's not the way the ranchers see it. This Dane here and her brother are on land that don't rightly belong to them."

"Then I must be too," she snapped back, "because they work with me. I'm Julia Gast, and I don't think we've had the pleasure of meeting." She noticed her name brought a spark of recognition to his whiskey-dulled eyes.

"Colin Norwell," he said with a slurred voice. "Never knew Rusty Gast had any brats."

"I'm his niece." Julia fought back the desire to let her temper get the better of her.

"You plan on running the place?" he asked.

"For now my plans are to work my pottery business and raise a few horses." She wondered why she was even wasting her time trying to explain. The man was obviously too inebriated to understand, let alone remember anything.

He belched. "If I were you, ma'am, I'd plan on moving into town as fast as I can. There are a lot of men who's had their eye on that property for a long time, and they'd stop at nothing to get it."

"Is that a threat, Mr. Norwell?" This time she didn't try to hide her irritation. Her hand reached down to grip the reticule hanging at her wrist.

"Listen, lady, don't be a fool!"

"What he says is partly the truth, miss," a voice behind her said. The man touched his dusty hat, shading sullen, dark eyes. "I'm Tom Morton, foreman for the Flying N. But it's the Indians that I'd worry more about. There are bands all over the area, and they're not choosy about whose stock they steal and whose goods they plunder."

"Why, they've been given government land to the southwest," Julia said. She knew Kit Carson himself helped arrange the treaty.

"That's true, Miss, but the government can't keep a redskin under control when he doesn't want to be. The renegades who don't take kindly to being pushed out are still roaming about, and they're armed."

"Then I shall have to be careful, won't I?"

"Careful?" Tom Morton snorted. "If I were you, I'd carry a shotgun to draw a bucket of water from your well. Indians aren't choosy about who they rape or kill either."

"I appreciate your candor, Mr. Morton." She glanced at Colin Norwell. He had a death grip on the side of the wagon. His face was white, and he looked like he was ready to tumble in the dirt at her feet. "It looks like your friend could use some assistance."

"What he needs is help finding his horse and a bed. If you'll excuse us," Morton said. He snagged Norwell under his armpit and led him away, toward the livery stable.

When the two men left, Julia felt a surge of relief. Glancing up the street, she spotted a small café where a peeling weathered sign above the door read, The Iron Skillet.

"Let's get some coffee," she suggested. "There's so much I have to tell you."

"Oh, yes, let's!" Anna replied, brightening.

Inside the café, they chose a seat beside a fly-specked window facing the street. The interior was cramped and dingy, with scarred chairs and grease-smeared cloths covering the tables. The lingering odor of burnt food permeated the room.

"Coffee and something sweet," Julia said as soon the serving girl made her way to where they were seated. She was a pitiful-looking child in a threadbare gray dress much too small for her budding figure.

"Sorry, ma'am, we're clean out of pie and donuts."

"Just coffee will do."

The girl nodded and disappeared.

"This lawyer you saw," Anna said leaning forward and whispering, "he was able to fix everything, ja?"

Julia shook her head, relating what had happened in Greenfeld's office.

"So, you see," she said finishing, "until I find out what Betsy Ashmore plans to do with her half of the ranch, there is nothing we can do."

"Surely it will all work out?" The Danish woman looked at her with hopeful eyes.

Julia sighed and gnawed on her lower lip. "Money, Anna, is our first concern. There is little left, what with buying the ranch and stock, securing our passage out here, and shipping the pottery. We have only enough to get some supplies to tide us over, unless I sell the engagement ring Bloomington gave me."

"No!" Anna's response was swift and sharp. "You must return it. The man would consider that thievery."

"I can't return it until I can find someone heading East, someone I can trust. Bloomington must never know where we are, you know that."

"Find a courier, and find him quickly," Anna said insistently, "get that ring returned before Bloomington decides to come looking for you. If that happens, you'll wish you were never born."

The serving girl returned, interrupting their conversation, and they sipped the strong, bitter brew in silence, each lost in her own unsettling thoughts.

Moments later, the door opened and a small woman with pale blonde hair sailed through. She made her way to the kitchen doorway, cocked a hip against the jamb, and spoke to the serving girl. "I'll need more eggs by tomorrow morning, Marcy, and tell your Pa to make sure they're clean, not like the last batch. Clean, you hear? There's no excuse when your well is right outside your back door."

Julia saw the young girl reluctantly nod. The blonde woman removed some coins from her apron pocket and handed them to her. "Oh, and when you stop by the store, be sure to remind me about those dresses I've been meaning to give you. Land sakes, child, you're growing like a bad weed!"

She patted the girl on her shoulder and turned to leave, her eyes circling the room. "Well, I'll be darned," she said and made her way toward Julia, "if it isn't the potter! I'll bet we have the whole town buzzing."

Taken off guard, Julia stared at her.

"Oh, excuse me, I'm Betsy Ashmore. Do you mind if I sit down?"

"Please do," Julia said, coming to her senses. She waved at the vacant seat across from her. "I was hoping to meet you. Do you prefer Betsy or Elizabeth?"

"Betsy is just fine." She laughed and her voice, animated and light, sounded like the tinkling of bells. "My pa said if I was abandoned next to his best mule, I might as well be named after her. I thank the dear Lord every day I wasn't left beside Erastus, Pa's other one."

Julia relaxed in the warmth of the girl's gentle humor. Like her brother Marcus, she was prone to smile a lot, showing a set of perfect teeth.

"Is your brother around?" Julia asked. The last thing she wanted was to have another confrontation with Flint Ashmore.

"Flint? Oh, heavens no, he rode back to the ranch as grouchy as a bear with a stomach ache. Not many people are able to catch him off-guard, but you've already done it twice. You have my admiration."

"Sympathy, you mean."

Betsy Ashmore let out another ripple of laughter. "Well, maybe that, too." She propped her elbows on the table. "It's about time Golden City got themselves a potter. Everything I sell down at the store, from milk pans to mugs, has to be shipped in from the Mormons in the Utah territory. Why, half of it is broken before it even arrives."

"You're forgetting one detail," Julia pointed out.

"What's that?"

"Your brother wants the ranch."

"No, it's the water rights that has him all fired up. He can get by without the house or grazing land." Betsy leaned closer and spoke in a hushed voice, "Just between you and me, there are a lot of people who had set their sights on that property."

"So I've heard. I've spoken with Mr. Norwell."

"You've already talked to Frank Norwell?"

"I suspect it was his son or brother."

"Colin?"

Julia nodded.

"His son. His only son. The Norwells own the land that curves like a backward C around yours. If they get their hands on it, they could lock up the entire town and make life miserable for every small rancher along the creek."

"Tell me," Julia said, studying Betsy warily, "did you personally approach my uncle about buying his property?"

"Me?" She shook her head. "Heavens no, it was Flint he always dealt with. It was Flint who signed the bill of sale. But I can assure you, Rusty never once hinted there was anyone else involved or that he had named only me on the deed. He died before all the paperwork was transacted, and we just assumed it would be in order."

Her gaze darkened momentarily. She slumped back in her seat. "One thing I can tell you is that Rusty rarely did anything that he didn't think through. Why he ever decided to pass the ranch to two women is beyond me. Yet, I'm inclined to believe he must have had his reasons."

She looked at Julia mystified. "But I have the feeling either he was headed for trouble. . ." She paused and rose from the table. "Or we are."

Startled by her frankness, Julia stared at her. Her stomach felt like she had swallowed a rock. Somewhere overhead her she heard a fly angrily buzzing, searching for a way out of the four-walled, grease-smelling tomb.

"Why do you think that?"

"Now, now, I didn't mean to cause you alarm," Betsy said. "Rusty was a close friend of my father's. It just doesn't make sense why he'd arrange to sell the ranch to you *and* Flint, but put only my name on the Ashmore half of the deed and not tell any of us."

She patted Julia's hand reassuringly. "Don't worry, it'll all work out, and don't you fret about that brother of mine. Flint has a tendency to act like a jug head, but he's been known to have a few lucid moments in his life. As the oldest, he's always had to bear the burden of keeping us all together with a roof over our head. He's actually the most fair and honest man you'll ever meet. Although I do admit that this ranch has had him in a foul mood."

Julia nodded weakly and watched Betsy walk away, stopping briefly to greet an old couple seated at a table nearby. She thought about what Betsy had told her. Fair and honest? Maybe all wasn't lost after all.

Five

Daylight had barely arrived the next morning as Flint lay sprawled on his belly in the dew-laden grass peering down into a ravine. Marcus was stretched out beside him. Below them, the creek on Gast property wound down through a draw and twisted itself into a half loop before winding through a small valley and spilling onto Norwell property. In the distance, three men were driving some young stock from his property toward a hidden draw where two men waited beside a small, smokeless fire.

"I'm getting too old for these kinds of games," Flint muttered, tossing aside a blade of grass he was chewing on. "I have half a notion to ride over to Frank Norwell's and shoot him through the heart."

"Easy, man, have you taken leave of your senses?" Marcus whispered, "or are you just needing a tad more sleep? Pull a fool stunt like that and you'll be decorating a cottonwood on the spot. We don't know those rustlers down there are Norwell's men."

"No? Well, tell me Marcus, who else would want to cripple our herd count so we'd pull up stakes and move on? Name me another man who wanted Rusty Gast's ranch as much as we did?" He elbowed Marcus. "Would you look at that, they're going to steal our cattle and brand them on our very own land!"

Marcus chuckled. "Our land? Betsy's and Julia Gast's land, you mean. That potter sure is a comely gal."

"She is," Flint agreed. And Lord, she had hair most women would die for. He remembered his father telling him to shy away from red-haired women. Meaner than a sack of rattlers when riled he had said, and act just as crazy. But Julia Gast was different. She could come to a full boil and still be a thinker.

"You still plan to meet her at noon?"

Flint nodded.

"You know, there's a solution to your problem with the Gast ranch," Marcus whispered. "You could marry her, and it would all be ours."

This time Flint snorted.

"Maybe it'll be easier than you think," Tye said in a hushed voice, crawling up behind them so silently they simultaneously flinched in surprise. He pointed to a low knoll to the left of the draw. A good mile out, Julia Gast was on horseback and heading straight toward them. "She may get her head blown away when she stumbles onto the little celebration below. This could be mighty interesting."

Flint groaned and swore softly under his breath. "Anyone have a plan? Speak up now." He knew they had only moments to make a move, and he also knew that men who stole, killed or rustled cattle had no desire to be caught in the act, especially by a woman.

"Nope," Marcus said and crawled backward noiselessly. He stood and spat on the ground. "We never had one before, don't know why we should start now."

He looked at Tye who was checking his rifle. He shrugged. "Don't look at me. I'm along for the ride."

"Maybe that's our problem," Flint said and eased himself from the ground, stepping back into the security of some leafy aspen. He stretched the dull soreness from his shoulders. "We need to start making more plans."

Julia Gast headed toward Golden. She had saddled her horse in the early morning light and decided to ride into town to check out the General Store before her meeting with the Ashmores. The ranch was low on supplies, and an empty stomach was no way to win the respect of newly hired help. She needed to find a place in town willing to sell the pottery she had brought from Pennsylvania. It was putting no cash in her pocket scattered on the shelves in the shed, and soon she would have to buy a mule to work the clay pit.

Selecting a small trail that looked like it was used by deer or wild horses, she headed toward Cherry Creek. She planned to study every inch of it and find the best clay deposits. This was as good a time as any to begin her search.

The sorrel she rode was a strong gentle one, sure-footed and accustomed to grass sliding under his belly and wildlife darting from under his hooves. He was among the few she had refused to sell when she moved West, hoping she could start a string of prime stock in Colorado.

The morning was already growing humid, promising another sweltering day. She found herself thinking about Flint Ashmore. He was a tough man, one other men would not easily cross. Yet, he was a gentleman, too. She smiled remembering the astonished look on his face when she tore the deed in two. He looked like he wanted to explode. Her uncle had mentioned him only once in his letters. He had said he was one of the most honorable men in the territory. She hoped he had not lied. She needed the ranch. She had no place to go and no one to turn to.

A thin trail of smoke rising from the trees along the creek ahead of her caught her attention. Curious, Julia headed toward it, reaching the ravine where she turned her mount west and picked her way carefully down a rocky slope into the draw. A quarter mile upstream, past a stand of aspen, she found the spot.

Five heads shot up when she rode into sight. The men stared at her, then fanned out from their positions around the fire. A bawling calf, recently branded, skidded away, tail flying. The stench of singed hair rose in the air.

She halted her mount several yards away.

A big man with a broken nose stepped forward. "Howdy, ma'am, nice day for a ride."

"It is," she agreed. She studied the men thoughtfully for a moment, her eyes darting to the spot where their branding iron lay abandoned. A rough-looking man stood several feet behind it and was rolling a smoke. Beside him, a young man dressed in an elbow-worn shirt rocked back on his heels nervously. Two others nearby held a roped calf.

"What spread you working for?" she asked the big man. She was aware everyone was listening. Not a man, nor muscle moved.

"Who says we work for a spread?"

"Who hired you?"

"What makes you think we're hired?" He rubbed his fat lips with a grimy hand. Yellow eyes on a jowly face sneered up at her. "These cattle here are ours, and we're just slappin' a brand to their hides before we drive them out."

Trying to suppress her irritation at the man's lack of manners, she said, "Polite people introduce themselves, sir."

"Lady, we don't need to be polite, and we don't need to be no one as far as you're concerned." The men behind him snickered.

"You do if you're collecting and branding cattle on this property."

"Who says?"

"The owner."

"Who might he be? I ain't seen no owner since Rusty Gast passed away." The man smirked through tobacco-stained teeth.

"You're looking at the owner. Julia Gast."

The man's chin dropped, and his face blushed an ugly red. He started toward her, and Julia swung her horse abruptly to face him broadside. She pulled out a bullwhip that would skin the hair off the top of a man's scalp.

"Back away," she warned him. She spoke to the others in a stern voice, "Gather up your things and get off my land. Leave the cattle."

"We could shoot you, lady, right here." The words barely left his mouth when a bullet whistled through the air and clipped a piece of his ear. He grabbed at the side of his bloody face, threw a wild look up to the ravine and screamed, "Renegade Indians! Run for your lives!"

Suddenly, gunfire erupted around them.

The man stumbled toward Julia, and she instinctively knew he meant to knock her from her saddle and take her horse. The sorrel, startled by noise and the lurching man, squealed and shied backwards. The whip she held slipped from her grip and fell into the dirt. Seconds later, horse and rider were tearing off down the draw.

Frightened, Julia clung to her mount and managed to gather the reins. Unfamiliar with the area, she allowed him to choose his own course, only veering him once when she spotted a small incline that left the draw. Yards beyond, he headed into a stand of pine and slackened his pace. She drew up and slid from the saddle, slumping against the trunk of a large pine. Trembling, she gulped mouthfuls of air, listening to the distant sound of gunfire.

Suddenly, just when she thought she was safe, a brown hand snaked out from behind and clamped itself over her mouth, the other encircling her chest. The attack was so quick she didn't have time to scream.

Unaware who her opponent might be, Julia fought wildly against the viselike hold, scratching at the strange hands to free herself. She drew a foot back and kicked her attacker in the shin. He staggered slightly, tightened his hold, squeezing the breath from her lungs. With no air and no strength left to match him, Julia realized she had no recourse except one. She stopped struggling and waited, heart thumping.

The hand at her mouth relaxed.

She sunk her teeth into the fleshy part of the palm and screamed, propelling herself away from her assailant who howled equally as loud.

Spinning around, she was astonished to discover she was face-to-face with an Indian. Tall and straight, he wore his greasy black hair loose, falling to his shoulders, and he smelled like he had slept with his horse for a year.

She raised her forefinger and shook it menacingly, shying backwards. "Don't you dare touch me!"

Sharp eyes glittered in his mud brown face. He laughed, then grunted something she didn't understand. She noticed he was missing his two front teeth. Drawing his knife, he stepped toward her feigning a jab. She darted sideways and realized it was she who had now grown careless. The Indian moved sideways with her, reached out, yanked her by the hair, and dragged her toward him. He shoved the knife against her ribs.

Beside her, Julia heard a deep voice drawl. "I wouldn't do it, Two Bears. Let the lady go."

Flint Ashmore stepped out from behind a tree. Seconds later, Tye followed and stood beside him. Both men's faces were bland and expressionless.

"Let her go," Tye said, then repeated the warning in the tongue of the Ute.

The Ute rattled what appeared to be a question.

"Speak English, Two Bears," Flint said in an exhausted voice. "I'm not wasting half the doggone day listening to Tye translate."

"You know this one?" The Ute directed the question to Tye.

He nodded.

"She your woman?"

"Yes," Tye lied.

The Ute grunted. "She too tall for you, Tye Ashmore. Much too tall. You need woman more like a sparrow. She need a man like Two Bears."

"All right, all right," Tye said, rolling his eyes skyward. "She really belongs to Flint here."

An oath of appreciation slipped out under Flint's breath.

The younger man shrugged. "Might as well hand over the reins to you, big brother. You were the one so all-fired up to kick those rustlers' backsides clean to the coast and rescue the little lady. Go ahead, give it your best shot. Use one of your new fangled plans." He suppressed a smirk.

"Marcus is right, Tydall," Flint snapped back. "Ever since we moved out here you have become wild and disrespectful. Ma and Pa are rolling over in their graves." He resisted an urge to reach out, snag his brother by his buckskins and shake him good.

Before Tye could open his mouth to defend himself, the Indian spoke, "Enough, you chatter like squirrels."

Silence fell around them while they glared at each other. Finally the Ute asked, "What will you give me for your woman, Flint Ashmore?"

Flint glanced at Julia. The Ute had a strong grip on her hair, but she had not uttered a sound, despite the pain. She looked desperately at him with wild, frightened eyes.

"What makes you think she's worth anything?" he countered, hoping the renegade wouldn't sense his concern. Two Bears was the leader of one of the most ruthless bands left in the area. He had little respect for most whites, and none for men who showed any weakness, red or white. Julia Gast, Flint feared, was becoming his weakness, whether he liked it or not.

"Give him something!" Julia hissed through clenched teeth. "For God's sake, give him something!"

Flint removed his hat. "Good hat. Almost brand new. Will keep the sun and rain from your head." He threw it at the Ute's moccasins and it landed in the dust nearby.

"Pfft," the Ute said. "This is woman with hair the color of the red fox. She worth much more! Much, much more."

Flint moved to his horse and untied his leather coat. "This will keep you warm on cold nights." It sailed through the air, following the same route of the hat, and fell to the ground beside it.

"So will woman."

"The coat doesn't cause as much trouble and never needs to be fed."

The Ute grinned. "This is true, very true. But coat no good without matching vest."

37

Flint sighed wearily and shrugged off his vest. It was his favorite, a present from his sister. Reluctantly, he tossed it on the pile.

What else you give me?" the Indian asked. His greedy eyes flew to the horses.

Flint turned to Tye. "Now it's your turn, little brother."

"Whoa, just a damn minute." The palms of Tye's hands flew upward and flat. "You're the one who always makes the deals in this family."

"The ring flask on my saddle," Julia groaned. "Give it to him!"

Tye moved to her horse, removed the flask and held it out. Two Bears stared at it curiously.

"Take it," Flint urged. "You don't want the woman. She's a little sick in the head. She likes to play with mud. Two Bears would have to stay near a river to keep her happy."

The Indian pondered his words, then looked at Tye. "Is this true?"

"Look at her hands," Flint urged.

The Indian let go of Julia's hair and grabbed her wrist in his filthy hand, inspecting her fingers where small traces of clay, difficult to remove, ringed the beds of her fingernails.

The Ute grunted, released her, slid his knife into his moccasin, and accepted the ring flask from Tye. Puzzled, he turned it around and around in his hands. "You have cut its heart out," he said and held it before his face. A dark eyeball peered through the round opening at her.

"It's supposed to be like that," Julia explained and crept sideways until she was standing beside Flint, safely out of Two Bear's reach. "It's to keep water in when you're far from a stream."

Two Bears grinned and inspected it again, then uncorked it and took a sip. He held it out in front of himself proudly. Suddenly, his eyes darkened. "But this is not from your man, Red Fox Woman."

"Oh, yes," she replied quickly. "I made it for Flint as a present. Take it. Please, take it."

"You can make these?" The Indian looked skeptically at her.

"Hush up, Julia, while we're ahead," Flint said in a low hiss and shot her a warning look. "Keep spouting off and you'll become valuable again. In case you haven't noticed, I'm about out of clothes."

Three calves, scattered from the ruckus in the draw, walked out from the grove of trees and started grazing several feet from the group.

The Ute gathered his goods and glanced at Tye. He stood tall and proud, but his eyes held a glint of sorrow and shame. "My people are hungry."

The words hardly left his mouth when Flint's gun flashed in the sunlight. He pointed it at the Indian's chest.

The Ute drew back, surprised. "You are a man of honor, Ashmore. We made a deal."

"You tried to steal my woman. Maybe I don't want you to try again."

"Ah, Flint, no. Don't do it," Tye pleaded. "Please put the damn gun away."

"You can't shoot him!" Julia screamed just before the gun exploded.

A lone calf beside Two Bears tumbled to the ground.

"For God's sake, Flint, I hate when you do that." Tye shook his head from side to side. "Scares me enough to consider becoming a priest. Someday, you're not going to jerk that gun fast enough sideways and you'll put a hole in someone's gut."

"Take the calf, Two Bears," Flint instructed tonelessly. "It's worthless to me wearing a Norwell brand. Feed your people."

The Ute hurriedly gathered his belongings, threw the calf over his horse and mounted.

When he left, Flint turned his attention to Julia. The color was still drained from her face and she was trembling. Her fingers were threaded through her hair as she kneaded the side of her aching head.

"You going to make it?" he asked and moved beside her. He stroked the back of her head, her hair was soft and silky as he imagined it would be. "Take a few deep breaths," he instructed. "Please don't faint on me."

She swallowed hard, nodding. "That Indian was odious and the stench too offensive to describe!"

"A man on the run can little afford the luxury of a bath. If it makes you feel better, Two Bears has never been known to harm a woman or child."

"Thank goodness you both came by," she murmured.

"Thank goodness you have a healthy head of hair."

That brought a wan smile to her face. Recovering her composure, she stepped back, away from his touch. "I want to thank you both."

"Our pleasure," Flint replied.

She hesitated a moment, then asked, "The rustlers back in the draw, did the Indians kill them?"

"There were no Indians, except for this lone renegade," Flint replied.

"But I heard gunfire for several minutes."

He grinned. "Oh, that. We left Marcus behind to finish target practicing on them. He just bought a new Winchester this month. Marcus isn't likely to kill them, but he'll pop a few buttons off their shirts."

While they talked, Tye had gathered their horses and brought them to where they stood.

"Since we're headed for the same place, we might as well ride together," Flint suggested. He paused, resting a hand on the pommel of his saddle and stared at her. He promised himself he was not going to ask the silly question that had rolled around in his head over and over for the past half hour. Yet, he had to know. "Tell me, Miss Gast, was it true what you said about that ring flask?"

"Julia," she said. "I prefer Julia."

"Julia," he repeated in a soft drawl.

"No," she said. She looked down, embarrassed, and studied the ground before her green eyes came level with his. "It wasn't true."

Her hand touched his upper arm and he felt his heart leap to his throat. Easy, Ashmore, a voice inside his head screamed. She wants your ranch.

"Now don't take this wrong," he heard her say. "The flask was actually a gift for Tye since he admired it so much the first day we met."

Flint stared at her while the words registered. "You mean Tye just let that redskin walk away with a present meant for him?"

She nodded sheepishly.

The corner of his mouth turned upward, and he threw back his head and let out a peal of laugher. His deep baritone voice rippled along the silent land, rattling like leaves in the summer breeze.

"Ah, dang it, Flint, it's not funny," Tye muttered sourly and threw a leg effortlessly over his mount. "You knew I took a shine to those flasks."

He looked at Julia. "I sure wish you'd have told me earlier, ma'am, that it was intended for me."

"Why?" she asked, curiosity getting the better of her.

Gathering the reins, he threw her a teasing grin. "Because I would have shot that thieving Indian."

Six

The town of Golden was deserted when the Ashmore brothers and Julia Gast arrived near noon. The overhead sun was brutal, baking the streets and wooden facades and forcing inhabitants to scurry for the cover of curtain-drawn parlors and shaded porches.

Flint left Julia at the front of the General Store and proceeded to the feed mill while Tye led the horses to a watering trough before delivering them to the coolness of the local livery.

He was troubled over Rusty Gast's request for him to make good on his bills. The old man was never one to be beholden to anyone for any reason, nor to be in debt. Furthermore, he had been far from destitute. His thoughts needled him the entire way to the far corner of town where the feed mill was located.

Syrus Bentley was seated outside when he arrived, propped in a chair in the shade of the overhang of the roof. The smoke from his pipe curled lazily upward to encircle his head. Bentley was old as dirt and one of the first to make a strike in the early '50s. He was sitting on his gold mine now. Every penny he had mined had gone into the feed mill which now supplied grain for the entire area and the Army's stock as well.

"Howdy," he said. "Good day for sleeping, eating and sitting."

Flint propped his boot on the top step of the wide loading platform which surrounded the mill on three sides.

"Good day for fishing and swimming, too."

"For you young-uns, maybe. Not for old folks like me." Bentley laughed. "What can I do for you?"

"I'm told that I've a bill to pay for Rusty Gast. Figured since I'm in town, I'd see how much Betsy would need to scare up."

"I'd write you a bill, Flint, just to see Betsy. Sure is a purty lookin' gal. Can't figure out why she hasn't grabbed herself a husband yet. What with all these miners underfoot, she could have her pick of the lot. Rich one, too. If I didn't have my old hound dog, I'd marry her myself." The old man chuckled. "She's not still waiting for that rascal Luke to settle down, I hope? Heard he's roaming around somewhere up north."

"I don't think Betsy waits for anyone or anything, including for the sun to rise. She flits around like a dust mote."

"That she does, that she does." Bentley rose and ambled into the mill. "You know, Rusty's bill is paid."

"It's paid, you say?" Flint followed the old man inside where the smell of grain and burlap was strong and pungent.

"Yup, Rusty settled up with me just before he died."

Syrus Bentley moved to a dusty shelf behind the counter and removed a soiled envelope. "He told me if you stopped by to be sure to give you this."

Flint scowled, took the sealed envelope, folded it and shoved it into his pocket. He would read it later in private. There was little that Syrus Bentley didn't know about the lives of people in Golden and very little that he didn't pass on. Flint wasn't about to share his affairs with the entire town.

"Ain't you gonna read it?" The old man sucked on his pipe and blew a perfect smoke ring into the air that floated above their heads.

"No, it's probably just instructions about the equipment I bought."

"He sold you his wagons, did he? Wonder how that potter is going to get along without them? There's another purty one, too."

Flint bit back an inward groan. The entire town must know about the potter taking up residence on his ranch.

"I'm sure something can be worked out," he assured Bentley and left quickly, retracing his footsteps, and stopping under a leafy elm beside the blacksmith shop before he opened the envelope.

Inside, a letter with a bank note read: *I'm sorry, Flint, you and your pa have always been my friends, but I owed Betsy. Gretchen would never forgive me. I hope you understand. I never meant to hurt either gal.* It was simply signed, Rusty G.

Flint stared at the bank note. Five thousand dollars. The exact amount he had paid Rusty for the ranch. Perplexed, he read the letter again. What did Rusty Gast owe his sister, Betsy? And what had happened to Julia Gast's money and the money for the equipment? He assumed Gretchen was Rusty's wife who had died the year before Flint moved here. What connection did she have with Betsy? And why did Rusty feel obligated to please her, or for that matter, Betsy?

Still sorting his thoughts, Flint tucked the letter back in his pocket and watched a wagon plod by, sending dust flying into the air. Crossing the street, he entered the telegraph office and wired a note to his brother, Luke. There were some advantages to having kin whose name was famous throughout the territory--or notorious, depending upon what side of the law his boots were planted on at any given moment.

On his way back to the General Store, he tried to remember everything he knew about the old man. His memory was dim. He knew Rusty Gast had shown up at his father's plantation about seventeen years ago, searching for horses to buy. Flint was about ten years old at the time, but he vaguely remembered a heated argument in his father's study. Rusty had left with some of his father's best stock and at rock bottom prices. The men had made occasional contact with each other over the years, and it had seemed natural for his father to look him up when he moved the family West.

Up the street, he caught sight of Marcus about to enter the saloon and signaled to him. Within minutes the burly man was beside him. He was holding Julia Gast's bullwhip.

"Ah, Flint, I was just gonna wet down my throat so I could spit. You missed a funny sight back there at the ravine. Five grown men putting that fire out with the seat of their britches." He squinted at Flint. "Where's your hat? You're gonna fry your brain."

"Probably riding around the bushes with my coat."

"You lost that brand new coat you just bought? Holy bells, man, how'd that happen?"

"Swapped it with that renegade, Two Bears, for Julia Gast."

Marcus's laughter was full and rich, rumbling up from his gigantic chest.

"What's so funny?" Flint asked gruffly.

"I think Two Bears got the better deal."

Still grinning, he took the envelope Flint shoved under his nose and growing serious, quickly scanned the letter.

"What do you make of it?" Flint asked.

Marcus shrugged and shook his head. "Don't rightly know, big brother."

Flint removed the bank note and replaced the letter in the envelope. "I don't think anyone needs to know about the money just yet."

"Fine with me." Marcus nodded. "At least, it'll put us flush with the loan we took to buy the dad-burned place. If we could just get the old homestead sold back East, we could sure ease our money problems."

And buy Julia Gast out, Flint thought.

The last time he had been back to Virginia, over a year ago, he had arranged with a lawyer to sell the property to the first man with some cash in his pocket. It might have been worth something, if the damn Yanks hadn't burned every building to the ground, just like his father predicted. Now all he could do was wait until he received word from their Aunt Mildred about its disposition. The War had punched a hole in a lot of people's lives.

"You know we have to get dibs on that Gast place," Marcus warned.

Flint knew. With supplies running low and bills running up, the last thing he needed was for the water to run out. He tapped the letter on his palm. "Let's find Betsy, maybe she can make some sense of all this."

"Last time I saw her she was down at the livery stable stirring Tye into a frenzy," Marcus admitted with a grunt. "I think she wants to buy another horse."

"Confound it, Marcus, not another one."

"Hey, don't yell at me, yell at her."

Flint rubbed the back of his neck. He disliked having to spar with his sister. One, because he hated to deny her anything; and two, because her twisted logic defied the most rational thinking known to mankind. "Why do I always have to be the one who sets the brakes on her?"

The huge man grinned. "Because she already has Luke, Tye and me wrapped around her finger. She'll listen to you."

Flint snorted. "Right. Listen is about the extent of it. In the end, she'll do as she pleases."

"Most women do," Marcus said and followed it with a chuckle. Together, they turned on heel and headed toward the other side of town.

"Did you get a good look at the men who were branding?" Flint asked. He swore softly under his breath, still angry from the confrontation.

"They weren't Norwell's regular men, Flint, if that's what you mean. Hired men, nothing we can pin on Norwell or anyone else for that matter."

"They were using his brand!"

"Ah, you know that doesn't mean a darned thing."

Flint knew all right. Men would brand with whatever kind they were able to lay their hands on when they were moving cattle illegally and needed to get out of the territory fast. Many of them were even mighty handy with a cinch ring. Phony bills of sale weren't hard to come by either.

Minutes later they approached the livery stable.

A ripple of giggles floated from the open doors, and Betsy came sauntering out, her arm wound tightly around Tye's waist. In her other hand, she held his knife, glittering in the sunlight.

"Tell her to give the knife back, Flint," Tye said in a pleading voice, "before she gets hurt. I'm tired of her fast hands."

"Do like he says, Betsy," Flint ordered. "It's sharp enough to split hairs. I wish Luke had never taught you such silly nonsense like how to pickpocket."

"Not until Tye promises to look at a horse over at the blacksmith shop." She unwrapped herself from her brother, but still held the knife. "It's an Appaloosa, and looks like it could run from here to Texas without a rest."

"No, absolutely not, we're not buying a horse."

"You haven't even seen it, Flint."

"No, and that's final."

Betsy slapped the knife into Tye's palm and crossed her arms at her chest, the toe of her shoe tapped out a rapid beat in the dust.

"The horse race is next month, and word has it there's a two hundred dollar prize for first, a hundred dollars for second, and fifty for third place. That's without a little serious betting on the side. I aim to have a horse in that race. Those silly miners will be laying down gold like it was water. We could use the money."

"Have Tye race your black," Flint suggested, "it's one of the fastest around."

"No, I won't risk it, she's still healing from a stone bruise. Anyway, Tye wants to race one of his own."

He stared at her in dismay. "You're not thinking about riding in that fool race, are you? Why, if mother was still alive--."

"--Pa would have talked her into it," she countered defiantly. She nudged Marcus. "Tell him, Marcus."

"Pa would have relented," Marcus agreed, "except for a race like you're talking about. This one may not be by the rules. Those miners use every dirty trick they know to unseat a rider and take the purse. Flint is right. It's no place for a woman."

Before they could start quibbling, Flint reached into his pocket and drew out the envelope. "Does this make any sense to you?"

She read it quickly, squinting in the glare of the bright sunlight. When she finished, she looked at him, perplexed. "Rusty Gast never owed me a thing that I know of. I baked him an apple pie now and then, and mended some of his socks and shirts. That's all."

"What did he owe the store?"

"A small bill for three boxes of shells and a new pair of boots he had ordered in from Texas. Said he would pay me next week, but he was gone by then." Her voice trailed away and her eyes lost their vibrancy.

Flint looked at her thoughtfully. It wasn't difficult to see why everyone was attracted to his sister—even an old man like Rusty Gast. She was strong, resilient, funny, and beautiful. Moreover, she was the kindest person he'd ever known. Yet, was there some other piece of information Rusty Gast knew and they didn't?

"Come along, we promised to meet Julia Gast at the store," Marcus said. "I don't relish roasting myself like a stuffed chicken in this heat and the longer I do, the meaner I get."

His words made her brighten. "You're hungry, right?" she asked.

"For such a little thing, you've got a whole headful of smarts," Marcus answered and steered her toward the store.

Julia Gast was pleased the Ashmores had left her alone at the General Store. It afforded her the opportunity to browse at her leisure. The two-story building, built of rough lumber, commanded the center of town, serving the local inhabitants for miles around.

Inside, barrels of salt pork and pickles, led to a counter where oil lamps and tins of tea sat amid glass jars of candy.

Perpendicular to the counter, a long table stretched half-way down one wall and was piled high with bolts of brightly colored calico and more subdued shades of broadcloth. A painfully thin man with stooped shoulders was waiting on a lady selecting ribbons and lace. Julia suspected it was Finley, the proprietor.

Skirting a keg of nails, she moved to the back of the store, where the smell of leather was sharp from the harnesses and tack. She was so caught up in the sights and smells that she backed into a man standing in the shadows. He had a broad face with an aristocratic nose. Powerfully-built, only his head of cloud-white hair belied his age.

"Pardon me," she said, startled, as his hand reached out to steady her, "I should have been more careful."

He spoke, "You must be Rusty Gast's niece, the potter. Hard to hide a pretty woman in these parts. Harder to hide a red head."

His smile was friendly, but his gray eyes were distant and hard. "Frank Norwell, ma'am. I believe we're neighbors, temporarily, at least."

"Temporarily? Are you moving, Mr. Norwell?"

There was no denying this was a rancher of wealth and power. His boots were of the finest leather, and his coat from the finest imported wool. His stance, manner and voice radiated wealth as well.

"Please call me Frank, ma'am. No, I just assumed that once you saw those run-down shacks of your uncle's you'd be looking for a buyer."

"Oh my, certainly not yet." Julia smiled. She remembered the sound of the rustling aspen outside her bedroom window and the clear, clean water in Cherry Creek as it gurgled and tumbled its way over rocks, singing like a lullaby. She loved the soothing hoot of the owl at night, and the sweet song of the sparrows in the morning.

"I dare say, that ranch is no place for a woman. It's too far out where even stray Indians can steal you blind."

"Or rustlers branding cattle that don't belong to them," Julia said and fixed a gaze on him. On the ride into town Flint Ashmore had revealed his suspicions about Frank Norwell to her. If he was involved, he revealed nothing, except for his eyes which narrowed at her mention of rustlers.

"I'd be careful, Miss Gast," he warned.

"I will," she assured him, "and I've told my men to shoot at anyone who looks like he shouldn't be on my land."

Frank Norwell managed a wane smile. "If you should change your mind and decide to sell, please come and talk to me first. I'd be willing to pay you a more than decent sum. The springs alone are invaluable."

"Thank you, but I think I'm staying awhile," she said. She wondered whether Frank Norwell had heard the town's idle gossip and if he knew Betsy Ashmore owned the other half of the ranch. She wondered if he would make the same offer, once he found out. For now, she decided against telling him. He would find out soon enough.

Norwell turned to leave, stepping around a row of saddles slung over a crude sawhorse. He inclined his head and spoke, "Maybe we could have dinner some evening. I have a son about your age, and a cook who can make the best dishes the West could offer."

Not wanting to seem impolite, she replied, "That would be nice, once I've settled in."

"My son and I will look forward to it." He nodded and walked down the aisle toward the front of the store.

Julia watched him go. She remembered the brash, drunken young man who had accosted her and Anna on the street the other day. She already had her fill of pompous, mean-spirited men. She had fled from one in Lancaster, the last thing she wanted was to go running into the arms of another. In fact, since her father's death, it had been men who stood between her and the things she wanted the most. This time, she was determined to follow her dreams if she had to battle every man who stood in her path, starting with Flint Ashmore.

Seven

The Ashmores were waiting at the General Store when Julia returned an hour later, having taken a quick tour of the town in the company of old man Finley. A loyal friend of Rusty Gast, Finley was a permanent fixture in Golden, just like Syrus Bentley at the feed store.

Much to Julia's surprise, he set to work inviting everyone, including himself, to partake of the fried chicken Betsy had earlier prepared. A table in the back of the store was quickly set and piles of food were shuttled from the kitchen.

Julia quickly realized that the eating habits of the West were far different than what she had been used to back East. To her dismay, the group ate in almost eerie silence, with full attention to the food placed before them. They were hardly interested in lively conversation, certainly not at the expense of nourishment.

Mountains of buttermilk biscuits and chicken vanished within minutes except for one drumstick which remained like a lone sentry to guard the empty platter.

Julia's eyes circled the silent group cleaning up the smallest traces of food. Only Flint seemed disinterested.

"You ought to see them when they're not holding back," Betsy said, catching her astonished gaze. "These men can put a pack of wolves to shame."

Marcus raised his head and smiled. "A good gun, a good horse, and a good meal. What more could any man want?"

"A good woman," Betsy said wearily, "to take the burden from my shoulders."

Poker-faced, Marcus spoke, "Ah, Bets, you wouldn't know what to do without us." He speared the last drumstick with his fork and began to devour it with gusto. "What's that I smell? Apples?"

"My mother used to say this one had a nose that could smell baked goods from a mile away, but she was mistaken," Betsy said, throwing him a hopeless glance. "He has a nose that can smell baked goods from any corner of the entire territory." She rose and disappeared into the kitchen, emerging with a pan of warm cobbler.

A half hour later, Finley rose from the table to tend the store, and Tye followed wordlessly behind him, heading toward the front door.

It was Julia who spoke first, swallowing and looking tentatively at those remaining. "It seems we have a problem. I dare say my uncle has placed us in a sorry state."

"That," Flint said, idly pushing his dessert around his plate with his fork, "is hammering a nail home without wasted motion." He laid his fork aside. His dark eyes found hers, and she dropped her gaze to stare at the crumb-covered table. His anger was all too apparent. His fingers drummed irritably on the table in the oppressive silence. Beside her, Betsy and Marcus sat motionless.

"So, how do you plan to resolve this?" he finally asked.

"Me?" Julia looked up, startled.

"Yes, you," he repeated and made a sound of disgust. "You are the one who's living on half a ranch, in half a ranch house, and using equipment you don't own. You are the one who moved clear out here on only the good word of your smooth-talking uncle."

Julia's chin lifted. She took a deep breath to steady the nerves that were flailing around in the pit of her stomach like jumping beans.

"Allow me to rattle your memory a bit. Mr. Ashmore. You were the one who was so sure your bill of sale was legal, and mine was not. You have rights to half the house, so by all means, pack your belongings and come take up residence in the vacant bedroom. I can't vouch that my cooking is as excellent as your sister's, but I can assure you that Anna Holberg is capable of making some very tasty dishes."

She heard Flint snort his dissatisfaction above Marcus's long, low chuckle.

"How much would it take to convince you to sell your half and choose another tract of land?" he asked.

"You don't have enough."

His eyebrow lifted in surprise.

She added, "Anyhow, I'd need to find land with clay deposits as easily accessible as those on my uncle's property."

"Does that mean you're willing to sell?" He leaned forward and looked at her intently. "And how much would you bleed me for should I make an offer?"

"Not one fiendish drop. Someone else has already made one."

That brought Flint upright in his seat. He gave her a hard, long look. "Let me guess. Frank Norwell?"

"And I must say, he was much more charming about it," she replied defiantly. Inwardly, she was pleased Frank Norwell's offer gave her some leverage. She knew the springs that fed the creek on Rusty's land were the main source of water for Ashmore stock and everyone down stream. Right now, Flint Ashmore needed her as much as she needed him.

Flint scowled to hide his embarrassment.

"I've been thinking--" he said after a long moment of silence.

"For you, Mr. Ashmore, that could be a very dangerous activity."

"Flint," he said softly.

"Flint," she repeated, looking at dark eyes which were so powerful she felt like a flower wilting in the sun. There was something about this man that made her want to run to him and away from him at the same time.

"I was thinking," he repeated, "we should be able to come to a sensible solution which might benefit both of us. Temporarily, of course, until we can reach a suitable agreement. How many wagons do you need?"

"Just one," she managed to say, forcing herself back to the subject at hand. "You may have the other two, and half of your tack as well. I'd be willing to pay you for your generosity, but at the moment I have very little cash until I sell some pottery or my horses. In fact, I have barely enough to buy feed and pay my hired hands. If you're willing to let me remain at the ranch and take the clay, I'm willing to allow you to avail yourself of the water. I'll even warn you beforehand of any muddy water washing downstream when we work the deposits."

He chuckled. "Julia, I fear you have a brain which ticks faster than my pocket watch."

"I'll take that as a compliment," she replied, brightening. "I also need to secure a mule to help me work the clay pit. One that is not given to having temper tantrums, either. And a goat, a young one, not prone to arthritis or full of parasites."

"To keep the mule company?" Marcus asked, grinning.

"No, to keep Anna happy. She swears she will be able to provide the best pies and confections in the area, if she has one."

"I'll keep my eye out," Marcus assured her. "There's always a miner who goes belly up, or just decides to cash in while he's ahead. Mules are bought, sold and traded on a regular basis around here."

"Tell me," Julia said to Flint, "how did my uncle die?"

"He had a bad heart." Flint pushed his chair from the table. "He always had trouble when the heat was overbearing. He even complained about how hard it was to breathe. We found him on the floor next to the supper table clutching the locket of his wife, the one he willed to Betsy. He obviously had been overtaken by an attack; his head was bruised when he fell against the table. He must have known he was getting worse because he arranged all his affairs in a matter of a few days."

Grimly, Flint rose, "I am sorry, Julia, despite this little mix-up, Rusty was a good neighbor. We all miss him." He reached up unconsciously to adjust his hat, discovered he had none, and ran his hands through his unruly hair instead.

"Get me a new hat next time you put in an order to Denver," he said to Betsy. "I seem to have misplaced mine."

Julia felt her face flush. "Please put it on my bill when it comes in."

"That's not necessary," he said.

"No, I insist."

"It's my loss, Julia, not yours."

"It was my scalp, I'll pay for it, and for the vest and coat as well."

Betsy's chair scraped against the floor and she rose. "Why don't you two haggle over the clothes when they come in?" She waved her hand toward the door. "Come, Julia, I'd like to show you where I planned to display your pottery. You can even send some ring flasks down to the feed store. I'm certain Syrus will take at least a dozen to sell."

"From the sounds of things, I gather you've already discussed business operations," Flint said.

Julia's gaze slid to his. "The pottery? Of course. We worked out the details while we were ladling the food. Betsy assured me we'd come to terms with the ranch."

Flint's expression soured. "Well, the least you could have done was to tell me and eased the worry. My entire meal was ruined."

"Good thing." Julia laughed suddenly. "The way the others were shoveling it down, I was afraid there wouldn't be enough to go around."

Glumly, he sat back down. Retrieving his fork, he reached for his abandoned plate. But to his dismay, Marcus had taken it, scraped off the cobbler and was devouring the last bite.

Later, that afternoon, in the stillness of an empty store, Julia and Betsy studied a shelved corner just inside the door and tried to decide upon the best means for displaying the redware.

"Marcus recovered your whip," Betsy told Julia. "It's under the front counter."

"I must be sure to thank to Marcus." Julia smiled and pushed back a tendril of hair falling across her face. "It must be wonderful having all those brothers."

"It is, 'though sometimes I wish I had a sister to share secrets with."

"I know what you mean, my mother died when I was young and I was raised by my father's eldest sister. Flora never liked children underfoot, so I rarely had friends visit. That's how I learned to use the whip, from an old German stable hand."

"At least your dolls were safe. Mine were forced to swim in mud puddles, fly from hay lofts and wear sweaty bandannas. Tye once strapped my favorite one onto our old collie dog, and she was dragged through the dirt for an entire morning before I finally found her."

Julia smiled, imagining the scene.

Behind them, a door opened and Colin Norwell swaggered in, his guns tied low, twined around his bean pole figure like a vine. Behind him, Tom Morton followed.

"Well, well, so we meet again," Colin said to Julia.

Julia smiled. "Actually, I didn't know if you would remember."

"But of course," he replied, "no one forgets someone so lovely." He turned to Betsy. "Would you excuse us? I'd like to talk with Miss Gast."

"Certainly, Colin." Betsy nodded. "I just remembered I have a new shipment of sugar that needs my attention."

"Well, get to it. I'm sure Finley doesn't pay you to lollygag around and chat."

Despite his terse manner, Julia was surprised Betsy Ashmore didn't seem the least bit disturbed. Instead she rewarded him with a token smile and looked over at the ranch foreman. "Come, Tom, help me get a sack of sugar to take back to the ranch." She laughed good-naturedly,

"'Though I doubt we have enough in the territory to sweeten his sour mood." She hurried away before he could formulate a retort.

"Ashmores! The whole wretched lot of them ain't worth a nickel and a lame horse." Colin sneered, and around him the air vibrated with his open disgust.

Even though the light was poor, Julia could see his face was pale and his eyes, still bloodshot. She surmised he had a walloping headache to match.

"Actually, I'm rather fond of Betsy," she admitted. "She has a lively way of keeping the kettle bubbling."

He ignored her remark. "My father tells me you still plan to stay at the ranch, despite his advice."

"Yes," she admitted.

"It's going to take a lot of time and money to get that place in order. Rusty never seemed to care about the upkeep."

She nodded. "Well, I certainly have the time, that's for sure."

"And the money?"

She shrugged.

"You might consider offering your land for grazing," he suggested. "It could get you some ready cash, right fast."

"It's an idea," she agreed. Earlier, she had learned from Finley that ranchers in the area were scrambling to enlarge their herds as fast as possible, speculating that with the building of the railroad into Denver, beef would be a top commodity to sell and ship to the Eastern states. "I guess I should talk to Betsy about it."

"Betsy Ashmore?" He looked at her wide-eyed. "Why Betsy Ashmore?"

"She owns half the ranch."

He took an impulsive step toward her. "You mean two women now own that ranch?"

She nodded, and he emitted a shrill, almost derisive laugh. "God Almighty, old man Gast must have been plumb crazy."

Julia bristled, and for a fleeting moment she wished she had her hands on a fistful of clay. She would wipe that slick grin from his face, or break her arm trying. "I assure you, he was not."

Silence followed, tense and uncomfortable.

Finally Colin Norwell spoke, "Forgive me, it was a surprise, that's all."

"I'm sure it was. I understand how odd it might seem." She

scrutinized his face. He certainly didn't look regretful. She sensed he was a rash and unstable man, accustomed to saying and doing what he pleased. The thought made her feel uneasy.

"Allow me make it up to you," he offered. "I'll take you riding tomorrow and show you the layout of the land near your ranch. Some right pretty sights."

When pigs learn to pray, she thought to herself. She wasn't about to spend even a minute longer than necessary in his presence if she could help it. She stepped forward to skirt around him and hoped Betsy Ashmore was somewhere nearby. She wanted to get away, end the conversation as soon as possible. There was something eerie about this man, something she didn't like. "I'm sorry, maybe some other time. There is still so much to do at the ranch," she said apologetically.

"But you must, I insist." He clamped his hand around her wrist, halting her.

Julia glanced at his knuckles, then looked up. For a long moment their eyes held, measuring each other's mettle. She was relieved to hear someone approaching from behind.

"Let me go," she said softly.

"Only if your change your mind."

"You're too late, Colin," Betsy Ashmore said, joining them. "I've already offered to show her the whole blessed countryside." She held a sack of nails that jingled and jangled with her every movement.

"This is none of your business, Betsy." His eyes were strangely animal-like, wild and reckless.

"Why Colin Norwell, that's sheer nonsense. Everything that happens in this store is my business," Betsy said. "Now let her go, or I'll drop this blasted sack on your foot. I mean it."

"You'd better check with old man Finley first," he growled. His hand held fast. "You could lose a good customer. Our ranch does plenty of business here. Leave us be, you hear?"

"Oh, all right," Betsy agreed much to Julia's astonishment.

What happened next, she was totally unprepared for. Betsy Ashmore heaved the sack against Colin's chest. It split open and a shower of nails flew into the air, raining down over them, clinking and clanging like a chorus of bells.

She squealed.

Colin yelped, releasing her wrist.

"Now look what you've done, Colin." Betsy brushed past him and rounded a flour barrel, wiping her hands on the side of her white canvas apron. Seconds later, she dropped to her knees and began to dump fistfuls of nails into the front pocket. She muttered as she worked, "I'll be picking these out of the goods for the next two months, thanks to you."

Finley appeared at the end of the aisle. "What in Sam Hill is all the ruckus about?" His old fox eyes assessed the mayhem.

Speechless, Colin Norwell seemed more confused than angry. He removed his hat and more nails fell down melodically upon them from their hiding place in the brim.

Julia spoke first, "The sack broke and took us all by surprise, Mr. Finley." Blushing, she squatted quickly and began to help Betsy. She fought hard to control the laughter of relief that was welling up in her chest.

"Humph," Finley grunted. "I can see that. Norwell, if ye'll not be lending a hand, I'd suggest you quit pestering these ladies and be gone. There's work to be done around here."

From her position on the floor, Julia caught Betsy wink at her as she continued to jam the nails into her pocket.

"Guess it wouldn't be neighborly of me," she grumbled, squinting up at Colin, "if I didn't warn you my brothers are roaming the town."

He snorted above her head, resetting his hat. "That might be rather entertaining. I'd like to see if that oldest brother of yours is as fast as everyone says he is."

"Oh, no you don't," Finley spoke up sharply. "There'll be no gunplay here. I'll not have my establishment torn to shreds. Get on with you, skedaddle!" He turned and shuffled away, his stooped shoulders sagging.

Frowning, Betsy stood, shaking the dust from her skirts. "You know, Colin, if you bray like a mule all the time, people have the tendency to believe you are one. I'm amazed you're clever enough to use two guns at one time, and not get confused and shoot your foot off."

"Confused? Why, you never get confused." Colin Norwell's hands dropped to his holsters, but his right hand came up with thin air instead. A look of horror spread across his face.

"I swear I was wearing it when I walked in here," he said.

Betsy shook her head. "Yeah, and I'm immensely surprised you haven't forgotten your name."

"I know I had that gun," Colin insisted. His voice was near a childish whine now.

"Okay, okay," Betsy agreed. "I'll tell you what, I'll search the store as soon as I finish here, just to be sure. It's a pity when you lose a gun from a matched set. Women, I dare say, understand these things, 'cause we have the same problem with earrings."

"Earrings?" This time he all but shrieked out the word. "Earrings? Are you crazy, woman? How can you compare a set of cheap baubles with expensive Colts?"

Red-faced, he turned, stumbling over a bag of grain to reach the door.

When it closed behind him, Julia exhaled a grateful breath. The man was everything she had earlier come to believe. Cocky, reckless and frightfully stupid.

From the other side of the aisle, Finley's voice rose, then faded as he ambled to the back of the store. "There's a saying that a man's greatness is measured by his deeds. But here's another. If you want to wallop a polecat, swing lower and use a sturdier sack."

Betsy laughed, then moved to the dusty flour barrel and dipped her hand inside, sending a cloud of white billowing upward into the room. Seconds later, she fished out the Colt, dangling it from her index finger.

Julia glanced from the gun to the flour barrel and back again. Suspicions began to form in the back of her mind.

"I wonder how it got there?" she asked.

Betsy gingerly wrapped the gun in the torn cloth bag. "I suspect it must have fallen in when he was trying to tear your arm from its socket."

Hoisting herself onto a covered barrel, Julia studied the girl intensively for a few moments. There was a lot more to Betsy Ashmore than met the eye. She surveyed the damage that still needed to be rectified.

"Tell me," Julia said. "Do you know how to operate one of those things?"

"A gun?" Betsy glanced down at the cloth-wrapped weapon, then set it aside. She reached for a broom and began sweeping the scattered nails. "I have four brothers, remember?"

"Is Colin as fast as he says he is?" Julia asked.

Betsy stopped and pursed her lips a moment. "Colin? He's fast, I guess. Not as fast as Flint, and he'll never be as fast as Luke." She glanced at the door as if she expected him to return any minute, and then began to sweep once again.

"Sometimes I feel sorry for him," she continued with a grim expression, "he's got some pretty big boots to fill. Frank Norwell built a cattle empire and is counting on him to take over, but he doesn't have the brains of a tree stump, nor the know-how to do it."

"When will you tell him you found his gun?" Julia asked. It would be sheer enjoyment to linger around and hear the exchange.

The sweeping stopped, and Betsy looked up. A mischievous twinkle fought to surface in her blue eyes. "Ah, Julia, don't be ridiculous. I'm not that crazy, nor that neighborly."

Eight

Flint Ashmore sat at a corner table in the saloon, his back to the wall as he watched Marcus order whiskey at the bar. Normally, he avoided the saloon as much as possible, but he was indulging Marcus just this once. It was the end of a long week, and in an hour they'd be riding back to the ranch as soon as Betsy finished at the store.

The saloon was deserted and quiet, but he knew by nightfall it would be filled with the tinkle of glassware and the tinny sound of the old piano, never tuned since the day it arrived on a freight wagon a decade ago.

Marcus walked to the table, two glasses in his meaty grip and a bottle of whiskey in the other. Between his teeth he held an unlit cigar.

"I hope you're not going to light that thing." Flint groaned.

Marcus plopped the glasses on the table in front of them, sat down and poured them each a generous amount. "Ah, come on, Flint, you know how Betsy hates it when I try to smoke one of these any place within fifty miles of her."

"If you broke down and bought a decent one, maybe it wouldn't stink like pig dung." He removed a battered hat from his head and threw it down on the table. "And this, Marcus, you call this sorry thing a hat?"

"I don't see how you can afford to be fussy about borrowed goods when you gave yours to an Indian."

"Good Lord, if I had offered him this heap of felt, it would have been an insult."

"Yeah, and Julia Gast would be pumping out pottery in a teepee."

Flint scowled and let out a strange sigh. "She's only part of our problem. I talked with Tye and we're missing more than three dozen head of young stock from the northern valleys."

Marcus shrugged. "Cattle move around, look for better feed. Unless you want to go out, hunt 'em all down and number them with a can of paint, we have no sound evidence they're missing or someone's taking them. Maybe you ought to have a talk with Frank Norwell and ask for his help."

"Oh, yes, I'm sure he's staying awake each night waiting to lend a hand."

"Not if you confront him with that mulish attitude."

"I have a better idea," Flint said. There were a few of Norwell's hands who were honest enough men. "Maybe I'll just have a talk with Jess Williams."

Marcus shrugged noncommittally. "He's been working for Norwell long enough. Hey, what ever happened to that little widow you both were courting in Denver some time back?"

"Word has it, she married a gunsmith."

Marcus chuckled. "Must be she didn't cotton to either of you or ranch life."

"Must be," Flint agreed, not wishing to discuss the subject further. He had never had much luck with women. Most of them yearned for a soft life near town. Certainly not the kind a rancher could provide—with long tiring days, bone-chilling winters and summers that blistered lily white skin to gingerbread brown.

He looked out the front window where a veil of dust rose and pushed its way steadily up the street like a giant gray wall. Harness rattled above the clamor of hooves and snickers of horses. The afternoon stage, slung low to the ground with its springs moaning their displeasure, rolled past. From his vantage point Flint could see that every available space, including the roof and boot, was piled high with packages, boxes and baggage. Since the discovery of gold in '58 and the end of the war, people were flocking into the territory.

"They keep piling in," Marcus said as if reading his thoughts, "hoping to make that big strike that will keep them from getting dirt on their hands ever again. Pa always said if there was an honest, clean and easy way to make money, someone would have discovered it by now." He bit off the end of the cigar and lit it.

The swinging doors of the saloon opened and the stage driver entered, a mailbag slung over his scrawny shoulder. He strolled over to the table where they sat and pulled out a chair. Despite his crusty looks, Flint knew the old codger to be one of the best drivers on the line. He handled his six-hitch team Yankee style, with three of the six reins threaded between the fingers of each hand allowing him to separately maneuver each horse.

"Tye told me I could find you here," he said through tobacco-stained teeth.

Marcus laughed. "And I suppose you just figured right quick, we'd be cooling off, sipping a glass of mint tea, huh, Charlie?"

The old codger tossed the mailbag over the back of a vacant chair, sat down and rubbed his whiskers. "Just like your pa, Marcus, slick and quick with the words, but not the cash. Good friends dig deep into their pockets now and then and buy a few rounds, just to keep some warmth in the friendship, mind you."

Flint pushed his untouched glass toward the man. "Be my guest, Charlie, I'm in need of a clear head for tonight. I promised Betsy a round of poker, and I don't want her to clean me out."

"Is she still snatching things from poor unsuspecting fools?"

"I sure hope not," Flint replied dryly. "I sure wish Luke had never taught her how to pickpocket."

"Ah, but what a charming pickpocket she is." Chuckling, Charlie leaned back in his chair and took a long sip from the glass, smacking his lips. "Heard about old man Gast, must have been a blow to her, what with them being so close. He was good man, real good man. Used to sit a lot and jaw with him when I came in from a run."

"Did he ever mention he had any money problems?"

Charlie sucked on his front teeth a moment. "Well, not really, Flint. Few days before he died, he sold me these boots of his." The old man propped a dusty foot on the chair beside them. "Said they were genuine Texas leather, toes were genuine Texas alligator."

"Did he ever mention any family?"

The old codger shook his head and lowered his bowed leg. "Once mentioned a brother back East, but he never said too much about him. Oh, about once a year he gave me a letter to post from Atchison."

"Why from Atchison?" Marcus asked. He blew a puff a smoke backwards over his shoulder.

The old man shrugged. "Guess he didn't want anyone knowing his business."

Flint leaned forward. "I don't suppose you ever read the address?"

"Sure, I did. It went to a lawyer's office in Georgia. Why, something wrong?"

Flint shook his head. "No, just being curious, I guess." There was no sense in getting half the town riled up, he decided, because a crazy old fool sold his ranch twice and left it to two women.

Charlie guzzled the remaining glass of whiskey and rose. "Can you boys see to it that the mail gets to the post office? It's been a long day and I'd like to find me a soft bed."

"Will do," Flint assured him.

As soon as he left, Marcus looked over, frowning. "Well, all those details just left the pond as clear as mud. You figure this Gast gal will last?"

"I don't know. I'm hoping she runs out of money first. Lord knows she won't run out of mud."

"So what's your next move?"

"We'll send Luke East, have him check on the homestead and try to shake a few trees. Maybe there's something Aunt Mildred might remember."

"That's one conversation I'm gonna hate to miss. Sour-puss Millie and slick-talking Luke. Oh, to be the fly on the wall."

"Luke can handle her."

"Sure, there ain't a woman he can't sweet talk."

Flint smiled, genuinely amused. "Well, well, if that isn't a coyote poking fun at a fox."

Marcus laughed. "Now, Flint, you know me better, I have my priorities."

"And let me guess, learning Danish is one of them." He pushed himself upright and fished in his pocket to check his watch. "Just keep in mind, Marcus, that's the enemy's camp you're toying with." He hefted the mailbag over his shoulder. "Let's gather up Betsy and head for the ranch. Finish your drink, I'll wait outside, and for Pete's sake—"

"I know, I know, snuff out the smoke stack," Marcus said, grinning.

On the walk, Flint paused. Beside him, he heard a wagon plod by, harness rattling above the squeak of an axle in need of grease. A shaggy dog with sorrowful eyes trotted up and stopped to sniff his boots. He knelt and patted it on the head. Everything Charlie had just told him was pretty run of the mill, except for the letter to Georgia. Rusty Gast had always been a private man, but for him to post a yearly letter outside Golden just didn't make sense. It could only mean one thing. There were people in town who didn't need to know about it. But who? And who was he sending the letter to via the lawyer's office?

"Well, well, if it isn't Flint Ashmore," a voice said, interrupting his daydreaming, "and his best friend!"

Flint scowled, recognizing the voice. Colin Norwell. He rose, looking up, a sour smile tugging at his lips. He noticed the kid was wearing two mismatched guns. "Yes, Colin, dogs and horses, man's two best friends. I've always had a fondness for both. I can't say I always feel the same about mankind."

Colin Norwell sneered and tossed his head. Dirty blonde hair tumbled into animal eyes that were anything but friendly. "Lost your hat, eh, Ashmore?"

"Yes, but luckily not my gun," Flint drawled. "It must be tough trying to gun sling without it."

Colin Norwell blushed. "I just misplaced it, Ashmore, I'm sure it will turn up." His eyes flitted to the mail bag. "Golden's mail? What luck, hand it here."

Flint frowned. "Since when did you appoint yourself postmaster?"

"I didn't." Norwell snorted. "My father is expecting some important letters."

"Sorry, but you and he will have to wait, just like the rest, until it's sorted."

"Now just a minute. Who gave you the right to take charge?"

"This is U.S. Government property, Colin, and I'm delivering it as required." Eager to be rid of Norwell, Flint stepped off the walk and into the street beside a hitching rail where a horse, a skinny dun with long legs, was tied.

Without warning Colin stormed after him, stumbling over the dog and sending it howling up the walk. A look of scorn blazed its way across his face.

"Your sense of duty is touching, Ashmore." His hand shot out and grabbed for the bag. "I'm ordering you to give it here."

Ordering? Flint stopped and stared at him. That was all he needed to put a lid on his day. The last thing on earth he needed was for some wet-behind-the-ears kid, who couldn't even hang onto his guns, to order him around.

He seized the young man by the front of his shirt, lifted him off his feet and propelled him backwards like he was slinging a bed pillow.

Colin staggered and caught himself against the rail.

Nostrils wide, the dun whinnied and nervously danced sideways, kicking up a cloud of dust.

"Don't kick the dog or shove me," Flint warned in a low voice, "and don't rile the horse."

Norwell stared at him barely a second before he lunged with flying fists. Both blows intended for Flint's head missed, but he followed them with a plunging dive that knocked them both onto the street.

Hatless now, they rolled free and came to their feet, each man unbuckling his gun belt simultaneously.

Flint searched the walk for a familiar face. Cigar wedged between his teeth, Marcus pushed his stocky frame through the saloon doors and sauntered to the edge of the walk.

"I sure hope that's not a clean shirt you're wearing, 'cause Betsy will be hopping mad if you bloody it and give her more laundry." He snagged the gun belt Flint held out.

"She'll get over it."

"Not unless you win." Marcus stepped gingerly out of the way, backing up against the building to watch from a safe distance.

Flint turned his attention to Norwell, circling him cautiously. There was nothing he liked better than a toe-to-toe slugging match. He had spent many childhood hours back in Virginia sparring with his brothers. Yet, he surmised the match would not be as he had hoped. Norwell was moving in a sluggish gait. Fists held at awkward angles barely covered his face or stomach.

Swinging a hard right, Norwell came at him again. Flint stepped aside and delivered two solid punches to his middle which sent him reeling backwards.

A crowd quickly gathered, but Flint hardly noticed, his eyes fastened only on his opponent. He had never found much enjoyment in fighting in public. He had no appreciation for cowardly men who never tasted blood, who loitered outside the ring, and cheered and jeered at those who did.

Norwell backed off to catch his breath before he moved in again, storming him with upraised fists. His right connected solidly, barely missing Flint's eye, but his left was much too slow. Flint ducked it and sent each of his into Norwell's mouth and left ear.

The kid staggered backwards, spitting blood. Instantly, Flint knew he'd get no satisfaction from pounding the kid senseless. Norwell was shorter, lighter, too slow and much too inexperienced.

"Give it up, Colin," he said, panting. "Stick with cattle rustling. That's what you do best."

Norwell grunted. "I wouldn't waste my time on those scrawny things you call beef!" He swung again.

This time Flint planted another fist into his middle that sent him flying flat onto his backside in the dirt.

Fists lowered, he turned to leave. Behind him, he heard a startled gasp from the crowd, and he whirled around in time to see the kid scramble up, lunging again. He slammed him in the solar plexus, bringing him to his knees.

"Give it up, I said. This is foolish."

"I'll kill you, Ashmore," Norwell groaned.

When the kid drew himself up for the third time, Flint realized he had no choice. He smashed him hard in the left side of the jaw and sent him spinning down into the street where he lay unconscious.

With short brisk motions, he brushed the grime from his clothes, picked up his relic of a hat and shoved it on his head, then moved to retrieve his gun and the mail bag. Beside him, he heard the sound of hooves and Marcus's deep voice, "Better load up your dusty carcass and let's head for home. Best we get going before Norwell's men start drifting in. I'm not getting my knuckles skinned before supper defending you and the U.S. Mail."

Flint mounted his bay and swung it in line behind Marcus. He could feel the heat of the fight along with the warmth of the afternoon sun on his back and shoulders. Yes, it was best they were leaving now. In a few hours it would get hotter still, once Frank Norwell discovered he had flattened his insolent son and left him lying in the street, coughing up dust. Now, at least one thing was clear. He could count on the kid to come gunning for him.

Nine

Julia sat at the kitchen table, the sketch book she was working on thrown aside, hopelessly abandoned. The light from the lantern cast faded rays onto her new design. It was a pitcher. Around the edges of the paper, a group of scrawled computations encircled the page like a frame. No matter how she had tried to juggle the figures, she realized she was in desperate need of cash. There was barely enough money to last until the end of the month.

As she rose from the table to tidy the room and prepare for bed, she could feel the strain of the last two weeks. They had been long and tiring ones. With the help of Sven she had fired a load of clay she had brought with her from Pennsylvania, and for three days they had carefully tended the fireboxes of the new kiln, gradually bringing the intensity of heat to the glaring temperatures needed to harden the greenware properly. Not one piece had collapsed or been damaged in the process.

They had also spent a week digging a supply of clay from various locations along Cherry Creek and storing it in the underground cellar beneath the ranch to season. Every muscle in her body ached from the long back-breaking hours of shoveling the coarse raw earth into the wagon bed and later into the huge storage vats below. And they had collected stone. Piles and piles of flat rock. A huge pit had been sufficiently hollowed out beside the shed and now required only a snug stone liner before it was complete.

Yet, despite all this work, she was far from developing the income she needed, and she was worried. Her pottery had only begun to show signs of becoming profitable, and the few horses she owned would not provide an income for another year, unless she could increase the herd. That too, took money. Money she didn't have.

Her only consolation was that Flint Ashmore was not pressing her to settle the fate of the ranch. If he should, there was no way she could come up with any cash to bargain with him. She only hoped he was unable to lay his hands on some extra funds either.

Outside, the night was balmy and warm. A faint breeze rustled the leaves. Julia could hear the mares in the corral restlessly snort to each other.

She had given the two hired hands a well-deserved free night in Golden City, and Anna and Sven had left for Denver to collect the last of their belongings sent from the East.

It was almost strangely peaceful to be alone. She was falling in love with the land already. It was a beautiful one. Lush valleys of grass nodded in the fragrant, clean breezes that swept in from the mountains. The low ridges surrounding the ranch bore clusters of blue-green spruce and silver aspen, their tops swaying and skimming the clouds which seemed suspended from an inverted bowl of cobalt blue. And she had even become fond of the sweet song of the larks as they flitted from branch to branch and called to their mates.

With a jumble of thoughts still stirring in her head, Julia extinguished the light and headed for her room. Normally, she would have taken the lantern to prevent a fall, but in the three weeks she had spent on the ranch, she had come to know the house well, and a full moon shining through the side windows shed a soft golden glow over everything.

She barely crossed before the front window when the sound of distant gunfire punctuated the still night air. Three more shots in rapid succession followed, each growing increasingly louder. Seconds later, a bullet slammed through the front window sending a spray of glass flying through the air to land like ice crystals around her feet.

Heart thumping wildly in her chest, she dove onto the floor. Hooves thundered in the front yard. Another bullet whistled in the air and embedded itself in the thick oak door with a frightening thud.

Still on her hands and knees, Julia half-crawled, half-scrambled toward her bedroom door, silently berating herself for her carelessness. Over the last two weeks, she had faithfully practiced with her uncle's revolver under the scrutiny of Betsy Ashmore. The tiny, single shot derringer, bought from a gambler for her trip West and perfect for her reticule, was hardly sufficient protection for a ranch the size of hers. Yet, she had neglected the first basic rule Betsy had taught her: A weapon is useless unless it's loaded and within reach.

Outside the noise grew deafening. Amid more gunfire, horses whinnied and screeched. The few chickens Anna had recently bought fluttered and squawked, scurrying for cover. But it was the sound of redware shattering and snapping among the harangue that made Julia's teeth clench in frustration. Her attackers were now blindly shooting at everything in sight, including the barn, the corrals and pottery shed.

With gun in hand, she crept back to the window and peered over the sill. Several yards away in the dim splatter of moonlight, two men galloped back and forth across the front yard. A third man on a dark gelding had unlatched the gate to the corral and was herding her horses through it.

Afraid to shoot for fear of hurting the stallion or one of the mares, she hesitated, then cocked the gun and fired a shot high into the air above the man near the corral. Instantly the first two men spun their mounts and sprayed bullets at the window. Ducking beneath the sill, she heard more panes of glass explode and rain down upon her. Splinters of wood flew from the frame.

Above the din, a drum roll of hooves moved past the side of the house, then silence. Eerie silence.

She scrambled up and tore through the door. Shards of glass which had hitched a ride in her hair and on her clothes fell soundlessly onto the ground around her feet. Dust like a shroud swirled around her, and she quickly realized the yard was deserted. Squinting into the black night, she saw her attackers disappear, chasing six of her horses before them. Gun still in hand, she emptied the remaining chambers into the air.

"No, please!" she screamed at them. "Not my horses!"

Frantically she looked around. The doors to the shed, battered open, were hanging askew on torn hinges. In the moonlight, piles of broken earthenware littered the straw beneath the shelves.

With fear and anxiety clawing at her, she ran to the shed and searched the shelf above the work table. Her tin box was gone! Along with it, the torn deed and all her cash from the few pieces of pottery she had sold.

Slowly she sank to her knees, gritting her teeth to staunch the tears beginning to race down her cheeks.

"Ashmore," she said aloud as a sudden thought struck her. Only Flint Ashmore knew where she kept the tin. She had never wished to harm anyone in her entire life, but suddenly she felt a rage that made everything seem different. She stumbled up and covered the short distance to the barn where she removed a halter from the pegs along the wall.

Outside again, she whistled shrilly. A little gray mare came prancing toward her from a cluster of maples below the barn. Julia had raised the foal since birth when its mother had died. Hand-fed, the mare was more a pet than good breeding stock. It would take more than a few brazen men with noisy guns to chase Sugar away.

The horse danced toward her, and she called her by name, softly coaxing until the mare nuzzled close enough to slip the halter on. She led her to the fence and stood on the bottom rung, then hoisted herself up. The horse, accustomed to long rides without a saddle, responded as soon as she settled herself and nudged her with her knees. Together, they raced into the night.

Fifteen minutes later, when she finally drew her lathered horse into the silent front yard of the Ashmore ranch, only one lone light flickered at the far end of the sprawling, one-floor dwelling.

Sliding from her mount, Julia stared at it, fury building again in her chest like a raging river out of control. It was bad enough to try to ruin the ranch and steal her horses, but to destroy her pottery and take her money was insufferable. She picked up a fist-sized rock and heaved it toward the lone gleam of light. It sailed through the air and hit its mark, shattering the silence with the tinkling of broken glass.

A low curse followed.

The window went black.

"I'll kill you, Flint Ashmore!" She raised a threatening fist into the air. "I swear I will."

The front door flew open, and Flint Ashmore's broad shoulders appeared. He was bare from the waist up, and was still buttoning his trousers when he stepped onto the wide porch.

"What in tarnation--" he shouted, then stopped short when he saw her standing in the moonlight, waving a gun at him.

"Hold up. What's got you so riled?"

"You!" she screamed. "You stole my horses, shot up my pottery shed and ranch, and took my money. Don't deny it."

A yellow light from a lantern appeared behind Flint, and Betsy Ashmore stepped through the door. She was barefoot, in her night clothes, a thin wrap wound around her slender waist.

"Julia," she said calmly, "my brothers and I have been here all evening. In fact, I just cleaned up from a poker game about a half hour ago. How could they have possibly ridden to your place, drove off your stock and returned?"

"The tin is gone," Julia said insistently, "with my money from my pottery and the deed for the property. No one knew where I kept it, except Flint. He saw me remove the bill of sale the first day we met at the ranch." She continued to point the gun at his chest.

Flint stepped off the porch and walked toward her.

"I'm warning you, I'll kill you," she hissed. Tears began to trickle down her face and fall into the dust at her feet.

"I didn't take your stock, I didn't take your money, and I didn't vent your shed," he said evenly. "Please tell me why on earth I'd want to ruin half of my sister's holdings, Julia?"

"You want me off the ranch."

"Wrong, I want the water."

"You want your equipment, too."

He sighed. "I've gotten along quite well without it even while Rusty was still alive. Now put the gun down or use it."

He stopped a foot in front of her.

She lowered the gun to her side, and he eased it from her grip and checked the chambers.

"Next time you plan to kill me, you'd better reload."

She stared blindly at him, then suddenly let out a series of racking sobs, burying her face in her hands.

She felt his strong arms surround her as he pulled her toward him. He held her close until she gained control of her emotions. She could hear his heart hammering against her own. Somehow, it seemed so right standing there, feeling warm and safe, wrapped in his huge arms, her head against his naked chest, his hand gently stroking her hair.

"Now tell me exactly what happened," she heard him say as he led her to the porch and released her to sit on the bottom step.

Marcus appeared, leaned against the railing and gallantly offered her a handkerchief.

While she related her story between tearful outbursts, Betsy Ashmore scurried inside and reappeared with Flint's shirt, vest, hat and guns. He finished dressing while she continued, Marcus spewing questions at her like he was cross-examining her for murder.

Within minutes, Tye led two saddled horses into the yard. "They'll head south, toward Bear Creek, toward New Mexico. We get rain, we'll lose their tracks. We ride now, or we don't ride."

Flint nodded and strapped on his gun belt, barking orders to everyone in earshot. "Marcus, take Julia home, round up as much stock as you can. Betsy, get us enough food for three days ride. Tye, make sure we have sufficient ammunition."

Julia stumbled to her feet, swiping her palms across her tear-streaked face. "You're not going without me. They have my best stallion, the sorrel."

Startled by her voice, Flint swung around to face her. "Where we're headed is no place for a fancy Eastern lady, Julia. It's hard riding, rough terrain and there's plenty of wildlife." He glanced skeptically at her horse. "Besides, that little mare doesn't have a saddle and your hide won't have much skin after a few short hours. It's rugged, mean riding. This is no time to slow us down."

"I have to go," she said. The horses were the only thing she really owned. She had no money, no real home to call her own, and the fight was more hers than it was his. She looked at him with pleading eyes. "I've ridden all my life. I can keep up if you have to ride to hell and back. I promise I won't be a problem."

Tye spoke up from the shadows, "Here, she can take my Indian pony. I can catch up with you after I give Marcus a hand for an hour or so." He walked over to the pinto and slipped his rifle from his saddle scabbard and untied his saddlebags.

He glanced at Julia, then to his sister. "Better round up some decent clothes for her, Bets."

"Confound it," Flint barked, "we're wasting precious time. Throw the blasted clothes into a sack, will you? She doesn't have time to primp."

He gave her a quick, harsh once over. "If you're so hell-bent on going, I'd suggest you shuck some of those fancy petticoats. Flapping around in the breeze, they'll scare your poor horse half to death and add twenty pounds if we get wet."

Julia looked up to see all three Ashmore brothers staring like she was a freak in a traveling circus.

It was Marcus who came to her aid. He stepped forward, grabbed her gently and shoved her behind his broad back. "Get to work, you heard the man." He crossed his arms and stood like a solid wall.

Hands trembling, Julia hoisted her skirt and nimbly unfastened the thin satin ties underneath. A heap of white frills fluttered to the ground around her ankles.

In the meantime, Betsy materialized with a hat, a saddlebag full of clothes, a sack of food and a rifle.

"Give her a quick breather to change her clothes once you find the tracks," Betsy said to Flint in a tone that defied him to disobey. "Once you sink your teeth into a task, Flint Ashmore, you forget about everything and everyone around you."

She handed the saddlebag to Tye who proceeded to tie it behind Julia's saddle. The rifle followed, slipping noiselessly into the scabbard.

Julia heard Flint mumble something unintelligible beneath his breath, but he bent submissively toward his sister and allowed her to give him a quick hug before he mounted.

Betsy moved beside Julia as soon as she was astride and handed her the hat while Tye adjusted her stirrups. "I'll take care of the ranch, and see that the Holbergs and your men know what's happened," she said.

Marcus stepped forward and laid a gentle hand over hers. "Let this irksome piebald do the work for you, Julia. He's the kind that will still be running when the best are down, just give him lots of rein. Let that surly big cuss on that bay do the thinking for you, but I'd suggest you keep a tight hold on your temper 'cause Flint's a bear when he's missin' his sleep. Everything will be in order before you get back, I promise."

"Thanks, Marcus," she said, sniffling. "I owe you both a splendid meal, complete with dessert.

Marcus winked at her. "Anna's cooking? Now that's a fair trade."

She forced a weak smile. "Do you think we'll get the horses?" Silently, she begged for a glimmer of hope.

"Oh, you'll get them all right," he reassured her.

Her eyes strayed to Tye.

"Yeah, it's possible," he agreed. "If you don't kill each other trying."

"Come on, partner, enough blabbering," Flint barked out and turned his horse southward. "You still determined to make your home out here? You think this is God's country? Well, I'm about to show your some of the most god-forsaken parts of this beautiful land--if you can keep up."

"I can keep up," she replied stiffly, "but I'm not your partner, Flint Ashmore."

Suit yourself, Miss Gast, but we need to ride now." Undaunted, he thundered away, not turning once to check if she was anywhere behind him

"Oh good God, please help them to at least get along," Marcus quipped, throwing his big hands upward and looking skyward for heavenly intervention.

Betsy patted the big man's shoulder, "Marcus, they'll be just fine. Once they've ridden their hides off for a while, they'll come to terms with each other."

"Yeah," Ty muttered softly. "Like a union of two rabid dogs."

Ten

They rode relentlessly for the first few hours, angling toward the south, pushing the horses into the moonlit night and slowing them into a walk only long enough for them to regain their wind. Flint had never known any woman who could ride as well as Julia. She maintained his driving pace despite her cumbersome apparel, and she handled Tye's mount with a skill that could only come from spending endless hours in the saddle.

He was certain the rustlers would push the horses toward the foothills, away from familiar territory. Once they reached the mountains, they could lose themselves forever in the dense forests and intricate maze of canyons.

They stumbled onto the tracks an hour later at the entrance to a long valley sweeping between two sharp mountain ranges. Flint reined in his horse sharply under a cover of trees and stepped from the saddle. The night was cool, a few stars tossed in the sky.

"Why are we stopping?" Julia asked, drawing up.

"We have the trail and only two hours until daylight. It's time to get some sleep."

He watched her dismount wearily, almost losing her footing when her boot touched the ground. She grabbed the saddle horn to steady herself.

"What about Indians?" she asked, stifling a yawn.

"The horses will let us know if anyone's about."

She started to strip off the saddle.

"Here, I'll do that."

"I can pull my own weight," she said in a testy tone.

"Then pull it under a tree over there."

She started to say something, then remembered Marcus's instructions, thought better of it, and trudged away, choosing a spot strewn with pine needles at the base of a large pine.

Flint found her curled in a ball with her arm for a pillow when he returned from staking the horses. She looked like an angel, her red hair flowing over the forest floor and blending with the scarlet needles. He gently covered her with a blanket, then stepped back and sat down several yards away, studying her. He wondered what she truly thought about him. There was a strong physical attraction between them, he was certain of it. As much as it scared him, he hated to admit he might be falling in love with her.

He dozed, awakened, then dozed again.

The sky turned a misty gray, the sun still hiding beneath the horizon.

Awakening again, he saddled his bay and rode out from camp for about a half mile or more, scouring the area. The trampled trail was not difficult to follow. Obviously, the rustlers felt no one was following and had made no attempt to conceal their tracks. The trail dipped down and wound through a small grove of aspen, then crossed a noisy stream beyond.

Flint was almost ready to turn back when he checked the ground again. What he found sent an icy chill up his back. At least a half-dozen more horses had now joined with the stolen ones. They were unshod.

Grimly, he headed toward camp, his mind puzzled. Had the rustlers stolen a string of Indian ponies as well? Or had a band of renegade Ute joined them?

Julia was still asleep when he rode in. He tied his horse several yards away and quickly put together a small smokeless fire. Then he sliced bacon into a pan and took out two biscuits from the sack Betsy had prepared.

Occasionally while he worked, he glanced to where Julia lay in a heap almost hugging the base of the tree, but she continued to doze. It was the smell of coffee that brought her to her feet.

She came to stand beside him as he squatted by the fire. Her dress was dirty and crumpled, and covered with a layer of pine needles. She stretched, and he saw a look of pain flash across her face. Hard riding and hard ground were hard on the body.

He motioned to a sack several feet away, then to a gnarled oak ahead of him. "Best you change now. Past that yonder tree is a stream."

Wordlessly, she disappeared into the bushes and returned wearing a man's shirt, buckskin trousers that fit almost too perfect from Flint's perspective, and a fringed buckskin coat that fell loosely to her thighs. Flint suspected the clothes were Tye's. Julia was much too tall to wear anything belonging to Betsy. She had washed her face and fashioned her hair into one long braid that fell down her back like a thick silky rope.

Her crude trapping only accented her beauty.

She knelt before the fire, and he handed her a plate with food.

"Eat," was all he said.

"Are you always so talkative in the morning?"

He grinned at her. "Are you always so inquisitive when you wake up?"

A faint laugh bubbled through her lips. "Frankly, no, I hate having to carry on a lengthy conversation the first thing in the morning."

She accepted the scalding coffee he handed her and drank. "The horses, how far ahead of us?" she asked.

"There you go again." He looked at her with a smile in his eyes. He wondered whether he should tell her about the tracks he had found earlier, but decided against it. The girl was no fool. Only a blind person would miss them.

He drained the coffeepot and spoke, "I imagine we have less than a day's ride, if we're lucky. If they take their sweet time, maybe late this afternoon."

He watched her look at the sky with worried eyes. The sun had still not shown its rosy face. Instead, thick gray clouds floated high above them.

"Rain," she said. "Of all times for wretched rain."

Flint looked at the sky and merely grunted. Of all times for blessed rain, he thought. It would make the going tough, slow the horses and possibly wash away some signs, but it might also force the rustlers to hole up for a while and give Tye a chance to catch up with them. An extra gun always helped put a man's mind at ease.

They cleared the camp quickly. Before they mounted, Flint handed Julia her gun.

"It's loaded this time. You sure you know how to use it?"

Julia pushed a stray tendril of hair behind her ear. "I made a grave mistake the first time when I let those thieves ride away with my stock. I guess I was afraid to harm anyone. I won't make the same one again."

They mounted, swung the horses southward and rode steadily.

"Where did you learn about horses?" he asked suddenly.

"My grandfather raised them. Later when he died, my father continued where he left off, though not as seriously, what with his pottery business. As an only child, it was only natural to seek fun and companionship down in the stables with the animals."

"And speak Danish?"

"When I was young my father made frequent trips to Copenhagen to learn the trade. I spent my time in the streets with the children. I thought I was playing, and never realized until later, I was learning as well."

They arrived at the place Flint had earlier scouted and dismounted, carefully checking the trail.

"The sorrel is still with them," she said, pointing to a hoof print that showed a chip in the front shoe. "I planned to have him shod this morning." Her eyes stared curiously at the other tracks, but she said nothing.

Flint stepped into his saddle. "I take it you are not afraid of what you see."

"I've harbored fears all my life," she said. "I was afraid when my father died. I was afraid to move West. I was afraid that I wouldn't have a home, that my pottery business might not prosper. I've worried that everything I own will be taken from me, and lately it seems, my fears have been justified. What more could I possibly be afraid of?"

"Death, Julia, is something many men fear. Even I get a little skittish when I stop and think about it."

"But you still came," she said, "even though this fight is not yours."

He had no good answer for her so they rode in amicable silence, crossing a long grassy area and another small stream. In front of them, the sky turned to the color of lead and a sweeping wind spilled down from the mountains far ahead. Minutes later, the sky was ablaze with bolts of jagged lightening. Thunder rolled from the belly of the horizon.

Flint turned his horse down a long slope, sheltered on the right by a wide bank of earth and rock. His eyes searched the land until he found what he had been hoping for. An old abandoned mine lay within sight, and he urged his horse along a brush-lined trail toward it.

"This way," he yelled above the sharp cracks of thunder.

"What about the horses? We can't give up now."

"Unless those rustlers are plumb crazy, they'll stop somewhere and not move until this storm sweeps out. They've no desire to get cold and wet either."

They reached the giant mouth of the mine and clamored up the spoil pile in front of it just as the sky exploded and threw down a pelting wall of rain.

Inside the entrance, it was cool, but dry. They stripped the horses and started a small fire from the remainder of wood left by some poor soul who must have once taken shelter there as well.

Julia found a dry place on a flat rock that gave her a view of the entrance and sat down. Before her the rain poured down in a gray sheet so thick only a few feet was visible before her.

Flint threw some sticks on the fire. It caught and blazed up. "It wouldn't hurt to catch some rest," he said. "We still may have a long ride."

"I know," she said, "but I'm much too tired to sleep."

He nodded, thinking what she said made no sense and all the sense in the world. He had many times survived without sleep, solely on excitement--or fear.

"Your uncle," he asked, "didn't want to raise horses in Pennsylvania with your grandfather?" He thought it strange that Rusty Gast bought stock from his father in Virginia when his very own father and later, his brother, could have easily supplied them.

"Uncle Rusty and my grandfather were not very close," she said. "Rusty was the youngest, and Grandfather always called him wild and reckless. He was quite the lady's man, I'm told. When Grandfather died and left the ranch to my father, he created a greater rift between Uncle Rusty and my father than most could ever imagine. Uncle Rusty never felt the money he and his sister inherited was equal to what Father received."

"Yet, his devotion to the family couldn't have been completely frayed. He offered his ranch to you."

"Uncle Rusty always had a soft spot for me. The few times he came around when I was young, he would arrive with arm loads of presents, as if he understood the loneliness of an only child. Maybe it was because he had no children of his own, maybe because pampering someone else's helped take away the loss he felt. Then my father passed away."

Flint leaned back against the wall of the mine, opposite her and stretched out his legs. "So you decided to come West."

"Yes, but not at first." She hesitated, her voice faltering as she stared at her hands. "I have a surviving aunt, recently widowed, in New Orleans who urged me to visit her."

"You don't like New Orleans?" He noticed the subtle change in her demeanor, and he instinctively surmised there was more than she was telling him. Was she running from something? Or someone?

Julia shrugged. "After being raised on the outskirts of Lancaster with miles of fields, wildflowers and forests, New Orleans just seemed too stifling to even consider. Anyhow, there was no shortage of potters there, so I wrote to Uncle Rusty and asked if he knew of any land I could buy near Denver, and he suggested I buy his ranch. He was agreeable to run the stock for me in exchange for room and meals. He said it was about time someone else shouldered the worry."

She looked at him with somber eyes. "I never expected he would also pass away so quickly, before I had a chance to see him."

She rose and squatted by the fire warming her hands. "My uncle, did he ever mention me to you?"

Flint shook his head. "To be honest Rusty never said too much about anyone in his family, including his late wife."

"Rusty married when he was much older. From bits of family gossip I heard, I understand the match was not made in heaven. Rumor had it, Rusty once loved a young Southern woman who spurned him, and later married a Confederate officer. The war back East had a way of ripping families, friends and lovers apart. Thank God, it's over."

"Yes," Flint agreed, "thank God, it is." He thought about how it had ruined his family. After his mother was killed, his father was never quite the same. He had lost his zest for life, his sense of humor had waned, and his faith in mankind and religion had all but been destroyed. Even swift revenge had not been enough to sustain him. He died with his sons and daughter surrounding him, yet he had died a lonely man, still pining for his wife, still searching for a handful of happiness.

The crashing downpour continued for two more hours. Flint and Julia took turns feeding the fire and staring out into the hazy curtain before them until both grew weary and dozed.

The soft snort of Julia's mount brought them awake instantly.

"There's someone out there," Julia whispered and rolled silently to her feet.

The pinto pawed the ground and swished his tail restlessly.

Flint reached for his gun at the same moment a figure, appearing more like an apparition than a man, came barreling through the wall of rain and into the mouth of the mine. He slipped on the slick muddy ground and fell, then rolled past Julia.

She screamed and her voice echoed deep through the hollow mine. The horses shied and snickered in alarm.

The man was wearing a poncho and when he rebounded onto his feet, water spewed all over them.

"Don't shoot!" he shouted. "For heaven's sake, don't shoot." His unarmed hands flew out from the flapping garment.

Muttering a short expletive, Flint Ashmore released the hammer on his gun. "What men will do to get a little attention. About time. What took you so long?"

Before them the shivering form of Tye Ashmore slumped down near the small fire to gather warmth.

"I was hunting for a little water to fill my canteen," he shot back, rubbing his hands briskly over the flames. Water poured from his poncho and puddled on the cave floor.

Moments later, a monstrous gray horse the same color as the rain came crashing in, brushing its stout body past Julia in its haste to join the other animals and escape the weather.

Caught by surprise a second time, Julia jumped back and let out another series of blood-curdling screams.

Flint's eyes flew to her. Her back was pinned solidly against the wall. Her eyes were wide and wild, and so incredibly green, they shined like cat's eyes. She had her gun pointed in their direction and in her other hand, she held a fist-sized rock.

"It's all right, Julia," Flint said quietly. He stood motionless, afraid to make a quick move. "You can put the gun away. It's only Tye's horse."

"Uh-oh, forgot to warn you about him," Tye said, looking up. "I didn't feel right about forcing him up that slick spoil pile, so I dismounted below. I knew he'd follow me."

Rooted to the spot, she continued to stare at them, her face ashen, her hands still clenched to the gun and rock.

"Julia, listen to me," Flint urged gently again, "it's all right, put the gun down."

Slowly, she lowered the barrel of the pistol to fall parallel to her side.

"And the rock, too," he urged.

She unclenched her hand and the rock tumbled to the ground with a thud.

"Holy cow, Julia," Tye said, squinting up as the rock rolled past the fire and his feet, "you sure have an odd way of greeting folks."

Eleven

The storm continued, showing no signs of abating. There was little to do, except rest and wait in the safety of the mine.

Julia found a dry spot, farther back from the cavern's leaky mouth and slept. Tye poured water into a pot and set it over the fire, then curled into a heap and also dozed.

When the water was boiling, Flint dumped in some coffee and sat down, the cold rock wall offering a pathetic backrest for his weary body.

He was restless, and he knew sleep would not come quickly or easily. Soon he would be facing a stand-off, one that was not his. But he had accepted it, had even been drawn into it, believing it to be the right thing to do. Men like they were pursuing were ruthless, driven men who thought nothing of stealing or killing. He knew that he might have to use his guns, or even kill someone in self-defense, but it was of little consequence.

So what in tarnation was bothering him?

Julia Gast. Plain and simple.

Until recently, he had never given any serious thought to what he wanted from life. But now with the ranch starting to flourish and the cattle multiplying, he knew something was missing. A woman. He needed someone to stand beside him. And she would have to have fortitude and spunk. An agile, creative mind. He needed someone like Julia Gast.

He went to the fire, poured himself a cup of coffee, then returned to his cold stone seat. Both Tye and Julia were awake now.

Julia arose and came to sit beside him. He offered her his coffee and she took a sip, passing the cup back to him.

"I've been thinking," he said quietly.

"I've told you before not to do that," she said and smiled.

He laid a hand over hers. Her skin, fresh from sleep, was warm to his touch and felt good. She did not try to pull way, but looked at him with serious eyes.

"Julia, we have no idea what we might be getting ourselves into. It might be best if you stay here and let Tye and me go on ahead." He hoped she would be reasonable.

She was instantly on her feet. "No, I'll not stay here in some God-forsaken mine and wait until you return. You forget, those horses are mine."

"Come here," he said gently, "sit down and hear me out."

Instead, she stomped to the mouth of the cave, leaned a shoulder against the rocky wall and sullenly stared at the sheets of gray rain.

Flint glanced at Tye. He had staggered up, his muscles stiff and sore from the cold ground, and moved to the fire to pour himself a cup of coffee.

"What? What did I say wrong?" Flint asked, throwing a hand upward in the air.

Tye's eyes met his over the rim of his cup. "If you can't figure it out, I'm not going to tell you."

Irritated, Flint pushed himself erect and walked to where Julia stood, her back turned. She stiffened as his boots crunched on the gravel behind her, and he felt a drop of chilly water overhead slip down the back of his neck. He squinted upward and grimaced at the leak, cursing his rotten luck.

"Julia, I'm sorry if I injured your pride. I know you're no quitter, but you don't understand. Someone may get hurt or God forbid, killed."

"So you'll leave me here to wonder who?" she asked angrily, turning.

She stared at him. Her eyes were like green pools and he felt like he was drowning in them. It dawned on him then, like a hammer splitting his skull, that she cared about him much more than she wanted to admit. The leak was steady now, dripping on both of them, but neither could tear their eyes away from the other.

"I have an idea since you two don't seem to mind getting wet," Tye said, shattering the solitude. "If you're up for some wicked riding, we might be able to get the horses and keep our hides in tact."

"Tell us," they both said together.

"Gather your gear," he replied and splashed the remains of the coffee over the fire to douse the flames. "Explaining will only waste precious time we don't have."

They rode out into the sweeping storm, the rain showering them with its sharp stinging needles and the wind slamming against them so hard, it took Julia's breath away. The horses, disgruntled with the weather, had to be forced to follow the trail Tye chose, but after a while shouldered themselves along without being urged. The pinto Julia rode was so well-trained and sure-footed, that it plowed boldly through swirling eddies of muddy water and over rocky inclines, and she knew why Tye Ashmore valued him so highly.

The storm eased, and by the time they reached the mouth of a small canyon an hour later, it had stopped. Overhead, the sun was trying to break through and chase away the sulky gray of the sky.

Tye led them up a steep narrow trail which brought them out high above the small canyon. They halted among an outcropping of rocks and boulders strewn with brush and scrub pine. Beside them, the face of the canyon wall climbed upward to meet ragged red cliffs jutting over the floor below.

They stepped down from their saddles.

From where she stood, Julia could look clear across the canyon and into a lush valley which seemed to stretch forever before it disappeared at the base of a series of jagged blue mountains beyond. The sight was breathtaking.

"Oh, my," she whispered in awe.

"Yeah," Tye agreed. "Luke and I used to hunt horses in that valley. Funny thing, sometimes a man spends so much time trying to scratch a living from this land, he forgets to appreciate its beauty." His hand swept the rocky boulders. "There's no other way for those rustlers to pass into the foothills unless they use this route. You can have your pick of hiding places. Once they enter the pass, you make sure they don't turn back. You do know how to use a rifle?"

She shook her head. "Not very well."

"Doesn't matter," he said, undaunted. "Just point it at the face of that farthest wall and fire away. They'll get the idea quick enough."

He looked at Flint. "You get your choice, either guard the exit and me from the other side of the canyon, or I'll have the pleasure. One of us should be on the canyon floor to make some real noise."

"I'll take the canyon floor," Flint said and rubbed the scar above his eye unconsciously. "You're handier with that rifle, and I figure if you run out of shells, you can throw rocks."

"Don't blame me for marring that handsome face. I offered the other day to make you a matching scar to balance 'em out."

They grinned at one another.

"Do you think there's Ute with them?" Julia asked.

Tye shook his head. "If there were, the rustlers would be dead by now. Ute don't fancy honest white men, they have even less use for dishonest ones. From the tracks I picked out before the rain, there are only three men riding shod horses."

"The Indian ponies?" she asked.

"No riders on them."

"How long will we have to wait?"

"Half an hour or so, I reckon."

He gave her a cursory lesson with the rifle, then mounted his horse and rode back down the trail to position himself on the opposite side.

Flint turned to Julia, his face serious. "You sure you want to do this?"

"Of course not," she admitted, "but I've no choice."

"If anything happens to us, find yourself a hiding place in the brush and rocks up here and wait until everyone clears out. When you see them ride into that yonder valley, you hightail it hell-bent down this trail and back the way we came. Don't stop until you hit Golden."

He bent closer to her and she felt his warm breath fan her face. He smelled of leather, bay rum and rain. "Promise me," he said.

Julia's heart thudded in her chest.

"Promise me," he insisted.

"I promise," she said and felt his lips brush across hers as soon as the words were out. It happened so quickly, she was barely sure it happened at all. He turned before she could speak, mounted his horse and began the descent into the canyon.

She watched until he was out of sight. Carefully, she chose a well-concealed spot between two large boulders where an accompanying flat rock at their base provided a dry seat from the soggy ground. She knew it would take both men some time to find their positions, so she sat motionless, her eyes trained on the canyon floor.

Her thoughts turned to Flint Ashmore. He was a hard lonely man. Yet, beneath his tough exterior, he was a man who had his own code of ethics and wouldn't hesitate to stir up a little dust or grief if he felt someone was in trouble and needed a hand. It would have been easy for him to stand back and let her lose her stock, go belly up, and hasten his take over of the ranch and water rights. But that wasn't Flint Ashmore's way. Above all, he was an honorable man with a sense of values, fairness and justice.

Her eyes swept the canyon again, darting from the red broken cliffs across from her to the shadowed floor below. Suddenly, from the corner of her eye, she caught movement and she froze, not daring to move.

Several yards high above her, an Indian slithered onto a rocky ledge, peered over the edge, then slipped out of view. Silently, slowly, she wormed her way backwards into the thick cover of brush. She could hear her heart thudding in her ears. Her hands shook and she clasped them together, willing herself to stay calm.

Time suddenly took on new significance.

In a few minutes both Tye and Flint would be easy targets, in direct line with the brave above. Frantically, she scoured the area and discovered a small footpath winding upward through the brush. Did it lead up the mountain to the ledge or away from it? She had no time to think it through.

She set out, climbing the slippery trail, treading her way cautiously to avoid making noise. Once she slipped and fell, banging her knee on a protruding rock. As she lay sprawled, she found a broken limb the size of man's fist and picked it up, scrambling onward, ignoring the burning pain, knowing she couldn't risk firing a gun.

When, at last, she arrived near the top, she found the brave on his stomach, flattened against the ledge again. Movement below him had drawn his attention.

She crept closer.

Suddenly, like he could sense she was behind him, he turned and started to roll to his feet. Julia hefted the chunk of wood and struck him by the side of his temple. He fell to his knees, then started to rise, wobbling. She hit him again, and watched him collapse, slumping sideways, his rifle clattering on the rock beside him.

Julia grabbed it and hurried down the footpath. Quickly she tied the rifle to her horse and reached the cover of the boulders just seconds before the rustlers arrived, driving the horses before them. There were three, as Tye had earlier suspected.

They passed below Julia and rode straight toward Flint, crouched behind an outcropping of boulders. Without warning, a rifle barked and one men fell from his horse. The second man charged forward, but the third, a barrel-chested man, wheeled his horse and whipped him back toward the entrance. Julia jumped on her horse and tore down the mountain, reaching the bottom just seconds before he came plunging through.

Gun drawn, Julia blocked his path. He drew up several yards in front of her.

"Drop your gun," she ordered.

"Ah, lady," he said, his little piggy eyes glittering, "you wouldn't shoot me, would you?"

"Maybe, maybe not. You feeling exceptionally lucky?"

He urged his horse forward.

Julia snapped off a shot at his mount's front hooves, and startled, the horse reared suddenly and threw the man onto the muddy ground.

"Now, get up and drop the gun belt!"

The rustler stood and unbuckled it, letting it fall to the ground by his feet.

"Pick it up easy and fling it in that puddle over there." Julia gestured with her free hand.

"Why you little dirty--"

"You say one more thing or flinch even an inch when you reach for that belt, and I'll blow a hole in your chest to match your mouth. Fling it!"

She watched it hit the water with a splash. "Now," she snapped, "you can gather the reins from your horse and *walk* back into the canyon."

"Why can't I ride?"

"Because you weren't that generous to me when you stole my horses."

Minutes later, she found Flint sitting on a large smooth rock, his gun trained on the two rustlers. One, a slim fellow with a big ears, had taken a bad hit to his upper left arm and was staunching the flow of blood. The other, a youth Julia recognized from her encounter with the cattle rustlers, sat on a boulder nearby. Tye had not appeared.

She dismounted.

"It seems they don't know who they work for," Flint said. There was a mischievous glint in his eye. "Some sort of memory loss, I imagine."

"Hmmm." Her face took on a look of total disgust. "All right, all right. . .I say we just kill them. But I don't want to flip a coin this time to see who gets to do it. It's my turn, I need the practice."

The three men looked at her in astonishment.

"Now, just a second, lady," the barrel-chested one said.

"You can't be serious," the injured one piped up. His face was getting paler every minute.

The youth just sat there staring with wide eyes.

"She's pretty good," Flint said, rubbing his chin. "She usually tries to get you square through the heart, but sometimes she tries for the middle of the eyes. It's that head shot, that's where she loses her accuracy."

The injured man took a tentative step toward her and spoke, "We honestly don't know who hired us. We get our orders through a letter we pick up in Denver. We use the name Clyde Calhoon at the post office there. When we finish a job, we get our pay the same way."

"Liar," she snapped.

"No, honest," the youth said. "He tells it just like it is, ma'am. We had no idea we were stealing horses from a woman. All we were told was to run off the stock from the Gast ranch outside Golden City."

Somehow, she had the feeling the kid was telling the truth. "Just who is Clyde Calhoon?" she asked, facing him and eyeing him with a critical squint.

"A two-bit outlaw," the youth said, "who overestimated how fast he was with a gun. He was killed about a year ago in a saloon fight. It was Clyde who originally had the idea of getting ourselves hired without knowing who was providing the cash. We just continued with the ploy after his death."

Julia knew full well the world was full of men who were too cowardly to carry out their own wretched deeds, but willing to pay a great deal for someone else to, as long as they were never implicated.

She turned her gaze to Flint. His attention was trained on the shadowed far end of the canyon. He shook his head, drew in a disgusted breath and swore softly. "Company, Julia, best you break out your warm Eastern hospitality 'cause we're about to test it."

Julia's eyes darted to the spot.

Five Indians were wasting no time as they galloped straight toward them.

A knot tied itself in the pit of her stomach.

Grim-faced, she turned and looked in the opposite direction.

Four more Indians had slipped silently through the mouth of the canyon and were riding hard to join the first group.

Twelve

The Indians thundered through the open canyon, their erect bronzed bodies melting into the rocky landscape surrounding them. They drew their mounts to where Julia and Flint stood.

A tall Indian flew from the saddle like he had springs on his moccasins. His hair, straight and greasy, was held away from his dark eyes with a dirty, white rag wound around his forehead. The other braves held back a distance, and with grim, serious faces remained stiffly seated on their ponies. They were a ragtag lot, some dressed in grimy buckskins, others in tattered, stolen clothing of the white man.

He grinned at Julia with his toothless mouth. "Red Fox Woman?" He was wearing Flint's vest over his naked, dirt-covered chest, badly scarred from what seemed to be old, but ugly wounds.

Julia hid a smile. "I see you have not forgotten me, Two Bears. My name is Julia. Julia Gast." She thought she saw a hint of surprise flash in his fierce dark eyes.

"No man forgets a woman whose hair outshines the sun when it sets. I see you have recovered my horses, Jewel-lee-a."

"The ponies are yours?"

Two Bears grunted, his face twisting into a cruel, bitter countenance. His eyes were as cold as the rocky cliffs surrounding them. "All the horses are Two Bears! We tracked them for two days now."

"No, you've been tracking the ponies, the other horses are mine."

Two Bears laughed scornfully and thumped his chest. "Two Bears takes what Two Bears wants. I say the horses are mine."

Julia moved closer, her hand flying up in a frantic gesture. She hissed, "Six of those horses belong to me, Two Bears. You will *not* take them."

Two Bears nervously glided backwards. His gaze flashed to Flint. "I do not wish to talk to this crazy woman."

The click of a hammer broke the ensuing silence as Tye Ashmore stepped out from between two boulders, his gun leveled at Two Bears. A murmur rippled through the band and they shied their horses backwards a few yards. The animals stamped and snorted irritably under their tight reins.

"If I were you, Two Bears, I don't think I'd talk to the crazy woman either, I'd just listen," Flint suggested.

"There are more of us than you, Flint Ashmore. One signal from Two Bears and everyone could die."

"Not before Tye's bullet reaches you first. You decide whether it's worth it."

More calmly, Julia spoke, "Listen, Two Bears, I have been trailing these rustlers for over a day as well. They shot up my ranch, broke my pottery, and stole my horses. I've little doubt your ponies were also taken by these very same men. You may have what belongs to you, nothing more."

Suddenly, from the band of Indians, a young brave rode forward, shaking his fist threateningly in the air and muttering what sounded to Julia like obscenities. She noticed his temple was bruised and swollen, and caked with dried blood.

"Little Otter says you tried to kill him."

Julia's back stiffened. "Does Little Otter look dead?"

Two Bears only stared at her.

"I thought he was going to shoot at Flint or Tye," she explained. "He could have ruined the surprise we were planning for these horse thieves." She waved at the band of rustlers behind her who had now retreated a few paces and were huddled together near a pile of rocks adjacent to Flint.

Julia whirled and went to her horse where she grabbed the Indian's rifle. She strode defiantly to Little Otter, still atop his mount, and shoved it toward him.

"Tell him I am sorry for his pain. I didn't know he was scouting for your braves. I was only trying to take what was mine."

Little Otter stared at her, his once rage-filled eyes were now full of guarded caution. He nudged his prancing horse away from her.

"Tell him!" she insisted sharply.

Two Bears spoke quickly. The Indian nodded and rode forward only long enough to accept the rifle she held in her outstretched hand. He muttered another oath.

"What did he say?" she asked.

"He says you have shamed him."

"Horsefeathers! Because I'm a woman? He's a fool! When he's threatened by a rattlesnake, does he care whether it's male or female? Does he turn his back and walk away?"

Julia untied the ribbon on her braid and shook her hair loose. It tumbled down her shoulders in glittering curls of fire. "Tell him many white men say that women with hair this color have a head and heart that angers quickly. Quicker than the snake. But anyone, man or woman, who has had something stolen from him has an angry head and heart."

Two Bears nodded, and she watched as he translated. Little Otter jerked his head as if in agreement, then warily returned to the safety of the band.

"Flint Ashmore," Two Bears said, "why do you let this woman speak for you? Ute women know when to be silent."

Flint thumbed back his hat. "Your women don't have hair like fire, nor do they own a ranch or horses, or for that matter, wear pants."

"She should be taught to obey."

Flint grinned. "Granted, but take a look at her, a good look. Does she appear to be a woman who obeys?"

Two Bears eyed Julia curiously. Her clothes, covered in mud from her trek up the wet mountain path, were in a sorry state. She had tried unsuccessfully to brush the dried dirt from her coat and had only made huge brown patches of dark smudged marks instead.

"Red Fox Woman still plays in the mud?"

"Yes, and she's hauls buckets of it from the creek to keep in her shed."

"Does she still make the circles that carry water?"

Flint nodded.

Two Bears shrugged, like he understood the hopelessness of it. "These men, what will you do with them?" he asked.

"I don't know," Flint admitted.

"I will take them."

"And what will you do with them?"

"They will never steal again."

"No!" Julia interrupted, coming to the realization that their fate rested in her hands. "I don't want them dead."

"I can cut out their tongues," Two Bears offered.

Despite the revulsion crawling up from the pit of her stomach, Julia willed herself to stay calm. "It's a good idea, but it doesn't help us."

"I do not understand." The Indian looked puzzled. "They must be punished."

"No, not that way. They must be able to tell everyone for miles around that Julia Gast and Two Bears will not tolerate anyone stealing their stock."

Two Bears grunted in agreement. "It is a wise thing you say. How do we do this?"

Relieved, Julia suggested, "Why not take them to the edge of the mountains and drop them off with no horses? By the time they walk back to town, they'll understand how valuable horses are to themselves as well as Two Bears and Julia Gast."

Julia could see he liked the idea. A hint of a smile played on his lips.

"I will take their boots as well," Two Bear said smugly.

"Now just a moment, you can't--" the barrel-chested man piped up.

Julia turned on him and snapped, "He can do anything he pleases, you fool. One word from me and you could be dead, or wishing you were."

She looked at the youth. "You choose some pitiful friends. Your parents would be sorely disappointed."

"Ain't got no parents. Haven't had a family since I was twelve. You forget, ma'am, everyone needs a warm bed and a stomach that doesn't growl."

"An angry bullet can take care of that quick enough." Julia looked at Two Bears's nut brown face. He returned her stare like he was sizing her up. A slight breeze ruffled his hair making him appear wild and menacing.

"Leave their boots, otherwise we won't be certain one of them lives."

The barrel-chested man spoke again, glaring at her, "No one will live! Them Injuns are renegades. They can't be trusted. They'll kill us anyway."

Julia straightened her spine. "Do I have your word, Two Bears, they will not be harmed in any other way?"

"Yes, Red Fox Woman."

That was good enough for her. In many a white man's world rustlers were hung on the spot. These men had no idea how lucky they were. She moved to her horse and removed her ring flask. Stone-faced, she walked to the back of the band where Little Otter sat atop his horse. His eyes were still wary as she thrust the flask toward him.

"Tell Little Otter this is for his trouble. He is welcome to gather water at my creek whenever he is in need."

A slim brave broke loose from the group and raced up the canyon where three others held the string of horses. They led them to where Flint, Julia and Two Bears were gathered.

Julia heard Tye whistle and his gray came galloping through the mouth of the canyon, past the braves. He and Flint mounted.

She walked to the sorrel which was loosely tied with a woven lariat. She patted him on his stout neck and he snickered, shoving his nose into her shoulder. He appeared to be no worse for the wear. Beside her, Two Bears followed cautiously.

"What would you trade Two Bears for this fine horse?"

She shook her head. "I can't trade. The stallion was a present from my father before he died." She paused and gazed at the mounts the Indians rode. They were mostly pintos, piebald and spotted, with a few mustangs scattered in. A tough-looking lot, they were sturdy, well-fed. In the far recesses of her mind, an idea began to take form.

"You raise horses?" she heard Two Bears ask her.

"I'm trying."

"These horses of the white men," he said, "you do not want to take them?"

"No, you can keep them," Julia said, knowing full well a branded horse was of no use to her. It would be as good as stolen.

She moved to her mount and stepped into the saddle.

Two Bears stared at her for a long moment. "You are a strange woman, Jewel-lee-a Gast," he finally said. "Your magic is strong." He motioned to a brave. The warrior rode up and handed her the lead rope to one of Two Bears's ponies.

"I can't take--"

"Take it," Flint ordered in a low, harsh voice. "It's a present. Don't shame him."

She nodded curtly, and mounting, gathered the ropes from two of her own horses. She spoke, "You are welcome at my springs as well, Two Bears." She waited while Flint and Tye gathered the remaining horses. Then, she turned her mount toward the gaping mouth of the canyon and home.

The sun was rising high and the day, hot, when they finally stopped to rest an hour later. They had exchanged few words while they rode, wishing only to leave the Indians and the harsh hard land behind them.

When they found a grassy spot under some willows along a small stream, Flint set about picketing the horses while Julia and Tye started a small fire and dug into the sack of food.

"Do you think that Two Bears was telling the truth?" Julia asked Tye.

"About taking care of those rustlers?"

"He won't go back on his word, will he?"

Tye rocked back on his heels where he was kneeling, throwing together some coffee. "Most likely not, unless they give him some trouble."

Suddenly, the enormity of all that had recently transpired caught her full force and she sat down, hands trembling. What had she been thinking when she decided to make a place for herself in this strange land? She wondered what her friends would think of her if they saw her dressed in buckskin clothing and covered with mud up to her ears. And what would Charles Bloomington say if he learned she had just spent the night alone with a man she hardly knew, and a half hour arguing with a near toothless Indian?

Flint came to where they sat, dug into the sack and handed her a biscuit. "I got to say this for you, Jewel-lee-a, you sure know when to get fired up and when to back off. That hair of yours is like having a rabbit's foot in our pocket." He laughed, and Tye chuckled with him.

"I don't understand," she said, almost angered by their humor.

"Those Indians were afraid of your hair," Tye explained. "Two-Bears can't decide if you're crazy and magical, or just magical."

"I still don't understand." This time she didn't try to hide her annoyance.

"Two Bears thinks your ring flasks are clever inspirations from the gods. He already thinks your hair is a gift from them. To make matters worse, his people believe a part of your spirit goes into anything you make with your hands. So now both he and Little Otter are holding on to some very special ring flasks. Powerful medicine."

"That's crazy," she sputtered.

"No." Flint grinned, then snorted. "Two Bears thinks you are, and that only adds to the hilarity."

"What will he do with the horses?" She took a bite of the biscuit. It was dry, but served its purpose, and she was glad to have anything in her empty stomach.

"Trade them for what they need. Blankets, rifles, whiskey."

"Do they ever trade their own horses...with white people, I mean?"

"They do, but it's not a very wise thing for anyone to consider. You can't ever really trust those renegades, and the settlers around these parts get pretty riled." He rose from where he was crouched beside her. "You ready to ride?"

"Yes," she said, silently admitting she was anxious to find out how much damage would greet her at the ranch.

"Well, let's get out of here before Two Bears gets any ideas about becoming even more wealthy."

"And while we still have tongues," Tye said with a smirk.

Julia rose and began to gather their belongings. "He seemed like he could be trusted. In fact, he almost seemed like a gentleman, in a raw sort of way."

Flint's eyes met hers for a long moment before they darted across the landscape they had just covered. He started toward the area where the horses were picketed, then turned back and grabbed her roughly by the arm. Everything seemed to explode from inside him.

"No man, unless you know him well, should be trusted, Julia. Do you hear me? That's the first lesson you'll need to commit to memory if you're going to survive out here."

Julia frantically searched for something to say. "I only meant—"

"What?" he snapped. "Just what did you mean? What do you think would have happened if Two Bears had caught up with those rustlers before we did?"

Red-faced, he raged on, "I'll tell you what. He would have killed them right on the spot. And you know what else? The last thing your so-called primitive gentleman would have done was return your horses."

From inside his shirt, he withdrew a wad of bills and papers, obviously recovered from the rustlers, and slapped them into her open palm. A few fluttered to the ground.

"Easy, big brother," she heard Tye say. "It's over."

But to Julia's amazement, he offered not a word of apology. He strode off, still angry, leaving her staring at his broad back.

Embarrassed, she shoved the money into her pocket and reached to collect the rest of the money, the sack of food and her other belongings.

"Don't mind him," Tye said, kicking dirt over the fire. "Just give him a little space, a little time."

"Does he always act like that?"

Tye nodded. "Sometimes, when he's been in a tight situation, when he's needing a little sleep, or when he's protecting those he cares about."

"And what do you and your brothers do when he's like that?" she asked.

He shrugged, then smiled. "Most of the time we just sit around the bunkhouse thinking up ways to shoot him."

Thirteen

They continued to ride northward and from time to time studied their back trail, but there was no dust, no indication that they were being followed. They reached the ranch before sundown.

Julia, relieved to be home, was pleased to find the ranch in near perfect order. Repairs had been made to the pottery shed doors, and not a shard of broken redware could be found. Even the ground beneath the shelves was strewn with new layers of thick, fresh-smelling straw. After a few brief words with Anna and Sven, both Tye and Flint Ashmore begged off an invitation from Anna to stay for supper with the excuse their ranch needed attention first, not their hunger.

Julia was not surprised that Flint had barely said a word in farewell. The ride from the canyon had been a silent one, the afternoon dragging by slowly. The entire time he had been distant, irritable, lost in his thoughts. She knew he was still angry with her for being so trustful towards Two Bears.

After a warm bowl of stew and a hot soaking bath, Julia sat on her bed, combing the tangles from her wet hair. The crumpled wad of bills and papers lay beside her on her coverlet. Among them were half the torn deed and her pottery money, and an additional two hundred dollars, obviously taken from the pockets of the rustlers. She wished desperately she could use it to pay Flint for his wagon, but she needed a mule more.

A light rap on her door brought her from her thoughts.

Anna Holberg entered.

"I was wondering whether there was anything else I could get you."

"No, not unless you have a sack of money stashed somewhere. Come, Anna, sit down, tell me what's happened while I was gone."

"Oh, Julia, I was hoping to give you a few minutes to rest first." There was excitement in her voice. "Marcus thinks he has located a mule and a goat."

"Gracious," Julia said, "how will we ever afford them? The mule I may be able to swing. The goat, I'm not sure."

Anna face beamed. "Stop your worrying. Sven and I took all the pottery we could save into town. It's sold, Julia, all of it." She withdrew eight crisp ten dollar bills from her apron. "Here, look!"

Julia rose. "But how...why...what happened?"

Anna shrugged and shook her head. "As soon as everyone heard about your disaster with the horses, the pottery started selling like flap jacks. Syrus at the feed mill is completely out of ring flasks, and there's not one to be found in the store. Sven thinks we should make twice, no, triple the amount."

Julia opened her arms and tightly hugged the woman.

"Now, listen, that's not all. Marcus says the town is ripe for a bakery. He thinks we should open one."

"But what about the pottery?"

"That's just it, Julia, we could rent some space in the center of town, sell doughnuts, bakery goods and your pottery. We could take orders, too." She looked at Julia, eyes aglow. "Goodness, Julia, even you can see that little corner of the store is hardly enough space to display everything we're capable of producing."

"Anna, we have no money for rent," Julia reminded her, "and where would we ever find such a place?"

"Julia, Julia," Anna said and swiped her hand in the air, "in one week, we'll have the rent for a month. Marcus had agreed to help us locate a spot." She beamed. "We can even serve coffee to those who want to eat their pastry inside, away from bothersome flies and dust from the street."

"You don't understand, we'll need tables, and dishes and cups."

"Oh my, Julia, are you going daft? Sven can put together a few odd tables and benches with a few scraps of lumber. Dishes and mugs? We will make them, of course."

Julia stared at the animated woman. She had never seen her so happy and exuberant. Yet, everything she said made sense. The Iron Skillet was a nettle bed of dirt and grease, sluggish service, and paltry baked goods.

"I need to sleep on this, Anna."

"You sleep." The Dane patted her hand. "Sleep well. Tomorrow will be a very long day." She smiled and left.

Julia's head crumpled onto the pillow. A soft breeze blew in from the window, calming her swirling mind. She thought back to her days in Pennsylvania when the rolling green fields and dark forests brought solitude and harmony, where life seemed easy--and now, so far away. Had she made a mistake in moving to these high lonely mountains and wild endless valleys? Despite its beauty, Colorado was a bitter land. Could she ever get used to it, come to cherish it as much as she had Lancaster?

Restless, she tossed and turned on her lumpy mattress until exhaustion finally gave way to sleep.

The near-deafening noise of a disgruntled mule and bleating goats arguing outside her window brought Julia wide awake the next morning. Dressing quickly, she ran barefoot to the front porch afraid of what other disaster might have befallen her.

Marcus Ashmore stood in the yard beside a wagon heaped with bags of flour and sugar. Tied to the tailgate, a gray-haired mule brayed incessantly between the angry outcries of two skinny goats lashed to a ring beside him. One was black as ink, and the other had burnished red hair to match her own.

"You better tell me where to put them, before I put them out of their misery," Marcus shouted above the off-key trio.

Anna came through the doorway to stand beside her on the porch, and Marcus presented her with a smile wide enough to match a river in flood season.

The two women flew off the porch together.

"We'll put the mule in the farthest corral until he gets used to the horses," Julia said. "Where on earth did you find him?"

Marcus untied the lead rope from the tailgate. He yanked on it, but the beast refused to budge. "Come on, you stupid, no-brain," he pleaded, tugging again. "A miner needed some cash. Said he was pulling up stakes, going back to Missouri. He had two of these critters."

"What's his name?" Julia asked.

"Caesar."

"Like Julius?"

"Precisely." He looked at her, a twinkle in his eye. "The other was named Willard, but I saw more similarity with Caesar here, and he seemed a mite more chipper than old bag-of-bones Willard."

"He also appears to be stubborn."

"Naw, he just needs to feel welcome." Marcus jerked on the rope to no avail.

Julia stepped cautiously up to the mule and scratched his shaggy head between large, liquid brown eyes. "What a nice fellow," she crooned softly. "You just need a little attention, right? Maybe you need a friend."

The mule let out a lusty bray, and she skidded backwards in surprise. She heard Marcus roar and Anna giggle.

"Looks like he made one," Marcus said.

She gave him a scathing look. "Come on, Caesar," she coaxed and took the lead rope Marcus willingly offered her.

The mule belted out a series of complaints, then begrudgingly followed Julia out into the yard. She led him to the corral, opened the gate and unfastened the lead rope, but left the halter on. She had no desire to try to lasso him later should he prove to be belligerent. He trotted to a far corner of the corral and began to chew on some hay.

Julia made her way back toward Marcus and Anna, her bare feet padding through the filmy dust.

In the mean time, they had untied the goats and were leading them to the barn.

"How much do I owe you?" she asked Marcus, falling into step with him.

"Ah, Julia."

"Marcus, I won't take charity."

"The goats are a gift to Anna," he said, turning to wink at her. "The mule I got for a hundred, the supplies are around fifty."

Julia hurried to the house and took the bills from a drawer in her room. She met Marcus coming from the barn.

"They need a little time to adjust, I'd keep 'em tied a few days before I'd let them roam the yard," she heard him tell Anna, "and I'd be mighty careful around their flying feet."

"Here's for the mule and supplies, Marcus." Julia shoved the bills toward him. "The additional hundred is for Flint. I figure the wagon I'm using is worth at least two hundred."

Marcus shoved the money back towards her. "I don't know, Julia, best you take this up with Flint.

"No, please, Marcus." After Flint's explosion yesterday, she wasn't about to face him again. "I've inconvenienced everyone long enough." She had to tip her head to look up at him.

"Inconvenience?" Marcus chuckled. "Why, Julia, it's been a pleasure. You must know that Flint's taken a shine to you. He was itching to deliver these critters himself, only his God-awful pride got in the way. He's never been good at apologies or sharing his feelings. Why, he's worried about you being out here all alone."

Julia found herself secretly elated by Marcus's words. "I'm not alone. I have Sven and Anna, and the hands."

Marcus shoved his hands in his back pocket and shook his head. "Sven and Anna don't know how to handle a weapon. Your hired hands aren't always nearby." He looked down the road, past the barn and sheds, and studied the open meadows beyond. "To be honest, I don't like the idea of two women alone out here."

"Marcus, I thought you were on our side." Affronted, she stared wide-eyed at him.

He squinted down at her. "Now take it easy, Julia, I am on your side. But you got that stubborn pride of yours, just like Flint, that defies logic. You're as bull-headed as that pitiful mule over there, hell-bent to make it on your own without anyone's help."

"What's wrong with that?" She felt her temper beginning to simmer. She pushed the bills toward him again.

"Come, Marcus," Anna interrupted. She moved close and threaded her arm around his thick one. "You're going to fire her up as hot as that kiln we started out back. I have made peach cobbler and need your opinion. Maybe I'll sell it in the shop, ja?"

Reluctantly, he slipped the bills into his chest pocket.

Julia watched them walk to the house, heads together, sharing a laugh. So Marcus Ashmore was officially courting Anna Holberg!

Turning, she headed directly to the pottery shed. The next week she would have her work cut out for her and there would be little amusement in her life and little time to even think about something as silly as love.

The week seemed to blend itself into one long monotonous routine. From sunrise to sunset, Julia and Sven made and fired pottery. But always Julia's thoughts strayed back to the horses. If she could only find a way to secure enough money and double her herd, by spring she could double her profits.

One evening, while the moon played peek-a-boo with a cloudy sky, Julia stood by the corral petting Sugar. It was quiet in the yard, Sven and Anna already inside the house and her hired help in town playing cards. A bat swirled in the dim sky above her head, and somewhere far off in a distant tree, the owl she so loved hooted. The air smelled sweet with clover and wild roses.

"Jewel-lee-a."

The sound of her name, made her jump.

From beside the barn, an Indian moved silently toward her.

"Two Bears?"

"Your water, it is good, clear and sweet."

"It is not safe for you to be here, Two Bears," she said in a scolding whisper. "The Army has several detachments scattered about with the sole purpose of pursuing stray renegades."

"They chase their own tails in a circle, like a dog bedding down for the night." He chuckled and propped his elbows atop a splintered rail. "You have some fine horses here, Red Fox Woman."

"I need more," she said. "The winter will be harsh and I'll need money for supplies."

"This I understand well."

"I suppose you do," she mused. She thought about how horrible it would be to survive a winter, living on the run, without a stout roof overhead.

"Your home, it is many miles from here?"

"Pennsylvania, yes, far to the east."

"This Penn-sill-vane-ee-a, the winters there are not long and cold?"

"Oh, no, they are."

"Then why you come here?"

She frowned. She was not about to explain Charles Bloomington. "I don't know. I guess I've always wanted a place to call my own and since I was raised around horses, ranching seemed like the logical thing to do. Uncle Rusty promised he would help me get started."

"But you can fashion things from mud."

"Oh, the pottery," she said, smiling. "Yes, but it takes time to get started, to make enough and spread the word."

She studied him thoughtfully as his keen eyes darted over the ranch and yard like he was taking mental notes of every detail. Beneath Flint's now dirty vest, his chest looked like a map, the ugly puckered scars crisscrossing his leathery skin like trails. Julia had no doubt the wounds, when fresh, had once been very painful.

Something made him turn and he caught her staring. Their eyes held for a long time.

Finally he spoke, "You are not disgusted. Most women would turn their heads."

"I have seen many scars," she said and followed it with a sigh, "during the War."

"I have heard about this great war of the white men. I do not understand it."

She shook her head. "To be honest, neither do I. How'd you get hurt?"

"Grizzlies," he said. He thumped his chest boastfully. "Both are dead. Two Bears is not!"

Suddenly he cocked his head, listening. "Someone comes! Two riders." He stepped back and quickly faded into the long black shadows at the side of the barn.

Minutes later, Colin Norwell and Tom Morton rode in. They made no move to dismount, but sidled their horses close to the corral where she stood. Both were sweaty and dusty like they had ridden a long way.

"Evening, ma'am," Tom said. His hand went to the brim of his hat.

"You're far out of your way if you're night herding," she said.

"We're headed home from Denver," Colin said, "and just stopped to see if everything was all right. Heard the Army picked up a few renegade Indians north of here. Thought we'd warn you. You can never be too cautious."

Julia faked a smile. "No, I guess not. It's kind of you, I'll tell my men."

"Sure is going to make a muddle of Saturday night, isn't it?"

Perplexed, she stared at him. She noticed a faded bruise beneath his eye. She had heard he and Flint Ashmore had had a disagreement over the town's mail.

"Haven't you heard? There's a big dance at Finley's house on the edge of town. Everyone's invited."

"To be honest, Sven, Anna and I've spent most of the week working with the redware. We haven't been to town."

"Oh, you must come," Colin said. "Of course, you'll have to leave a few hands behind to guard the ranch."

"From what?" she asked.

"Those filthy renegades," Tom Morton said gruffly. "They'll steal you blind. Horses, cattle, anything."

Julia sighed wearily. She had already met a few white men who would do the same.

"Heard you had some trouble," he said as if reading her thoughts. "Lucky for you, you made out all right."

"Yes, well, the Ashmore brothers were certainly a big help," she admitted. "I owe them my gratitude."

Colin Norwell spoke, "I'd just be certain they don't have some hidden intent behind their kindness. I suppose you're aware they've wanted to lay their hands on this ranch since they moved here?"

She heard the icy contempt in his voice, but she had no desire to argue, nor prolong their visit, especially with Two Bears still prowling about.

Colin Norwell turned his horse and Tom Morton fell in line behind him.

"Have a good evening," he said in farewell.

Julia watched until they vanished into the western valley. Beside her, Two Bears reappeared, his moccasins silent on the dusty ground.

"Bad men." He grunted. "They would steal from their own mothers."

"Have you eaten lately?" she asked.

"Berries, some roots."

"Just berries and roots?"

When he nodded, she instructed him to wait inside the barn. She hurried to the house where she filled a tray with bread, meat and cobbler, and poured two cups of coffee. She slipped out the back door and into the barn where she set the food on an overturned wooden box.

Two Bears took the plate and sat crossed-legged in the clean straw, digging into the display before him, eating greedily with both hands.

Julia sipped her coffee, scalding hot like she liked it. She stood at the door, looking out at the night settling into a dusty deep gray. To the west, only a few rays from an orange sun fell over the land. Around her feet fire flies danced in the fading light. She wondered what she was doing, standing guard for a hungry Indian who over a month ago had almost pulled every strand of hair from her head. She remembered Flint's comment about Two Bears. He had never harmed a woman or child.

"Behind the shed," she heard Two Bears ask, "is that where you give thanks to your Great Spirit?"

Forehead wrinkled, she looked at him. "You mean--"

"Where the fires burn hot like the sun."

"It's called a kiln."

"Kiln," he repeated.

"It works like the white man's oven. The pottery must be baked with fire to be strong. Someday when no one is about I'll show it to you."

Two Bears nodded and took a bite of peach cobbler. His face lit up and he licked his fingers. "This is good! This is very good. You can make this?"

"No, Anna did," she admitted with a smile. "Tell me, Two Bears, why did you come here?"

"To help you get horses. Many horses."

"Horses? My goodness. Why would you want to do that?" It was the last thing she expected.

"Because you need them," he simply said. "Rusty Gast was a fair man. When he was young he found me shot by white men. He brought me here, hid me in this very same barn, and tended my wounds."

Julia crossed her arms at her chest and glared at him. "Do you have any earthly idea what would happen if anyone discovered I was dealing in stolen horses?"

Two Bears rolled to his feet. His face radiated the anger of a man gravely insulted. "Two Bears is no fool, Jewel-lee-a Gast. Stolen horses are only good to trade far across the borders, or to Cheyenne and Arapaho. No, I get wild horses from the valleys near the big mountains, many miles southwest."

"How could I ever pay you for them?" she asked, confused.

"I need supplies."

"Horsefeathers! I could get my neck stretched for that."

Two Bears grinned a toothless grin. "You get the money, Two Bears gets his own supplies."

"Around here?"

He snorted. "It is not so difficult."

Julia bit her lower lip. What he was proposing was ludicrous. Yet, if she was shrewd enough, she could have a good chunk of cash in almost no time at all. And she needn't do it forever—just until the ranch was on its feet, and the shop in town was flourishing. Who would know? What harm could possibly come of it?

"I have to think about this," she said. "This is dangerous."

"Life is dangerous, Jewel-lee-a."

She was silent for a moment, weighing his words, weighing the possibilities.

"Leave three small stones by the farthest post of your corral if you wish to talk to me again. We can meet at a gulch on Ashmore property across Cherry Creek ."

Julia nodded. "There's only one problem. I have no idea where I could sell the horses that quickly."

Two Bears grunted. "I know where you can sell them faster than Two Bears can get them."

"Where?" she asked.

The Indian's eyes flickered in merriment. He grinned his toothless grin. "To my enemy, Red Fox Woman. The Army."

Fourteen

Julia was drawing a bucket of water to use in the pottery shed when a deputy from the sheriff's office in Golden City rode up at the end of the week.

"Have a prisoner who says he knows you," he said without bothering to dismount.

"Me?" Julia frowned. "Why, I've barely been here a few weeks. Certainly, not long enough to know anyone who would get himself in trouble with the law."

"Didn't think so, ma'am, I knew the kid was lying," the deputy said. He was a tall gangly man, and his eyes were sharp and assessing. "Sorry to have bothered you." He turned his horse toward town.

"Wait," Julia called out. Her thoughts flew back to the young man in the canyon. "On second thought, tell the sheriff I'll stop by." She had planned to ride into Golden later in the morning.

"Want me to wait and ride with you?" he asked politely.

"No, that's quite all right, Deputy. I've a few more chores to do before I can leave."

"Suit yourself, ma'am." He tipped his hat and departed.

She went back to her work, listening until the rattle of hooves faded away.

Earlier, Anna and Sven had left for town with the first wagon load of pottery tucked securely between layers of straw. Flint had found a small shop in the center of town, abandoned by a seamstress who had moved to a larger house. The Holbergs had been eager to explore the place. It came complete with a stove and counter and seemed almost too good to be true.

The entire week she had pondered over Two Bears proposal and had finally decided, against her better judgment, that horses were in her blood, no matter how hard she tried to resist. She would have to plan carefully. No one must ever suspect she was working with a renegade.

Two hours later, she entered the sheriff's office, a low, wood-framed building on the east side of town.

Sheriff Anderson stumbled from his seat, rubbing his scraggly beard. He was a big man with a bigger stomach that hid his belt well, and he was obviously unaccustomed to having lady visitors. He shoved his stubby fingers over his unkempt head to try to flatten his hair.

"I understand you have a prisoner who's asking for me," she said.

The sheriff spoke, "The potter. Why, yes, of course. Strange kid, this one, can't seem to stay out of fights and trouble." He leaned toward her and added in a low whiskey-laced voice, "I think, perhaps, he's playing a game. This is the only place around that offers three square meals and a clean bed."

He led her to a room in back where four small cells lined the perimeter. On a bunk in the farthest cell, a slim young man lay sleeping. His lips were swollen and cut, and the left side of his face looked like it had been battered with a pick handle.

"Git up, Toby," the sheriff bellowed. "Got yourself a visitor." He leaned against the bars of the adjoining cell, but made no move to leave.

Julia watched the boy stagger up, swinging his legs over the edge of the cot, holding his side painfully as he stood. He was the same kid she and Flint had tangled with over her stolen horses.

"You!" she said. "I should have known."

He tried to grin, but only a painful lopsided smile emerged between his jaws.

"Ma'am, you are the only person I could think of to ask for help. Sheriff Anderson is threatening to take my horse, gun and saddle in payment for his kind hospitality."

"You're right about that, son," Anderson assured him and hooked his thumbs behind his belt. "I'm getting tired of playing hotel manager to a stupid kid who doesn't know how to stay out of trouble. Isn't it about time you found yourself a job?"

"Who'd hire me?" Toby touched his fingers gingerly to his puffy face and winced.

"That must be the second smart thing you've said all morning. Go South. There's plenty of ranches down in Texas where your reputation won't beat you there." He glanced at Julia and shook his head. "His pa must be doing belly flops in his grave. One of the best bronc busters in the territory before he died."

Julia gave Toby a sharp, penetrating look. "Just how good are you?"

"Almost as good as my pa."

"That's a stretch, if I ever heard it," the sheriff said. "He's only good if he can stay away from cards, rye whiskey, and fast ways to make a buck. First thing you know, he's going to get involved in stealing horses and I won't be able to help him. His neck will be stretched by a vigilante group. Men here don't cotton to horse thieves."

"How much does he owe you?" Julia asked. A plan started to form in the back of her mind. She would need a good bronc buster to tame the stock she sold to the Army.

"I'd let him go for ten, if he promises he'll never come back."

Julia pulled a gold eagle from her pocket. "Oh, he won't be back. I've got enough work at the ranch to keep him busy from sunrise to sunset."

"Now just a moment, I never said I would work for you." The words were uttered through a painful groan.

"Fine." Julia whirled and headed for the door. "How much you selling his gun for, Sheriff?"

"Now hold up a bit." Toby hobbled to the bars and gripped them, his nose pushed into the corridor. "All right, all right! I'll work for you—but only 'til the ten is paid."

Julia waited patiently while the sheriff set him free and rounded up his belongings.

Out on the street, she yanked him by his sleeve toward a quiet alley between two shops. "The first thing you do is get yourself cleaned up," she ordered and fished another coin from her pocket. "Then I want you to ride south to Pueblo and find out what price the Army is asking for fresh stock. Keep your ears open and that cocky mouth of yours closed. Get the name of someone who has supplied them in the past."

Toby squinted at her with puzzled eyes. "Crazy lady, what you're saying would make a coyote roll over and laugh."

"It's Julia, Julia Gast, and your job is to do as I say, whether it makes sense or not."

"What makes you so sure I'll do it? In fact, how can you be sure I'll even return?" he asked boldly.

Julia grabbed a fistful of his shirt and rattled him none too gently. He groaned out a painful expletive. "What are you trying to do, finish me off?"

"Now you listen up," she hissed. "You'll do exactly as I say, or I'll march right back into that sheriff's office and tell him you *are* a horse thief. The sheriff told you what they do to horse thieves in this town."

"I'll be long gone, lady, before anyone can even cinch his saddle." He pulled his body erect and attempted a smug grin, grimacing again from the pain.

"Horsefeathers!" She laughed and a smug look settled on her face. "You're as dumb as a mushroom. Try it, and I'll put a price on your head big enough to entice every bounty hunter in the territory to go looking for you." She watched his face lose its boastful luster.

"Now, go," she said, pushing him toward the main street, "and when you return, you're going to show me just how good a bronc buster you really are."

Flint and Marcus Ashmore were at the seamstress shop when Julia arrived an hour later. It was a spacious shop with shelves lining the wall behind the counter that must have at one time held yard goods, and spools of lace and ribbon.

Anna and Sven were already in the back examining what would be the kitchen and baking area.

"What do you think?" Marcus asked, confronting her before she had a chance to look around. "We could build more shelves against these two opposite walls. Diners could sit for a spell here in the center, eat, and have your pottery right at their fingertips to buy. Take only a day or two to construct the whole lot." He looked at her with hopeful eyes.

Julia remembered Sven saying that Marcus enjoyed working with his hands and had diligently worked beside him, helping to make the necessary repairs to the ranch after it had been ransacked.

"It looks perfect, Marcus, exactly what we need."

"You'll take it, then." He grinned. "Those miners will be standing in line to satisfy their sweet cravings, count on it."

"And count on Marcus Ashmore to be at the head of the pack," Flint said, smartly swatting Marcus on his huge, muscular shoulder.

The big man laughed heartily. There was excitement in his voice and energy in his step as he bounded toward the back. "I'll go tell Anna. We can get started on it today."

Flint inhaled deeply, then exhaled. "Looks like I'll be short a ranch hand for a few days."

Julia bit her lower lip. "I'm sorry. I didn't mean to cause you more trouble."

"We'll manage. To be honest, I've never seen Marcus so worked up for a long while."

"It may not be the bakery," Julia said and glanced up at him. He was tall and powerful, and he made her feel small, despite her height. "You're not angry with me?"

He smiled crookedly. "Should I be?"

"I don't know." She managed to return his smile even though she had the urge to reach out and strangle him. He couldn't have possibly forgotten his explosive behavior the day they recovered her horses. But then, Marcus had accused them both of being bull-headed and prideful. Maybe it was time to try some humility, she decided.

"I never had the time to properly thank you for helping me get my horses."

He shrugged. "So what's stopping you now?"

"Over coffee?"

"I'll buy. I know where the cheapest cup can be found."

"No, Flint, this is on me." Her gaze slid to the kitchen where the sound of Marcus's deep laughter mingled with Anna's cheery voice. "What about those two?"

Gently, his hand touched her elbow as he steered her toward the door. "Do you really think they'll even notice we've left?" he asked.

Outside, Flint and Julia walked in silence toward the General Store. Bright sunlight bathed the dusty street, and a light breeze carried the smell of hot grease and beef frying on a stove. A man loafing in front of the gunsmith's shop with a rifle in his hand looked up as they passed by. Farther beyond, two of Norwell's men stood outside the saloon.

Flint lifted his head and watched the townsfolk move about. Any other time, he would have felt pleased to have the company of a woman beside him as they walked together, but today, for some odd reason, he suddenly felt cautious and uneasy. His feelings did not go unrewarded.

A few feet ahead of them, Colin Norwell stepped out from telegraph office and turned to face them. Behind him, Tom Morton came sauntering up the wooden walk.

"Well, now, if it isn't Flint Ashmore," Colin said, his eyes shooting poison. "I've been looking for you for some time now."

"I'm never hard to find." Around him, Flint heard people scurrying from the area, getting out of the way of any gunfire. "You only have to ask one of my brothers. Most of the time they can pinpoint my whereabouts."

"We've a score to settle." Colin Norwell stood straight as a poker, his jaw so tight a tic flickered high on the side of his cheekbone.

Flint could see that he was itching for gunplay. He had replaced the Colt he had lost and now wore a matching set again.

"Sorry, Colin, not here. Not now."

The kid's face went black with anger. "Here's as good a place as any."

Flint stared at him a moment, then suddenly smiled. He stepped up to a post and leaned a shoulder nonchalantly against it. "No, not now, you see Julia has promised me a cup of coffee, and I don't aim to get shot before I get it. It's not often a pretty red-head is offering to buy, and I'm going to try to weasel a doughnut from her as well."

The remark caught Norwell flatfooted. Stunned, he looked blankly at Flint at a loss for words.

"Anyway, Colin," Flint continued, "I don't think either of us wants to risk dying for a few letters you've already read."

"Never figured you for a coward," Tom Morton snarled from behind Norwell.

Flint looked past Colin's stiff shoulders at Morton. The foreman's sun-weathered face was unreadable. Was he trying to urge the kid on and get him killed? Or was the slur merely meant to anger him and take him off-guard?

"I never figured you to interfere in another man's fight either, Morton. But then, I doubt you'd understand my reason, anyhow."

Baffled, Colin Norwell squinted at him. "Let's hear it, Ashmore." His earlier raw tension was now replaced with curious interest.

Flint knew he had him just where he wanted him. The kid was all ears. "Remember, Colin, when Golden City became the territorial capital and the town had the biggest celebration ever?" he asked. "Even bigger than the ones that followed some of the best strikes?"

"I don't follow you, Ashmore."

Flint grinned at him with a whimsical grin. "Ah, Colin, don't tell me you already forgot the gal you danced with that night?"

"Your sister, she'd just turned fifteen."

"Recall what she was wearing?"

"Sure, I remember, a green dress. She likes green."

"Yeah, pure silk, to be exact." Flint thumbed back his hat and raised an eyebrow. "Did it ever cross your mind how a poor rancher's kid could show up looking like the belle of the ball when her pa, still struggling to get started, couldn't even make feed payments for stock?"

Colin Norwell spoke, "Rusty Gast. It was Rusty Gast who scared up that dress, I remember her telling me."

"And where would Rusty Gast have ever dug up a dress so beautiful? Think, Colin, who in town was the same size, height and coloring as my sister?"

"My mother?" Norwell's voice rose in surprise. "So that's why my father was riled that night. I thought it was because I'd spent the entire night dancing with the poor rancher's daughter whose father had swiped the best prime grazing land right out from under his nose. But here Mother had supplied her with a dress."

Flint smiled. After the celebration, rumor about town was that Virginia and Frank had argued so heatedly and she was so angered by her husband's behavior she pitched him out of the house and made him sleep in the bunkhouse for a week. She was known to be a salty, little woman, maybe tougher than Norwell himself. And Virginia Norwell, had been an influential figure in all the church and ladies' groups about town. With one wave of her hand, she could have shut Betsy out, shunned her from every sewing circle and community gathering. Instead, she had done the opposite, even making arrangements to get Betsy hired on at the General Store so she'd have some extra cash. Her sudden death from cholera, two years ago, had taken everyone by shock, including Betsy herself.

"So you see, Colin, where we stand? I don't give a tinkers damn about you or your father, but I sure do have a lot of admiration for your mother and—"

Up the street Betsy Ashmore had stepped out onto the walk in front of the General Store and was staring curiously at them.

"—I've others to consider."

Colin Norwell looked over his shoulder and stared at the girl for a long moment. "I understand, Ashmore, another time," he said quietly, pensively, and stepped aside.

"What?" Tom Morton snarled. "You mean you're going to call off a fight because of a silly green dress?"

"Shut up, will you, Morton?" Colin turned on him. "This conversation doesn't concern you!"

The ranch foreman's face darkened in anger, but he obediently fell silent.

Colin Norwell tipped his hat to Julia. "I hope your coffee is still hot, ma'am. Sorry for the delay."

"I hope so, too," Julia said with a smile, "and it will be the last cup Flint will get free. Anna, Sven and I are opening a bakery, and in the next couple of weeks, we'll have fresh baked goods and hot, strong coffee for any man with a hunger and some cash. Spread the word, will you?"

Minutes later, Flint and Julia were seated in the back of the General Store. It was a quiet day, with very few people loitering about. They spoke briefly about the lingering hot weather, the water shortage, and the fact that Flint had still not discovered who had been responsible for stealing Julia's horses. He had regularly checked the post office in Denver over the past week. No additional letters had been delivered to Clyde Calhoon.

"You could have killed him," Julia said, referring to the earlier confrontation on the street.

"Colin Norwell? He could very well have killed me."

"But you didn't want to," she countered bluntly.

"Fight him?"

She nodded.

"No, the war between the Ashmores and Frank Norwell started way back when my father came. Frank Norwell never expected my father to settle where he did. It was first rate grazing land, but with little water. Well, Pa went to your uncle and bought a tract of his land that adjoined ours and stretched clear to the creek with the understanding that during dry times, Rusty would allow him to water his cattle."

"A clever idea," Julia said.

"Yes, unfortunately Frank Norwell was angry he hadn't thought of it. I suspect he wanted to bottle up Golden and own most of the land around it. With the railroad coming, no one would be able to get their cattle in without crossing his land, and for a price. I also think that was one reason Rusty Gast gave Betsy half the ranch. To keep our water rights secure."

"So you still think Norwell is behind the cattle rustling?"

"Who else? Who else stands to gain by crippling our herds in hopes of squeezing us off our land?"

From his chest pocket, Flint pulled the five twenty dollar bills Marcus had given him and tossed them on the table. "I never asked for any payment."

Julia stiffened and sat upright in her chair. "I know, but I'm using your equipment."

"Take the money and use it as an investment in the bakery shop."

"Oh, no!" She pushed the bills toward him. She owed him too much already. She couldn't afford to have strings attached to the shop as well.

"You'll need lumber, Julia, cloth for the tables, and silverware. This is no time to be proud."

"Proud? Why, right now you own almost everything on that ranch, except for a few horses and the clothes on my back."

"You're a beautiful woman, Julia," he said softly and leaned towards her. "Why not just marry me and have your pick of everything I own? It's not much yet, but we're square. In a few years, it'll be a mighty profitable spread."

Startled, Julia stared at him. She had never seen his eyes more grave and serious. Yet, she had never dreamed a marriage proposal could be so direct and emotionless. From somewhere outside she smelled the sickening scent of hot tar waft though an open window and her stomach began to churn.

"What's wrong?" he asked.

Fighting back tears, she forced herself to speak. "That has to be the most practical solution to my problems I've ever heard, Flint Ashmore."

"Julia, we're both very practical people, far beyond the age where blinding romance need be the only reason for marriage. I care a great deal about you, more than I have for any woman. Love, well, many people have a lot of definitions for it. My mother said admiration and caring must come first, then real love will follow with time."

"It wouldn't work," she finally said after a long uncomfortable pause.

"Why the devil not?"

"Because someday, when things have a way of getting rocky in a marriage, you'd wonder whether I accepted your proposal because I was penniless, without a choice. And I'd always wonder whether I'd sold myself short. Did I give myself a fair shake, enough time to make my own way in the world?"

"That's ridiculous." Annoyance clouded his face.

"I wish I was wrong," she said, "but I fear I'm not."

"I guess that's as polite a way as I've ever heard to tell a man to keep riding."

"No, you don't understand." She laid a hand gently over his. "It's not you, Flint, it's me. Don't you see, I gave up everything to come here? I have to try."

"How long?"

She shrugged.

"And what happens if you fail?"

She shrugged again. "Maybe I'll cash in, go East, back to a land and people I understand. Maybe South, to New Orleans. Who knows? And if that were the case, your generous offer might be for naught, anyhow."

His voice hardened. "But you can't just give up and leave—"

A hinge creaked and Betsy Ashmore appeared from the back room. Julia breathed a sigh of relief. Betsy's arrival couldn't have come at a more perfect time. It wasn't easy to hurt someone you respected and cared about, and maybe, even loved.

Flint rose glumly. "I've got some supplies to get loaded." His eyes found Julia's. "Take your time then, but think about what I said." He left the bills lying on the table.

As soon as he departed, Betsy spoke, "Please forgive me, Julia, I didn't mean to interrupt anything."

"No, no," Julia assured her. "Your brother and I were just discussing. . .some business." She smiled a tentative smile, "I need to get in contact with someone who's in charge of buying stock for the Army."

She expected Betsy Ashmore to ask a dozen questions she was not prepared to answer. Instead, Betsy gave an innocent toss of her shoulders and said, "That's not difficult, there's at least a half dozen brass buttons wandering the streets who can help you."

Fifteen

Julia hoisted a crate from the wagon tied outside the new bakery and felt a trickle of sweat drip down her neck. Above her, the blistering sun beat down unrelenting rays. Her hair, earlier pulled into a bun, had long since come undone and hung heavy on her shoulders like a blanket.

Without a doubt, she and Anna had chosen the hottest day of the year to move all the furniture, equipment and pottery into town.

Inside the bakery, a thundering crash split the still air, followed by a stream of colorful expletives. Julia lifted her head toward the disturbance, easily recognizing Flint's voice. Seconds later, the deep, rumbling laughter of Marcus rocked the room and floated out the door.

She sighed. Only Anna and he seemed immune to the intense heat. But then, it was obvious to everyone that they were in love. Silly, she thought, that the heat of passion could blind you to everything around you, including the weather.

Flint came through the bakery door, just as she trudged to the walk with the crate.

"Here, let me have that," he said, scowling. "You need to slow down before you pass out."

She was grateful for his help. Since dawn she had been up and about, unloading the kiln, packing crates and loading the wagon. She spoke, "Sounds like we had a little mishap."

He gave her a sour smile. "I think I just bought a set of plates and cups that no one will ever use."

He had rolled his shirt sleeves to his elbows and was drenched in sweat. His head, hatless, was a mass of wet dark curls, and he looked more like a disheveled boy than his usual cool and aloof self. Her heart skipped a beat and she had to resist the urge to reach out and brush the errant strands from his forehead.

"Don't worry, we can make more, now that Caesar, and Ludwig and Lucinda are doing their share."

"Caesar?"

"Yes, the mule. He is a real help."

"Ludwig and Lucinda?"

"The goats."

"You named the goats, too?" His face crinkled in amazement.

"I always name the animals."

In fact, she had named her pets and all the farm animals since she was a child back in Lancaster. She remembered Two Bears telling her that every living thing had a spirit. It helped her to feel less silly about the whole procedure, now that she was still carrying on the habit as an adult.

He grinned impishly. "Just don't start naming my cattle, Julia. I don't want to sit down to a steak dinner and wonder whether I'm devouring Blossom or Bessie."

"I promise I won't. I'd probably run out of names before I ran out of cattle." She laughed and followed him inside.

The room looked worse than the tool shed she had tackled shortly after she arrived at the ranch. Boxes and furniture were scattered about the room with only small pathways between. But she could see from the flushed exuberant face of Anna that the mayhem was heaven to her. She bustled about, giving orders to Marcus, Sven and Toby.

"How much more?" Toby asked, grumbling, looking up at Julia as she wound her way to the back of the room. He was unpacking a box of pots and crocks. "To be honest, ma'am, I'm a bronc buster, and this type of domestic work tries a man's patience."

"There are only a few more wagon loads left at the ranch," she said, hoping it would placate him.

Behind her, Flint leaned against a stack of crates and wiped the sweat from his forehead with the back of his wrist.

"It'll be easier with another wagon," he said. "I'll get my horse at the livery. Julia, you ride ahead to the ranch and I'll meet you there. At the rate we're progressing, we'll be wading through three feet of snow before we ever finish."

"That's a good idea," Julia agreed, following him back outside where they parted. Wearily, she reached for another crate.

"Need some help with that?" a familiar voice asked.

Frank Norwell looked down at her from the walk. A smile played on his lips. He looked anything but dusty and tired. A copy of the *Rocky Mountain News*, fresh out of Denver, was tucked beneath his arm.

"No, no, I can get it," she said, embarrassed that he should see her in such a dirty, disheveled state.

"Here," he said taking charge and signaling for two of his men farther up the walk. "You look like you're about done in."

As soon as his hands arrived, he spoke, "Unload this wagon and have the Danish woman tell you where to put the crates."

"Honestly, you really needn't do this," Julia said.

"Don't be silly." Norwell stepped onto the street and took her gently by the arm. "Come, walk with me, Julia."

She looked up at his old weathered face, framed by his signature snow white hair. "I don't think that would be wise." The last thing she wanted was to be caught in the company of Frank Norwell.

"If you're afraid, you can bring Anna," he offered gently.

"No," she replied, "it's just not a good idea."

"Come," he coaxed, "you need a break."

He looked toward the stables. "If it's Flint Ashmore, you're worried about," he said, as if reading her thoughts, "I assure you, I'll have you back soon enough."

Reluctantly, Julia let him lead her up the walk. They crossed the street and strolled, wordlessly, toward the blacksmith's shop, a faint breeze fanning their faces. Under the trees beside it, he ushered her to a small wooden bench where they sat down.

"If it's the ranch," she said. "I'm not willing to sell."

"It's not the ranch, Julia." He withdrew the newspaper, handing to it her. "I picked this up in Denver yesterday."

Julia quickly read the advertisement on the back page. *Reward: One hundred dollars for the whereabouts of a female potter from Pennsylvania. Tall with red hair. May be using the name Gast. Contact C. Bloomington, Lancaster, Pennsylvania.*

Julia felt her face go white. Her heart began to pound wildly in her chest, and a buzzing began inside her head. She willed herself not to pass out.

She stared at the article again. All her dreams and hopes for a new life shattered before her eyes.

"Would you like to explain?" he asked gently.

Her eyes filled with tears, and she turned away to hide them.

"Here, here," he said, patting her hand with his big, solid one. "It can't be all that bad."

No, it was worse, she thought. Charles Bloomington would hunt her down and ruin her. He was not one to take humiliation lightly.

"He was my fiancé," she managed to say.

"And you obviously didn't love him."

She nodded.

"Did he love you?"

"Oh, he loved me all right," she choked out. "He loved my horses, my farm back East, and every penny my father and I earned before he died."

She wiped away an errant tear about to spill down her face with the back of her hand. "I left him standing at the altar, a slight he's obviously not going to forget."

And now he was going to disrupt or destroy every plan she had for a new life. She remembered the engagement ring, still lying in a drawer in her bedroom. It would do little good to even try to return it. It meant nothing to him. He was a wounded man with a heart wrapped in ice. And he was obviously out for revenge.

"There's nothing I can do," she said wearily.

"You're giving up?"

She couldn't decide whether it was disbelief or a gentle scolding she heard in Frank Norwell's voice.

She spoke, "My choices are limited, Mr. Norwell." In fact, she thought, there weren't many at all. She could marry someone like Flint Ashmore and hope it would deter Bloomington, or she could try running. Perhaps change her name, go even farther West.

"You know," she heard Frank Norwell say, "this territory was settled by people who had a lot of grit and little cash. Ever wonder why you don't hear about the losers?"

She shook her head.

"Because they turned tail and ran."

"I don't understand," she said in an irritable tone. "I can bet that in less than a week, Bloomington will be sitting on my stoop. Any man would be a fool to let an easy one hundred dollars reward slip through his hands. I can't exactly hide with this red hair, either."

"Sometimes, my dear, a war is won by stalling for time to lay down tactics."

"I don't understand." She was confused.

"The newspapers will be arriving on the afternoon stage," he explained. "Why make it easy for someone to collect the reward?"

"Buy the newspapers?" she asked, shocked. "*All* of them?"

"It can be arranged."

"Isn't that a rather dishonest thing to do?"

"My dear, if the good people of Golden miss the news for a week, their lives won't be any more miserable than yours will be if they read that advertisement. And the editor of the *News* gets his money anyhow."

Their eyes met and held, and an amusing smile formed on his face. "If you like, I can take care of it."

"Why--why are you doing this?" she asked.

He turned and gazed at the distant horizon where rugged white peaks stood bold against the blue sky, in sharp contrast to the soft mounds of green valleys below them.

"Season after season, year after year, the land never ceases to amaze me," he said in a museful tone. "People come, people go, but the land never seems to change."

Her turned to her. "It's a beautiful one, don't you think?"

"Why, yes, yes it is," she agreed. For just a brief moment she was sure she saw something in his eyes, pain perhaps. "But why are you helping me?"

He sighed deeply. "Sometimes, Julia, it's not the winning that's the most enjoyable part of any war. Actually, half the fun is in the fight, the struggle, the plain-out stubbornness. That's what keeps a person young and alive."

He jerked his head toward the stables where Flint was emerging with her horse and smiled at her. "You'd better see to the moving, I'll see to those papers." He rose, tipped his hat and headed toward the stage station.

"Wait, I don't have any money!" she called out after him. But he was already out of earshot.

Minutes later, Julia raced her mount along the rutted road beside Cherry Creek as she headed for the ranch. If she hurried, she knew she could take a quick detour, cross Cherry Creek onto Ashmore property and reach a stone-walled gulch, ringed with steep ledges where Two Bears would be waiting. The night before she had left the three stones by the corral.

She splashed through the icy creek, ignoring the spray of water that splattered over her heated face and arms and sent a chill up her back. On the opposite bank, she stepped down from her saddle and quickly glanced around to be certain she wasn't followed. Behind her, she heard the gurgle of the water as it spilled over rocks and rushed southward. She scanned the ground barely a second before she discovered a patch of grass crushed by the hooves of a horse before her. Leading her mount, she headed for a stand of dense willow along the river bank.

Two Bears materialized from beneath the lace-trimmed boughs, grinning.

"You would make a good Indian, Red Fox Woman," he said. "Your eyes are sharp like an eagle."

"Detail is something that comes in handy in the work I do," she said, inwardly pleased he had noticed. "We need to talk, Two Bears."

"You need ponies?"

She nodded. "Yes, as soon as possible."

"It is done," he merely said.

She studied his dark eyes for a moment. "Only Toby can help, only Toby can know about this." She could well imagine the consequences should Flint Ashmore find out. Last night she and Toby had come to a mutual understanding. She would pay him more money for his work if he helped break the stock. The kid had become an easy confident. Her silence about his horse thieving went a long way to help convince him.

Two Bears spoke. "What did you bring me?"

She went to her saddle and withdrew a sack. The Indian opened it and pulled out a doughnut.

"What is this thing?" He held it out and poked his finger through the center. "You have cut out the heart again. *Why* do you do this?"

She laughed, and it rippled out, disturbing the quiet silence around them. "Try it, we call it a doughnut back East. They are similar to what people here call a bear claw."

He took a bite and grinned. "You can make these, Jewel-lee-a?"

"No, Anna, can. She's opening a bakery in town and will be selling them." She looked at the sun. "I can't stay, Two Bears. We're moving everything into town today, and I'll be missed."

"Wait," he said. "This Anna, she have a man?"

"Looks like it might be Marcus Ashmore," she admitted, with a smile. Lately, the Dane was radiant and content. No longer did she speak as warmly of Lancaster and Denmark since she met Marcus.

"Too bad," Two Bears said, finishing the doughnut and smacking his lips. "She be good squaw for Ute warrior. She make him proud."

"Why aren't you married?" she asked suddenly curious.

She was sorry she said it as soon as the words left her lips. A raw, cold look covered his face. She shivered, stepping backwards.

"I was. My squaw is dead."

Julia sucked in breath and looked away quickly, staring at the treetops and plentiful grass around them. "I'm sorry."

"You are sorry for someone you did not know?" he asked perplexed.

"I am sorry for anyone who can not smell this clean air, who can not hear the laughter of the birds, the sigh of the wind, or see the dawn break in colors of reds and golds on a clear morning. Yes, I am sorry for her death."

"You are a strange woman," Two Bears said, stepping toward her. He reached out and touched a tendril of hair, rubbing it between his grimy fingers.

She refused to shrink from his touch. She forced herself to stare into his dark, piercing eyes. His dark hair blew gently around his proud, straight shoulders.

"I am a poor woman at the moment, Two Bears."

"And what would riches bring?" he asked, withdrawing his hand.

"In a white man's world, freedom. Freedom to live as you please, do as you want."

He grunted. "Everyone—white man and red man—wants this."

Julia turned and climbed into her saddle. "So we have a deal?"

"Yes," he smiled, showing his missing front teeth, and held up the sack. "If you bring me more of these things without hearts."

"If I bring you more, you will get fat and lazy and will not be able to round up the ponies I need," she said, smiling. She reined her horse toward the river and cantered away.

She heard him laugh a deep rolling laugh, and shout after her, "No doughnuts, no horses, Jewel-lee-a!"

Later, when she drew her mount into the deserted ranch yard and hurried to the house for a glass of lemonade, she discovered an unexpected surprise.

Two bundles of newspapers, neatly tied with twine, were lying on her front stoop.

For a brief moment, she stared at them, wondering whether she should be grateful to Frank Norwell or suspicious of him. But one thing she knew for sure, there was now a chance she might not be discovered —and a glimmer of hope burned again.

Sixteen

Julia stood in a far corner of Finley's dining room and watched through the wide archway as couples waltzed gracefully over the polished oak floor in the spacious sitting room beyond. She had not planned to attend the dance, but once she discovered that several of the Army's officers would be present, she decided it was the ideal time to meet those in control of the Army's purse strings. It was also the ideal time to move stock. At this very moment, with the ranch unattended, Toby would be accepting at least twenty wild horses from Two Bears.

Betsy Ashmore, in a pretty blue gingham dress, crossed the room toward her. Julia quickly noticed the Ashmore brothers were missing. Panic surged in her chest. If they came late, they could easily cross paths with Two Bears, Toby and the horses.

"Flint and Marcus are not here yet?" she asked, trying to keep worry from showing in her voice.

Betsy smiled. "Yes, they're all here, even Tye." She pulled Julia close and spoke softly, "Finley is not fond of having liquor underfoot so the men have set up their own gossip corner in the barn. As soon as we arrived, they all suddenly had the need to trade news."

Relieved, Julia said, "I didn't know Finley was a man of temperance."

"He's not, really. When he first moved into a cabin here some twenty years ago, he brought his wife and daughter and son-in-law. A year later, a granddaughter was born. Finley left one day to visit a neighbor and returned to find his family killed, cabin burned, and the grandchild kidnapped by the Indians. He always blamed himself for lingering a bit longer than necessary to partake of some mountain mash."

"The granddaughter? Was she ever located?"

Betsy shook her head. "No, and for the past sixteen years now, he's been trying to find her. It's not an easy task with so many bands roaming the area. Ute have been known to trade their women and children for food and livestock. She could be clear into Canada."

"How pitiful!"

"Depends upon how you look at it. She could be faring pretty well, too. Women are often traded to bands that are wealthier."

"But the poor child, never being able to know her parents, never knowing a real grandfather even exists."

"I was abandoned as well," Betsy reminded her. "Sometimes you learn to accept what's dished up."

"You never wonder about your parents?"

"All the time. I wonder whether both were alive when they gave me away, whether one was dead and the other couldn't care for me." Betsy smiled a tolerant smile. "But what good comes of it? Other than to make your life more miserable? Look what God gave me! Four very handsome brothers who would give their lives for a sister who isn't even of the same blood."

Julia nodded, feeling awkward, sorry she'd brought up such a painful subject.

Betsy Ashmore touched her lightly on the arm and drew her farther back into the corner of the room, away from earshot of others. "I think you should know that a few days ago two Army officers stopped at the store. They said they were looking to purchase additional supplies."

"What's that got to do with me?" Julia asked. She knew the Army had the best supplies around from ammunition to canned goods. What they bought from Finley were just everyday staple goods. Flour, sugar and such.

"I don't think they were looking for supplies, I think they were looking for information."

"What kind?"

"Information about who might be supplying the Indians with goods."

Julia's voice was cool. "I still don't understand what that's got to do with me."

"All right, Julia, I'll spell it out," Betsy said, her voice a harsh whisper. "Anyone caught making deals with the Ute should understand the risks and hope neither the Army, nor the settlers, discover his shenanigans. That is, if he wants live a long life, even though it might well be in jail."

Julia Gast stared at her, her face grim. "How did you know?"

Betsy shrugged. "It comes as no surprise, 'though you might be amused to know your own uncle played the same game with Two Bears at times. Not a healthy one, Julia."

"You don't understand, Betsy. It'll take a lifetime to get enough money to build the type of breeding stock I want. A few dozen wild horses, a couple sales to the Army, what harm can come of it? Actually, if you think about it, I'm helping them."

"They may have a different view of the situation." Betsy smiled a tight, but reassuring smile. "Don't worry, your secret's safe with me."

"Do your brothers know?"

"Oh, heavens, I don't think so, although I can't vouch that Rusty's actions weren't suspect at times. They knew he had an alliance with Two Bears for many years."

Flint, impeccably dressed in a dark trousers and a black pin-striped coat, materialized from the crowd. He crossed the room in long strides and came to where they stood. His arm encircled Betsy's shoulders and he squeezed her affectionately. "Girl talk, I reckon?"

"No, actually I was telling Julia what gallant brothers I have," Betsy replied with mock sarcasm, "and how they literally dumped me at the doorstep and flew to Finley's barn for a piece of gossip themselves. The carriage hadn't even rolled to a stop, for heaven's sake."

"Deposited, not dumped, there's a difference, and the carriage was as still as a rock," he countered defensively.

Betsy touched an intricate oval locket that hung from her neck. "Look what John Greenfeld dropped off the other day. He told me Rusty wanted me to have it." Her fingers fought with the clasp.

"Here," Flint offered, taking the locket. He popped it open. A daguerreotype of a striking light-haired woman with delicate lips and soft eyes stared at him.

"Wasn't his wife beautiful?" Betsy asked.

Flint studied the portrait thoughtfully. "I thought Rusty's wife had dark features."

"Aunt Maggie did," Julia agreed. "Here, let me see it."

"Aunt Maggie?" Flint's eyebrows knitted as she maneuvered closer to get a good view. "I thought Rusty's wife was named Gretchen."

"No, I'm certain it was Margaret." She scrutinized the picture, then shook her head. "This isn't Rusty's wife."

"Who is it, then?" Betsy asked bewildered.

Puzzled herself, Julia shrugged. "I have no idea, Betsy, but she's certainly a beautiful woman whoever she is. Evidently, it wasn't just rumor that my uncle was a very infamous fellow."

"But this is Gretchen!" Betsy snapped the locket shut.

"You can't be sure of that," Flint said.

"No, listen to me, I removed the picture and looked on the back. It says: To Rusty. With love, Gretchen." She glanced from one confused face to the other. For a moment all three stood silent, each caught up in his own thoughts. Several seconds passed before she let the locket fall to her breast and said quietly, "Well, whoever she was, it was kind of Rusty to will it to me. It certainly is a very expensive piece of jewelry."

Julia watched Flint's face nod in agreement. He made a good try to follow it with a tight smile.

Behind her, a lanky young Army officer, sporting a neatly trimmed handlebar mustache, cleared his throat and spoke, "Betsy Ashmore? Little Betsy Ashmore from Virginia?"

"Hoot Owl?" Betsy whispered breathlessly, whirling abruptly.

The officer grinned. "Reckon this is my lucky day. Lieutenant Jamie Banes, at your service." He stepped forward to graciously bow when Betsy grabbed him unceremoniously by the shoulders and wrapped her arms around him, hugging him in a warm embrace.

"Mercy, mercy, Hoot Owl, don't be so darn formal! We know each other rather well, I'd say."

"Quite well, perhaps." Jamie Banes blushed.

"What brings you West?

"Chasing Indians. But if I'd known you were here—

"Stop it." She gave him a playful wag of her finger and turned to Flint. "You remember, Jamie?"

Flint chuckled lowly. "Yes, and you've certainly put on a few inches since we've last met."

Banes's face reddened again. "I've also learned to swing with my left, sir."

Betsy introduced Julia and explained, "Hoot Owl and I grew up together in Virginia. We were—"

"Ah, Betsy, please—"

"Good friends," she said, laughing, "and neighbors. Jamie and I spent most of our summer days riding instead of walking."

"That's why the Army sent me here. It seems they need more able bodied men who know something about good horseflesh."

"Then you and Julia will have a lot in common. She raised horses in Lancaster and is planning to start a herd again."

"I've just recently made plans to gather wild mustangs, break them, and sell them for mounts or pack animals," Julia explained quickly. "I'd be interested in discussing business sometime in the future."

"Of course," Jamie Banes said. "We can use as much stock as you can supply. Let's get together as soon as it's suitable for you. Tonight, though, I'd like to renew old times and swap some. . ."

"Tales, Jamie. Tales with Betsy, I hope," Flint interrupted, grinning. He cocked an ear toward the dance floor. The first soft strains of a waltz swelled from the sitting room. "Julia, I believe this is the dance I've been waiting for."

Seconds later, Julia found herself locked in Flint Ashmore's arms as he whirled her about the floor. He was an agile, light-footed dancer, and when she told him so, he merely laughed.

"My father insisted we all learn to handle a gun as soon as we could hold and load it. My mother, on the other hand, insisted that we learn to dance as soon as we could walk. Sometimes there were some mighty good arguments over whose lessons should come first."

"What happened then?"

"We'd take off for the fishing hole while they hashed it out. By the time we got back with a string of fish, it was too late for either lesson. I think that's how I learned to like fishing the best."

"I've never tried it," she admitted.

"Oh my, I must take you sometime soon. There's nothing more relaxing than a blue sky above, blue water in front of you, and a few half-hearted bites to keep you occupied until you're properly rested."

As they moved across the floor, Julia noticed Flint's eyes circling the room like a wary hawk. He frowned when he saw his sister and Jamie Banes stroll out onto the wide front porch and vanish into the darkness.

"Is something wrong?" she asked. "You don't seem enchanted with this Banes fellow."

"Oh, Jamie is a fine lad all right. Unfortunately, he's all grown up. Caught him behind the barn trying to steal some kisses from Betsy some years ago when they were childhood sweethearts. I gave him the thumping of his life. I just don't know whether I could do it again."

Julia laughed. "Well, Betsy is all grown up, too. I imagine she's more than capable of taking care of herself."

"Exactly what I mean," Flint said, grinning. "Somebody has to protect the kid." He pulled her closer to him.

Julia felt his hand at her back as he guided her effortlessly about the room. He radiated warmth like the summer sun. It seemed so right, so

129

safe, to be locked in his embrace. She lifted her head to look up at him and found him intensely studying her. He smiled and her heart skipped a beat.

"Now what's wrong?" she asked.

"Nothing, absolutely nothing," he said. "I was just admiring your freckles. Were you teased a lot?"

"As a child, yes," she said, smiling, "until my father told me freckles were a gift from the fairies and I was sprinkled with an extra handful of magical dust. Then everyone else wanted them."

The music ended and they crossed the room, moving toward a table heaped with platters of sandwiches and pastries.

"I didn't know you had planned to sell stock to the Army," she heard Flint say near her ear.

Julia tensed, afraid to look at him. "I guess I didn't mention it because I wasn't sure. But now with Toby on the payroll, I figure it might be worthwhile. The boy is supposed to be one of the best bronc busters around."

"What about the pottery, surely you're not going to abandon it?"

"Oh, my goodness, no." She tried to mask her nervousness with a lighthearted reply. "Sven and I would never think of undergoing Anna's wrath. We've promised to supply her with the needed plates and mugs for the bakery."

"I thought you were going to help run it."

"I'll help her get started. Anna's a very competent woman. Eventually she'll need to hire extra help, especially once her customers get a bite of her doughnuts and pies."

Julia was pleased for the change in conversation. It saved her from having to lie, to offer details about the stock.

Flint chuckled. "Well, we know who'll be Anna's most loyal customer."

"We certainly do," Julia said with a grin.

Tom Morton, Colin Norwell and some Army officers were at the refreshment table when they arrived, and Julia could see that Morton had made one too many trips to Finley's barn. His powerful body teetered. The cup of punch he held awkwardly in his thick hands, sloshed about and threatened to spill over the rim. Even from where she stood she could smell the whiskey in the drink.

"Well, well," he said. "You did come after all, Julia."

She smiled. "Yes, but I took your advice and left Toby behind to watch the ranch."

"Ruthless renegades," he sputtered in a slurred speech. "Some day they'll be all wiped out. Isn't that so, boy?" He nudged Colin Norwell.

"I guess so," Colin muttered uncomfortably as all eyes turned toward him. He set down his cup and hastily brushed past Morton, heading for the front door.

"Guess so?" Morton snorted and looked with blurry eyes at a young man in Army uniform standing nearby.

"We certainly hope so," the young officer agreed in an appeasing tone.

For some odd reason, Julia found the remarks of both men annoying. "Oh, for heaven's sake, you act like they're animals with no feelings. It's their land we're standing on this very minute."

Morton's eyes darkened in surprise. "God's blood, Julia, they have sixteen thousand acres west of here, guaranteed by treaty with the U.S. Government. How much more do you think they deserve?"

"I don't know," Julia admitted. "I only wish there were a better way." She thought about the settlers pouring in. How long would it take until the territory could hold no more, and pressured by the settlers, the government would welch on their deal and demand the land back, piece by piece? How long until every Ute in Colorado was chased clear into the Utah territory in the name of civilization?

"Well, I'll be darned," Morton said, lifting the glass to drink. He smacked his lips. "We have a highfalutin Indian lover among us civilized folk."

Jaw clenched, Flint lurched forward, but Julia laid a restraining hand on his arm.

She spoke, "I have, Mr. Morton, seen four long years of bloodshed between civilized men. White men, I might add, who were too stupid to realize that as the War between the States dragged on, their very own brothers would be killed or maimed. Now, the same men come West, using the Indian for their whipping boy instead of the Negro. Pray tell, when will all this fighting ever end?"

She paused and gave him a narrow-eyed look. "Nothing personal, Tom, but as long as we have ignoramuses like you underfoot, this land will never see peace."

"Now, just a minute, what's that supposed to mean?" Morton demanded. "What's an ignoramus?"

The sudden blast of a gun split the air, bringing an abrupt end to the conversation. A frightened hush fell over the noisy crowd as every eye skidded toward the porch and the darkness beyond.

Somewhere a voice, muffled but urgent, yelled, "Betsy Ashmore has been shot. Quick, someone get the doctor!"

Seventeen

The porch was crowded with curious onlookers when Flint and Julia pushed their way through to where Betsy lay prone on the weathered board floor. Jamie Banes knelt over her, head bent, his hand clutching her limp wrist. Above, Colin Norwell stood helplessly by, his face white and troubled. A drawn gun hung uselessly at his side.

It was Finley who spoke, "Shot came from out of nowhere." He gestured up the street into the inky blackness of the night. "We were just standing here talking about the upcoming horse race."

Julia heard Flint swear under his breath before he dropped to his knees beside Banes. For a moment she froze, then became suddenly alert, firing orders to those around her, requesting more room, more lanterns and some clean linens. She knelt across from Flint's dark figure and could see that his face was as white as Betsy's listless form.

"Pulse?" she asked, glancing at Jamie Banes. She felt her heart thudding in her chest and willed herself to be calm.

He nodded. "Weak, real weak, and she's barely breathing."

A small blood stain which had only seconds ago appeared on the girl's left shoulder now began to spread rapidly outward. It puddled, drenching the fabric of her dress. Julia took a clean cloth someone handed her and deftly pressed it over the wound.

"We have to move her to the doctor's office quickly," she ordered, "and without moving the shoulder or arm."

From somewhere Tye, Marcus and Anna appeared.

"Get a door," Flint ordered looking up at a circle of curious faces distorted in the dim yellow light of the lanterns, "and be quick about it!"

Minutes later, the girl was transported to Doc Silverstone's office, two blocks up the street, and placed on a table in the examining room. Faithfully, Jamie Banes had remained by her side and helped to carry her. Now he sat beside her, holding the cloth tightly over the wound with bloodied fingers while Julia bustled about the room. Beside him old man Finley stood wringing his gnarled hands. Tye Ashmore had only stayed long enough to determine his sister was alive, then silently disappeared into the haunting, dark night.

"A doctor!" Flint yelled at everyone, anguish in his voice and eyes. "Someone get the doctor."

Anna stepped forward. "He was sent out on a call at a nearby ranch for a delivery. It's at least a twenty minute ride one way." She made her way to the tiny stove inside the room, added wood to the dying embers and poured water from a bucket into deep pan, setting it on top to boil.

Julia saw terror flicker in Flint's eyes.

"Well, someone has to get him!" He turned to Marcus. "Hurry, go now."

"We haven't time, Flint," Julia said, trying to keep her voice steady. She knew the girl could die before he ever arrived. Time was of the essence.

"We have to get that bullet out and the wound closed immediately."

"Who. . .how?" He paced the floor and gestured wildly like a mad man. "Who's going to do it? We have no one capable here."

"One of us will have to," Julia said quietly.

"For God's sake, Julia, it's not that simple!"

"What do you suggest?" Her voice rose louder than she intended and she willed herself to remain calm.

He shook his head. "I don't know, I. . . I just. . .don't know."

"She's right," Marcus spoke up. "We can't wait for a doctor. What if someone rides out there and he's tied up with the birth, then what?"

"But how? With what? And who?" Flint asked. His eyes wildly circled the room. "We don't even have any instruments."

"He's right," Anna announced, rummaging wildly through the drawers and cupboards. "There are only some needles, thread and a scalpel. Everything must be in his satchel."

"Tweezers," Julia said. "We'll need tweezers." She looked frantically at everyone. When she received no replies, she said, "Think, for heaven's sake, think."

"A gunsmith," Marcus offered.

"The seamstress?" Anna asked.

"No, no." She paused, her eyes scanning the room to take stock of the supplies at hand. She noticed that the office was immaculately clean, and it gave her some comfort. During the War, she had heard of too many doctors whose filthy surroundings, even filthier instruments, linens and hands had helped to bring about anything but recovery for their patients.

"The watchmaker beside the bakery shop," Flint said, "would have every size we'd need."

"I'll go," Finley offered, rushing for the door.

A crowd had gathered at the entranceway of the waiting room, familiar faces of people who knew the Betsy Ashmore well, and Julia watched the old man shoulder his way past them. She could hear them murmuring as heads appeared and disappeared in the open doorway.

When he left, Julia took control again in a crisp voice, "Marcus, Flint and Anna scrub your hands with that lye soap in the sink and rinse them in that carbolic acid overhead in the cupboard. Anna, you'll take care of the instruments. Marcus and Jamie, you'll keep Betsy still. Flint, you're going to have to help get the bullet out."

Flint looked at her, his eyes distant and dim, his face full of anguish. "Julia, I don't know if I can do this," he said in a hoarse whisper.

"You can't be afraid of blood." She searched his face. "You're not, are you?"

He shook his head and dropped his face to rest in the palms of his hands. It was then that the thought struck her. He was afraid he might make a mistake and take his sister's life.

"Julia can do it," Anna said softly, moving to stand beside him, "if you help her." She laid her hand tenderly on his arm. "Trust me, she can."

Flint's anguished eyes flashed to her. "Have you done this before?"

"On horses," she admitted. "During the war, the Army would drop off wounded animals at the ranch. The stable hand and I picked out a lot of lead."

"Betsy is not an animal!"

Anna bit her lower lip and a look of despair spread over her face. "She lies. Tell, him," she pleaded. "Your secret is safe, Julia."

"Anna, please, that's enough," Julia ordered sternly.

In a low, hoarse whisper, he asked, "What does she mean?"

"I've also taken out bullets from wounded men."

"Where?"

Julia sighed. "It's not something I brag about. Before the war, many had the wrong color of skin, and during it, they were sometimes wearing the wrong color of uniform. God only knows who the real enemy was. The point is. . ." She paused. ". . the point is that all of them were wounded and needed a place to hide and recover. Our stables were beside a well-used route running North and South and seemed to be a logical place for some odd reason. So we'd patch them up and send them on their way."

"North?" Flint asked. "To spy?"

"Maybe, maybe South to join their ranks. I made it a point to never ask a soldier which way he was headed once he was back on his feet. An old priest at the parish helped arrange for their safe departure. Father McMillen willingly bore the burden of healing their souls and forgiving their transgressions, allowing me to concentrate on healing their wounds."

She looked across the room to see Jamie Banes staring at her in astonishment, and she shook her head sadly. She had prayed that it would never come to this, that no one would ever find out. "I know, Jamie, you fought for the Union, but I fought to keep all men alive."

Frank Norwell appeared in the doorway, hat in hand, his shaggy white hair glistening like snow. "Flint," he said. "I'm really sorry. Is there anything I can do? I can send a man into Denver for a doctor."

Julia saw red anger in Flint eyes as he lunged toward the big man.

"Haven't you done enough already?" he spit out as Frank Norwell stepped back quickly avoiding his flying hands. He ranted on, before the man could interrupt, his face still twisted in pain, "I want to talk to you Norwell, as soon as this is over, and if you or any of your men had anything to do with this, you better be wearing a gun."

Coming to her senses, Julia stepped between them. She could feel anger radiate from both.

"Yes, Mr. Norwell, there is something I need," she said. "Send someone to the seamstress shop to get the finest needle and most delicate white silk thread available, and hurry." When he nodded and turned, she continued, "Oh, and keep that crowd back. I don't care how many stack up in the waiting room, but no one is to come in here, understand? I don't want this room contaminated."

Frank Norwell's head nodded and seconds later, she could hear him barking orders as he pushed his way through the overflowing waiting room.

Julia turned to Anna. "As soon as the tweezers, needle and thread arrive I want you to soak everything in boiling water."

"Forget Norwell," Flint said. "We have needle and thread here."

Julia spoke, "Flint, if your sister recovers, she will be scarred."

"What difference does that make?"

"I don't want to make it worse than necessary. The finer the thread, the neater the stitches, the smaller the scar."

"Confound it, who cares about a blasted scar?"

Julia patted the area above her breast and smiled a weak smile. "Most women do, trust me, Flint. It's vanity, sheer vanity. And everyone one of us has a little of it."

When all the supplies arrived and were scoured and boiled to Julia's satisfaction, she set to work cleaning the wound, removing the bullet and stitching the damaged area closed. She knew the girl was in pain, even though she appeared to be unconscious. Once, when she tried to thrash about, Julia was forced to order both Jamie and Marcus to hold her down. Betsy had cried out, screaming for help and yelling nonsensical phrases. But always, through the entire ordeal, the name of her brother Luke was on her lips until she finally collapsed into an insensate state.

When she finished, Julia sent the men outside and gently washed the girl before placing her between clean sheets. As she worked, her hand unconsciously flew to Betsy's forehead and she silently prayed a prayer of thanksgiving each time it came away cool. Then, under the noise of rattling pans as Anna bustled about straightening the room and soaking the soiled clothes and utensils, Julia slumped exhaustedly into a chair beside the bed and closed her eyes, falling into a stupor like the patient beside her.

Flint Ashmore was not prepared for the throng of people who were seated in the waiting room when he appeared. Outside, many had gathered on the porch and were sitting or milling about, just waiting for word about his sister. Half the town was present, he surmised, as he quickly explained what he and Julia had done. Then he begged everyone to go home and get some rest, saying he would relate further word on Betsy's condition as soon as there was a change.

Only Jamie Banes and Frank Norwell remained. Banes was slumped in a ladder back chair, his hands still blotched with Betsy's blood. The young man's face was white, but Flint had to silently admit that Banes had more guts and stamina than he'd ever given him credit for.

"Get some sleep," Flint told him. "There are enough people here to take shifts."

Jamie Banes shook his head. "I'd rather stick around a while."

Flint shrugged wearily. "Suit yourself."

Frank Norwell rose from his chair. His face was gray, his eyes, sober, and his mouth, grim. He spoke, "Colin seems to think the bullet was meant for him."

"He doesn't exactly have a reputation for making friends around these parts." Flint admitted and shot him an icy glare.

"Agreed," Frank Norwell replied, "but neither do you."

Flint grunted. "To be honest, Norwell, you had the best reason. You've always wanted us off that ranch. We've been a thorn in your side from the day we arrived."

"Don't be ridiculous!" Norwell's tone was brusque. "Had I wanted you off that ranch I could have done it many times before this, and I'd surely not start by killing Betsy, not when you and your brothers are underfoot and easy targets. My late wife took a shine to that girl. Betsy would be the last person I'd hurt, you know that. You don't need to be told who'd be the first."

Flint stared at him. The man was ruthless and dangerous, but he wasn't stupid. What he had just said was closer to the truth than Flint cared to admit. Only a fool would harm Betsy and risk bringing the town and all four brothers down on his back.

Frank Norwell glanced at Jamie Banes. "In fact, it's quite possible that even Banes here was the target."

"Me?" Banes said, shooting out of his chair. "Now, just a darn minute!"

Frank Norwell ignored him. "You know as well as I, Flint, that there's a lot of sour-faced Army men mulling about these days. I'll wager none of them were any too delighted when the Army decided to bring in a stranger from the East to take care of stock they've been tending all their lives."

Flint Ashmore nodded. It was a possibility all right. Outsiders were not greeted with a warm welcome. How well he and his brothers knew. It had taken them years to fit in and be accepted.

He walked to the fireplace across the room which was cold and dusted with ashes since summer's arrival and leaned an arm on the mantel. He was tired. Dead tired. Tired of all the troubles the ranch had been having lately. All he wished for was his sister to survive and a little peace. He was getting old, he wanted to settle down. Peace, a little peace.

"Do me a favor, will you, Norwell?" he asked. "Keep your men from dogging my young stock at least until everything here blows over. If then, you want a fight, I'll be ready. Best man wins."

"My men have not touched your stock!" Norwell protested. "Any man who says they have is a liar."

"Someone has been stealing them. They just don't disappear into thin air."

Frank Norwell's bushy eyebrows lowered themselves over gray eyes which had darkened to charcoal. "I assure you, Ashmore, it's not me, nor my men. Think man, chasing you off is of no benefit to me. I'd only have to deal with some nester who might want to raise dairy cows, or God forbid, goats and sheep. I know as sure as the moon hangs in the sky you'd never sell that land to me even if you were at the end of your rope and on your last penny."

A half-smile appeared on Flint's face, and the old man knew he was right.

"What's the other favor?" Norwell asked gruffly.

"When you leave, wire Luke and tell him to get down here. He's marshalling up in Cheyenne."

"Your brother is a U.S. Marshal?" Norwell asked. His face clouded with uneasiness. "Egad man, you sure you want to do that?"

"I want him to see Betsy, just in case. . ."

"If she dies, Luke will tear this whole damn territory apart looking for her killer," Norwell warned.

"I'm counting on him doing it, even if she doesn't."

Norwell heaved a sigh. "All right, Ashmore, I'll do it. I guess it's your turn to make a few enemies, and bringing Luke down here will surely be a step in the right direction."

After he left, Flint looked over at Jamie Banes. "Speaking of enemies, Banes, Julia doesn't need any."

"She has to be reported. She's a traitor!"

Flint crossed the room in angry strides and grabbed Banes by the front of his shirt. "Now you listen to me, Jamie Banes," he said in a clipped voice. "She may have been a traitor by your definition, but she kept men alive. Alive! You hear me? Including slaves who would have been shot or torn to shreds by dogs." He pushed the young man away from him and watched him stumble backwards, then awkwardly regain his balance. "The War's over, Jamie. Accept it."

"You can't tell me what to do, Ashmore."

Flint stared at him through fiery eyes. "You think I can't? Let me tell you what I can do. I've played cards and shared some mighty interesting conversation with your good Captain. I know how he's short changed supplies, mishandled government money, and made deals with the Indians. I've got enough on him to send him to the most remote corner of any desert in the Utah territory."

He swiped his hand around the room. "And see for yourself, Jamie, the number of people here tonight. They're all Betsy's friends. One word from any of us, and you'll not be able to buy one blasted horse from anyone in a hundred mile radius. You'll end up right beside the good Captain, cleaning cactus spines from the seat of your britches."

Jamie Banes shifted uncomfortably. "I guess I can make an exception," he conceded grimly.

Flint chuckled and threaded his hands through his hair. It was amazing how smart a man could become in just a few short minutes, he thought.

Eighteen

Julia stopped by the front window and watched Toby working with the new horses in the corral. He had been up before dawn, eager to cull the best ones from the band to break for saddle horses. From her vantage point, she could see him moving about the corral with a natural self-assuredness that could only come from ingrained habit and experience.

A day and a half had dragged past and Betsy, though feverless, had slipped into a state of unconsciousness that couldn't be shaken.

She had not heard from Flint, but Doctor Silverstone had stopped by from his rounds and had praised her skillful work and quick thinking. Betsy Ashmore's unconsciousness he couldn't explain, yet he said he had seen it before with those who were badly injured. Sometimes a body just shuts down to rest, he conjectured, trying to reassure her.

In the kitchen, Anna was already up and about, sweeping the floor, washing dishes and setting the kitchen right. On a cooling rack near the stove, pans of warm cinnamon rolls gave the room a sweet, homey scent. She looked up as soon as Julia entered.

"Sven is taking me into town to deliver some goods to the bakery." She eyed Julia with a critical gaze. "You would do well, Julia, to spend some time in the pottery shed. Our best creations sometimes emerge when emotions are close to the surface, and it will do you good to do something besides mope around, waiting for a change in the girl. Open the window in the shed and let in the fresh air, ja? You must eat, too. I will leave a couple of warm rolls."

Julia shook her head. "Not now, Anna, maybe later. First, I'll help you load the wagon."

"Are you sure you'll be all right?"

Julia smiled a carefree smile she didn't feel. "Of course, Anna. Toby is here if I need anything."

The Dane carefully covered the pans with clean, white linen cloths. "I'll check on the girl and send Sven back if there is a change."

Julia nodded, pleased by Anna's thoughtfulness.

When the wagon was finally loaded, and the Holbergs on their way, Julia crossed the yard to the shed, flinging the doors open wide.

Inside, she unlatched the window and tied on a thick canvas apron before selecting a bolt of clay from the wooden shelves on the other side of the shed. She thought about Flint Ashmore as she took the clay to the wheel and slowly worked it in her hands. He had been so kind and gentle to her after they had removed the bullet, it almost made her heart ache, and she suddenly felt guilty she had turned down his offer of marriage. The clay beneath her fingers was soft and cool as she worked it, and she decided to make something special, just for him. Not a ring flask. He would be expecting that. Perhaps a crock with matching lid to keep in the spring house. Betsy had told her that he loved buttermilk.

Within the hour, she was so absorbed in her work, she never heard anyone enter the shed until the intruder was standing a scant three paces from her, and she caught a glimpse of his shadow from the corner of her eye. Her gaze instinctively fell upon his meticulously polished black boot impatiently tapping the hard-packed ground before it climbed up to meet his thin, sober face. Her potter's wheel shuttered to a stop beneath her fingers.

"Surprised, my dear?" Charles Bloomington asked.

"Why Charles, of course, I am," she said, sliding from her seat. She moved to the wash bucket on the table, scooped up a bar of soap and dipped her trembling hands in the cool water, rubbing away sticky remnants of red clay.

"What brings you to Golden City?"

The chilling laugh he gave her sent a series of shivers up her spine. "Surely, you are jesting, my dear? You leave me standing at the altar like an injured crow abandoned on a fence post, and you think I'd just pull in my broken wing and forget what happened?"

"No, Charles, I was hoping you'd realize that our future together was not to be."

"We are betrothed!" he shouted.

"I would have thought you'd also understand that the engagement was broken," she countered, dryly, trying to keep her emotions in check. She dried her hands and set the cloth she used aside.

"You still have the ring?" he asked.

"Yes." Julia took two quick steps toward the door, but he stepped in front of her. "Where do you think you're going?"

"To the house to get it."

"Likely story, my dear, but I've no intentions of letting you get away again."

Julia's heart thudded wildly inside her chest. *Get away again?* What was he planning to do? What did he hope to gain by thinking he could force her to marry him? There was no way they could ever share a life together. "I'll go to the house and get it for you," she repeated.

At the doorway of the shed, Toby suddenly appeared, hat in hand. "Do you need anything, Julia?" he asked. He looked at Bloomington with a wary, puzzled expression.

Not wishing to cause alarm, she waved him away with a sweep of her hand. "No, no, Toby, everything here is fine. Captain Bloomington is an old friend from Pennsylvania who stopped by to visit."

The boy didn't look convinced. He continued to stare at Bloomington like he was memorizing every fastidious detail of the man's elegant attire, right down to the silk cravat at his throat. The squeaky handle of the water pump handle outside brought him to his senses. He spoke, "Oh, by the way, a rider just came in from the north, riding hard and heading for Golden City. He says he needs to water his horse. Looks like a drifter who has put a lot of trail behind him. Horse looks done in, too. I told him he was welcome to use the pump and water trough."

Julia nodded. "Fine, see to his needs, will you?"

When Toby's frame cleared from the doorway, Julia caught the glimpse of a lanky, light-haired man working the pump handle. Sweaty and dust-covered, he had removed his shirt, but not the two Colts resting casually at the sides of his waist. Deftly, he splashed the bucket of water he had filled over his head and broad, muscled shoulders.

Julia's eyes turned back to Charles. His jaw was rigid, his face inflexible, and he stood with that arrogant stance she so remembered and so despised.

"Father McMillen, is he well?" she asked.

"As well as can be expected for an old man who swills wine," he volunteered with a sneer.

She watched his eyes sweep the shelves. Disgust marred his face. She wondered how she could have ever been attracted to a man who derived pleasure from the manipulation of others.

"I'm thinking about going to California to settle," he said, "perhaps near San Francisco. How long do you think it would take to find a buyer for this pathetic place?"

Julia faced him and folded her arms. "'Til hell freezes over?"

The remark caught him by surprise. He took a step backwards before recovering. "I'll not let you speak to me that way, Julia! Please try to remember your dutiful place, my dear."

"I'm not your dear, Charles, and I'm not about to sell anything, nor go traipsing off to California. Look around you. I've made a home for myself here."

He looked at her chapped hands instead. "Oh, yes, I can see you have. Why, look at you! You're half covered in mud. And this dreary shed and pathetic ramshackle ranch--you call this making a home?"

"Yes, I do." She tore the strings from her apron and flung it on a shelf, then whipped around. "This dreary shed is my life, Charles, can't you see that? It's what I do. It's what I know best."

The look he gave her made her feel like she was covered in spit. "You'll not do it any longer, that's for sure."

Before she could cross the shed to stop him, he strode to the potter's wheel and swept the crock away, upending the wheel. A deafening noise ensued as it fell, crashing over an array of already fired redware pans and jugs stacked nearby.

"No-ooo!" she screamed, rushing toward him. "Stop it! Leave it alone. Please, Charles."

A cool, deep voice from the doorway of the shed echoed into room, "Is there something wrong here, darlin'?"

Julia looked up, stunned, and found the drifter, shirtless, leaning calmly against the doorjamb. Droplets of water spilled from his unkempt hair onto his chest and denims. His hair was so pale yellow it was almost white, and his jawbones were covered with at least a day's growth of light beard. She knew she should be taken back by the endearment, but somehow, she suspected it was just his natural way of speaking. And there was no way he could know her name, unless Toby had told him.

"This is none of your business," Bloomington hissed. "Get on with you, man. Take your horse and keep riding."

"Not until the lady here tells me to," the light-haired stranger said. His voice was soft and controlled. Had he been dressed in anything but dust and trail clothes, Julia would have thought he was a gambler by trade. His whole demeanor was slick and smooth, but the tone of his voice sounded familiar.

"I'll have you know, sir, you are interfering with me and my fiancé.

The stranger raised a pale eyebrow. "Most men around here treat their womenfolk with a more gentle hand than you've got, mister." He turned his faded blue eyes on Julia. "Is he your man?"

"No, he is not." Julia replied sharply. "I was once engaged to him, but that was months ago, before I came West."

"She has my ring. She never returned it," Bloomington said smugly. "That still makes her mine."

"Do you have it?" the stranger asked, turning to her.

"Yes," she admitted. She covered her face with her hands and pressed her fingertips to her forehead, then fanned them out cutting the air as she spoke. "I had every intention of returning it. Truly, I did. As soon as I could find someone reputable to deliver it to him."

"See, I told you," Bloomington said smugly and crossed his arms at his chest.

"Told me what?" the stranger asked irritably.

"We're still engaged."

The drifter heaved a weary sigh and looked at her. "Are you telling me, miss, you've no desire to get hitched to this jackass?"

"None whatsoever, I assure you, sir."

"Then I suggest you hustle your little backside up to the house and find his ring. The sooner he leaves, the better everyone will feel."

Bloomington's hand suddenly dropped, reaching for his gun.

The stranger cleared leather so fast Julia never saw him move. He had Bloomington covered before he could pull his gun from the holster.

"Ah, now, why did you go and do that?" the stranger asked. His voice was so controlled and calm it could quiet a crying infant. He kept his gun trained on Bloomington's chest. "You've provoked the lady, and now you've riled me. Take the gun from your holster and drop it in the straw. Be easy about it."

He gestured with the point of the barrel toward the house. "Go get this old man's ring, will you? I think it's time he cuts himself a new trail." He stepped aside to give Julia access to the door.

When she returned from the house, emerald ring in hand, Charles Bloomington was already astride his horse. She noticed his gun was tucked in the stranger's waistband, although the man still had not holstered his.

She thrust the ring up at him. "I'm sorry, Charles, I was hoping you would be reasonable about this."

"Reasonable? I can assure you, *you will* be sorry. That's a promise," he said bitterly. He snatched the ring and turned to the bare-chested stranger, "You will be sorry, too, mister."

The stranger never flinched. "You can pick your gun up at the sheriff's office in Golden City later today," he said to Bloomington, "but I wouldn't suggest you even think about staying the night."

As soon as Bloomington rode away, Julia turned to him. "Thank you, my name's Julia Gast. I'm so sorry you had to get involved." She stared thoughtfully at him. Any fool could see he was at the brink of exhaustion. His eyes were red-rimmed, and his face, tired and wane.

"Here, let me get you something to eat," she offered. "I have fresh baked cinnamon buns in the house. Fresh lemonade, too."

The man holstered his gun, walked to his horse, and pulled a clean shirt from his saddle bags, shrugging into it. "I can't stay. I've someone I need to see in Golden City. I'm running late now."

"A lady?" Julia asked and blushed at her bold curiosity.

"Yes, and more beautiful than the first yellow rose of the summer."

"Your horse," Julia said, glancing at the lathered roan as he shoved his shirttails under his belt, "can't possibly be pushed a mile more, poor beast. At least let me loan you one of mine."

"Bones here has more staying power than he looks."

"Bones?"

"Yeah, when I found him as a colt, he was just a bag of bones. Filled out pretty good, don't you think? All the curves in the right places, just like a good-looking woman."

Julia laughed. She could listen to his smooth, sing-song drawl all day. "You must be an amusing person to be around."

"Some folks don't think so." He winked. "You know if I didn't have someone special in mind, I'd invite you to dinner in town sometime soon."

He paused. "Maybe I'm overstepping my bounds, but I'd suggest you find someone else right quick to take Bloomington's place. Never can tell what a man like that will do. A pretty little gal like you should have no problem throwing a saddle on some decent man."

Julia smiled. "Actually, I have someone in mind." As soon as the words left her mouth, she felt her face heating up. Why had she blurted that out? What was she thinking?

"Lucky man. Who is he?" the stranger asked. "There's still a few folks left around here I know."

Julia looked into his pale eyes and blushed even more. "Flint Ashmore," she said, realizing how good it felt to admit it to herself, let alone openly admit it to a stranger. "Do you know him?"

The drifter grinned a wide grin. "Crimany, don't that beat all. I broke a few horses with that sullen old coyote way back when."

Julia rose to Flint's defense. "He's not old. He's not even thirty."

"Well shoot, he's older than I am," he replied. He laughed and stepped into the saddle, then pulled his sweaty hat down to shade his eyes before he kicked his horse into a trot. "Good day, Miss Gast. Obliged for the water."

Julia watched him ride away before she returned to the shed. Inside, she found her potter's wheel turned upright. Obviously the stranger had put Charles Bloomington to work before he accompanied him to his horse. She wondered how Charles Bloomington reacted to soiling his hands and taking orders from a mere drifter. Deep inside she hoped it was the last time she would ever see the likes of Captain Bloomington, but she realized he was not the kind of man to give up easily.

Despite her fears, she smiled, thinking of the carefree man with a voice like silk. It was only much later, after she had fashioned the crock, when the thought struck her that he had never once mentioned his name.

Nineteen

The sun sent slanted rays of blazing light into the waiting room that fell across Flint's face, awakening him. For a moment he sat still, trying to remember where he was and why he was there. Then he realized he was in Doc Silverstone's waiting room.

He had decided that all three brothers would take turns keeping a constant vigil. Even if the bullet had been targeted for Collin Norwell or Jamie Banes, who had been standing near Betsy, he felt it was best not to take any chances. How could they be certain it wasn't meant for Betsy and someone wouldn't try again? His stomach growled, and he wondered when Marcus would return. He had stopped by an hour earlier to check on Betsy and promised he'd go to Anna's bakery and bring back some fresh cinnamon buns.

Flint pulled his hat down over his eyes and repositioned himself on the hard wooden chair. It was far from comfortable. Yet, there was little he could do except make the most of it. He had not gotten much rest since the shooting, and the short naps he was able to squeeze in were welcome.

He thought briefly about Julia. Besides her visible beauty, she was woman of strength and courage. He couldn't even begin to imagine the horrors she must have witnessed during the War. And yet, she had devoted herself to healing all those she could, regardless of which cause a soldier had chosen. Her hands were just as skillful in helping the wounded as they were in creating a delicate piece of pottery. She had removed the bullet in a totally efficient manner with true concern for Betsy's welfare and recovery.

If anything good had come from this ghastly incident, it was the realization that he loved her. He loved her more than he had loved anyone in his life. But why was it so difficult to tell her? Because he feared she would reject him. And she would reject him again and again, until she could prove to everyone and herself that she could make it on her own. She was a problem, he decided, a problem that he wasn't able to handle at the moment.

He dozed again, and a half-hour later, a sharp kick to his boot sent him flying from the chair, right hand on his gun handle.

"Whoa," Marcus's deep voice rumbled out before Flint's eyes could clearly focus on the two men in front of him. "You draw on this one, and you'll be playing tag six feet under with the gophers."

Beside him, a lanky man grinned and splayed his empty hands palms out.

"Edgy as always, big brother."

Flint recognized the Eastern drawl instantly. "For God's sake, Luke, can't you think of a better way to wake a man?"

Luke pushed his hat back from his forehead revealing faded blue eyes. "In my job the element of surprise counts for a lot."

He stepped close, clasping Flint's hand while the other beat him solidly about the shoulder. "You're looking good, real good. Ranching must agree with you."

"Wish I could say the same for Betsy."

"How is she?"

"See for yourself." Flint stepped into the examining room where Betsy lay motionless on a cot in the far corner of the room. Her eyes were closed, and her face so colorless and drawn, it seemed to evaporate into the bleached sheets around her. The room smelled of lye and bitter medicines.

"We've tried everything we know to try to bring her around, but nothing seems to work."

"The bullet?" Luke asked with grave concern.

"Came out with little trouble. She's lost a lot of blood, and Doc thinks her body just shut down from the whole ordeal. He says it's a good thing because she'd not in pain. I'd rather have her scolding us and yelling like a lunatic about our crude behavior than like this. Doc says when she does come around, it will take weeks before we can even find out if she can use her arm."

Flint noticed the anger on his brother's face.

"And you have no idea who did it? Didn't anyone see anything?" Luke asked.

Flint shook his head. "It's like picking ants out of gravel. Betsy had no enemies, everyone adored her. She could bring a pack of hungry wolves to a dead stop with that smile of hers."

Frowning, Luke squatted at the edge of the cot and took Betsy's hand in his, stroking it gently. "Well, let's see what we can do." He turned his full attention to her, his voice shifting soft like the wind.

"Hey, pretty lady, time to rise and shine," he coaxed. "Didn't ride my tail all night and most of the morning to get a welcome like this."

When she made no response, he sighed and continued, "Ah, Bets, I know you're sore 'cause I haven't written, but I promise I'll try harder next time. God knows, I was never good with pen and paper."

He looked up at his brothers, his brow arched. "How long has she's been like this?"

"A least a day and a half," Marcus volunteered.

This time he took both of her hands in his, taking care not to jostle her injured shoulder. "Listen to me, Betsy," he said in an insistent voice, "I promise I'll buy you anything your little heart desires if you just rouse up long enough to let us know you're all right. Anything, anything a'tall--fancy dress, fastest horse in the territory, new saddle, you name it, kid."

"I already tried that," Marcus muttered, "so far I've promised her everything except the shirt off my back."

Luke grinned, despite his weariness. "Well then, sometimes a man has to go the extra mile."

He turned to the listless form again. "Betsy, marry me, honey. Can you hear me? It's Luke. Marry me, and I promise I'll take you away from this flea-bitten town and show you the sights of cities you've only dreamed of."

"I've tried that, too," Flint admitted sheepishly.

This time Luke let out a rolling laugh. "Well, that's the problem, she won't believe anything you two jackels have to offer. The gal's unconscious, she's not feebleminded."

Betsy's eyes fluttered for barely a second, and all three brothers flinched in surprise.

"Keep talking, Luke" Flint ordered. "I don't care what you say, but don't stop. Recite poetry. Sing. I think we're getting somewhere."

"Oh, good God, pleeease," Marcus groaned, "don't tell him to sing."

"Hey, pretty lady," Luke said, "I need a bath and a shave and a hug." His blond hair melted with hers as he bent down and kissed her on her cheek. "Come on, Betsy, I'm hungry for some home cooked meals and your apple pie. If you don't come 'round I'm going to be forced to start singing. That'll make me more enemies than friends."

Her long lashes fluttered again against her blanched face, and she moaned softly. For the first time since the accident, Flint felt a surge of hope course through him. "Keep talking," he urged Luke.

Luke rubbed her hands more briskly. "Come on, Betsy Ashmore, I've got a real surprise for you. A surprise so big that even your ugly brothers, myself excluded, won't believe it."

Much to everyone's amazement, she opened her eyes slowly and groaned, "Luke. . . Luke Ashmore? Is that you?"

"Luke?" she repeated and clutched his hand weakly in hers for a brief moment, then reached up and touched his chest. "It is you. It's really you."

He grinned, breathing a sigh of relief. "Yes, yes it is. One trail-beaten brother here. And if you think I'm frazzled-looking, you ought to see my horse."

"Where are we?" Betsy asked in a strained voice. She tried to sit up. "Oh-h, dear Lord, my shoulder. . .it feels like it's on fire."

"Well that happens when you get pounded with lead." He pushed her gently back down. "We're at Doc Silverstone's. You need to rest, and later you can tell me why you tried to stop a bullet."

"I'm so tired, so sore." Her voice was barely a whisper. "I want to talk to you."

"Not now. Go back to sleep," he ordered in a soothing voice and pushed limp strands of golden hair from her forehead. "When you wake up, we'll round up the family and talk."

The three men watched her eyes flutter and close shut again.

Luke removed a tin star from his chest pocket and tucked it securely in the palm of her good arm, then covered her gently with the sheet. He rose from the side of the cot and rubbed his hands over his red-rimmed eyes and face.

Overjoyed, Flint thumped him on the back with several hearty whacks. "Good going, Marshal Ashmore. I knew you would be the ticket!"

"Lord a-mercy," Marcus said, "for a moment I was sure I was going to have to listen your god awful singing."

"Come on men, insults after food and sleep," Flint said. "I'll take you down to the General Store. You can use Betsy's room. Marcus can stand watch here."

"Where's the wild Indian?"

"Tye? He'll be here as soon as he hears you're underfoot. Trust me, this town will have the word out in an hour."

The two brothers headed toward the door.

Marcus piped up, "Oh, one more thing, Luke, I think I should warn you."

The tall man turned. "Yeah?"

"Flint is still cranky when he's tired. He didn't outgrow it."

Luke snickered. "Are you still miserable when you're hungry?"

The huge man nodded, looking sheepish.

"Some things just never change, do they?" Luke said, shaking his head and smiling as he pulled the door open.

Outside, the two men crossed the street and headed for the far side of town where Luke could check on his horse at the livery and gather his meager belongings. The sun climbed hot and clear, and dust swirled at their feet. Somewhere in a nearby tree a red-winged black bird cried out.

"She may lose some of the use of her right arm," Flint told him as they walked along. "We picked a bullet out deep in the muscle."

Luke shrugged, his constantly wary eyes darting about. "I'll teach her to use her left. She learns right quick."

They paused briefly to watch in amusement as two dogs played tag, tangling with each other over a sun-bleached bone.

"That ought to be right interesting. It took us forever to teach you to tie hitches and knots. Sure stretched Pa's patience thin, too."

A grin split Luke's face. "Happens when you have older right-handed brothers who don't know a tinker's damn about knots in the first place."

The sheriff stepped out of his office in front of them.

"Heard all you boys were in town together," Anderson said. He made a futile attempt to hike up his pants under his drooping stomach.

Flint could see that the surly man had already taken more than a few hits from the bottle, and it wasn't even noon. He spoke, "Guess word travels quickly, Sheriff."

The man belched. "I don't want any trouble here. You understand?"

"What have you found out about the shooting?" Flint asked, ignoring the question. There was nothing he hated more than a man who threw less than one hundred percent of himself into any task.

"Nothin' yet, been working on some leads."

"From the chair in your office?"

"Now just a minute, just because your brother's one of those fancy U.S. Marshals, doesn't mean I'm just a hick town sheriff. I do a right fine job."

"Yeah, then tell me, who have you questioned? Where have you been?"

The sheriff's face turned scarlet.

For the last couple of years, everyone in town knew the sheriff hid his bloodshot eyes in the dim light of his office, venturing out only when absolutely forced to. His deputy handled most of the daily business and skirmishes.

"Just as I thought," Flint said, coolly. "Good day, Sheriff."

"Hold up, you can't brush me off like that, Flint Ashmore. Hey, how do I know Luke's even a marshal? He got papers? He ain't wearin' no badge."

Ignoring the man's outburst, the men continued up the street.

"I said I want to talk to you," he bellowed after them.

Luke glanced over his shoulder. "When you've got some leads, we're ready to talk, otherwise don't waste our time standing around snapping at thin air."

Anderson mumbled a string of expletives and stomped inside, the door banging shut.

Farther on they passed the gunsmith shop and telegraph office.

"You really planning to marry Betsy?" Flint asked. That Luke had always been in love with Betsy didn't come as a surprise to anyone. He had left home soon after they arrived in the territory, preferring to keep a distance between himself and the family to shield Betsy's reputation from tarnish. All the Ashmore brothers knew he'd return someday to claim her.

"Been thinking of settling down, yeah. What about you? Find anyone willing to put up with you?"

"Thought I did, but it didn't go anywhere."

"I'll bet you've been wooing the gentle lady in your usual romantic ways, big brother. Showing her how to clean a gun, shoe a horse, muck out stables, and offering her stability and a ranch to tend." He punched Flint playfully on the arm. "Say, bet I can guess the color of her hair."

"Bet you can't."

"Half-eagle says I can, let's make it worth my while."

From his pocket, Flint pulled out a five dollar gold piece and flipped it in the air, deftly catching it.

"Do it again," Luke urged.

The coin flew up again, but Luke's hand snatched it in mid-air this time. He shoved it into his pocket.

"Hey, that's not fair," Flint sputtered. "You didn't even guess."

"Red!"

Baffled, Flint stared at him. "How did you know?"

He watched his brother adjust his hat at a rakish angle and grin from underneath the brim. "Lucky guess, I reckon. I thought Pa told you a thing or two about red heads."

"Pa told me a lot of things to shy away from," Flint agreed in a disgruntled voice, not pleased he had just lost a gold piece so easily. "Gunslingers and brothers who gamble, for starters. Did you know Jamie Banes is in town?"

Luke shook his head. "Banes? What's he doing here?"

"Working for the Army."

"Never thought the Army was that hard up for decent help." Luke's face took on a perplexed look.

Together they entered the dim cool interior of the livery stable. Flint propped himself up against a stall, hands crossed at his chest, while Luke threw more hay for his horse and gathered his belonging stashed in a corner.

"You know," Luke said frowning as he threw a bag across his shoulder, "you sure had me on a turkey hunt with that Rusty Gast message."

"You found out who Gretchen was?"

"In a round about way, yeah."

"What's the relationship?"

"You're never going to believe this." A devilish smile tugged at the corners of his mouth.

The door to the livery opened on its creaky hinges and both men instantly fell silent. Frank Norwell walked in, leading a handsome blood bay. His white hair gleamed full moon white against the rich, red color of the prancing horse, eager to reach some feed.

"Well, well, just the man I hoped to see," he said to Flint and nodded at Luke in acknowledgment. "See you made it."

Flint threw him a gloomy stare and pushed himself from the stall.

He waited for the man to continue, not wishing to encourage his presence.

Frank Norwell spoke, "I got to thinking of what you said the other day about your cattle, so I decided to ride out and check the herds myself. There's well over a hundred head or more of mine missing."

Flint felt himself bristle. "Are you saying they're on my land?"

"Take it easy, Flint, I'm not saying any such thing. I'm saying someone's working both our herds pretty hard. Problem is, I can't figure out how, with all my men over the range. Tom usually keeps a tight rein on everyone coming and going on Flying N land."

"As soon as we get the time, we'll check ours again," Flint said. He didn't know what else to say. He wondered why the old wolf was taking the time to tell him.

"How's Betsy?" Norwell asked.

"We'll know more in a few days. We can't tell about the arm for quite some time, until the healing begins."

"I hope you come up with the scoundrel who did it." Norwell paused. "I know a few good doctors in Philadelphia. I'm willing to send her back East as soon as she's fit to travel."

Startled by his generous offer, Flint looked at him. The man's face was grave and he sounded sincere.

"Egad, Ashmore, don't look surprised," Norwell said with a frown. "I've always admired Betsy. In fact, I was hoping that someday she and Colin might get together."

"Colin?" Flint's mouth opened in astonishment, but he couldn't come up with anything to say. He felt Luke stiffen beside him.

"Yeah, the kid could use a level-headed woman like Betsy to cool him down. A good woman will do that. I'm not going to live forever, and there's a lot of ranch to take care of. It'll need to be run by someone with a quick mind and firm hand. Your sister can take care of books, order supplies, handle a weapon, and ride better than most men I know."

Flint smiled, thinking of his sister. "Yes, she can, that's a hazard of having four brothers. But I've my doubts she'd ever consider riding along side your son."

"Maybe you boys would never consider letting her do it," Norwell countered. He stared at the ground, then looked up with distant, dim eyes. "Sometimes when a man gets up there in years, he starts thinking about other things besides money. Grandchildren, for example."

He turned and led his horse into an adjoining stall, and busied himself stripping the saddle.

Outside, Luke looked incredulously at Flint. "Is he going senile? Whatever gave him the notion Betsy would look twice at that hot head with a twisted sense that a fast gun will make him a man?"

"She'd have everything she'd ever want," Flint said. "Everything we could never give her."

"What about love?" There was sharp edge in Luke's voice.

"Fancy dresses."

"What about love, I say?"

"Fastest horses in the territory."

Flint looked at his brother's sickened face and resisted the urge to smile. It wasn't often he was able to find Luke's soft spot. "Then there's a new saddle and tack. Pretty dishes, jewelry, lace, things women get a hankering for."

"You still haven't mentioned love!"

Unable to bear it a moment longer, Flint laughed, a deep satisfying rumbling laugh.

Hand on hips, Luke swore under his breath. "Why you, good for nothing, low down polecat, you had me for a moment. If I weren't so doggone tired, I'd try my hand at giving you a good thrashing." He spun around, toward the direction of the General Store.

Still chuckling, Flint hurried to keep up with him. They walked quickly along, past a buckboard tied at the dress shop and horses standing three-legged at the hitching rails.

"Gretchen," Flint prompted.

"She's Betsy's mother," Luke replied. "Dead now, passed away a year ago, about the same time as Rusty Gast."

"How'd you find out?"

Luke heaved a long sigh. "It wasn't easy. I had to drag my tail all the way to Virginia to do it. After I lost my leads on Rusty, I decided to have a chat with Aunt Mildred. Thought for a while I'd have to shake it out of the tight-lipped ol' gal, but then this brilliant idea popped into my head."

"Go on, let's hear it."

Luke flashed a mischievous grin. "I told her Betsy was dying of an incurable disease, wasting away to nothing, and her last wish was to know who her real parents were."

"Oh, Luke, how could you?"

"It worked," Luke said defensively. "Well, almost. She caught on fast, grabbed me by the ear and said, 'Lukie, I expect more of an Ashmore than a sack full of lies.' So I ended up showing her the wires you sent, and she finally relented, saying that now that Ma and Pa were dead, there was no longer any reason for secrets.

It seems Gretchen's parents, wealthy landowners from Georgia, weren't too fond of Rusty Gast and arranged for her to marry a true Southern gentleman. The courtship lasted a few months when she found out she was pregnant by this so-called Confederate gentleman and fled to a relative's house in Virginia. Rusty killed her fiancé in a gunfight. Fair, I might add, although I can't vouch Rusty didn't instigate it. But that left Gretchen in a more shameful situation than before. Refusing to marry Rusty, she had the baby and abandoned it with Ma and Pa."

"This Gretchen never wanted to find her?" Flint asked astonished. He couldn't imagine any mother abandoning her child.

"Well, things got more knotted. She ended up married to another Southerner who later enlisted in the War. They had a child who died around the age of three. To go North at any time would have caused suspicion and alarm. Later, with the War, it was impossible and would have been fruitless since Pa had already moved us West. However, Rusty had promised he'd keep a watchful eye over Betsy's whereabouts."

"Pa knew all this," Flint said matter-of-factly, remembering the times he had supplied Rusty with horses at rock-bottom prices.

"Oh, he knew all right, but he made darn sure Mother never found out, and Rusty was sworn to secrecy. Pa was afraid the information would break her heart, and there was no way he'd ever give up Betsy, not after he raised her like his own. Of course, Rusty would never tell, because he'd have to admit he killed her father, and he'd risk losing Betsy's trust and friendship. He'd taken a real shine to her by then."

"That's why he gave us back the money for the ranch," Flint said, realizing the tremendous guilt Rusty must have lived with every time he saw his sister. It also explained the letters he posted from Atchinson. He never wanted Betsy to know. What it didn't explain was why he sold the ranch to Julia Gast. He looked back over his shoulder and watched Tom Morton enter the telegraph office.

"Did Gretchen have any next of kin? Anyone that can be contacted? Anyone that can offer more information?"

"Now, Flint, just like you to be the curious one. I figured it was none of my business. If Betsy wants to scare up some ghosts, that'll be her choice."

"Who's going to tell her?" Flint asked.

"Best if I do," Luke replied. "It won't break her, she's wanted to know this for a long, long time. Maybe now she'll quit fretting and get on with her life."

"With you?"

Luke shrugged. "Who knows? It won't be Colin Norwell or Jamie Banes, you can bet on it."

"Why not?"

"I'll find a way to send them packing," Luke said quietly.

"Hurry, Anna, or we're going to be late."

Julia placed the picnic basket by the front door. The aroma of fresh baked apple pie rose from under the lid and made her stomach growl in an unladylike fashion. Through the open bedroom door at the back of the ranch house, she heard Anna muttering to herself in Danish. The young woman had cloistered herself inside for the last hour, flinging armloads of dresses about, trying to decide what to wear.

It had been two weeks since Betsy Ashmore had been shot, and she was recovering at home. Julia, Sven and Anna had been invited to supper at the Ashmore ranch. Julia had little doubt it was their modest way of expressing their gratitude. From the amount of fussing Anna was doing over her appearance, she also suspected there might be another cause for celebration. Earlier, Marcus had stopped by, dropping off a buggy for them to use. Sven was already out front, waiting patiently.

Minutes later, Anna appeared, pinning a cameo to the front of her blue silk dress as she hurried toward Julia. "I look good, ja?" she asked. She fidgeted with the cuffs on her sleeves.

"Anna, you look stunning," Julia said. "However, I warn you, if you decide to change one more time, we're going to have to eat that apple pie on the way over to avoid starvation."

The Dane laughed nervously. "Ah, but I do not want to shame him. I am meeting his brother, Luke, for the first time."

"Marcus Ashmore has never been ashamed of you when you were dressed in gingham with flour on your face, so I doubt he'll be ashamed to have you meet his brother dressed as splendidly as you are."

"Ja, but he is important. Imagine, a U.S. Marshal."

"Then you're safe. I doubt he'll know anything about fashion. I would suggest you memorize some wanted posters of outlaws instead." Grabbing her by the arm, Julia propelled her out the front door and toward the buggy before she could change her mind again.

Their route to the ranch was a circuitous one as they rode between small hills, capped with spicy pine, and across Cherry Creek, meandering in long, looping curves through the flat green valley abutting Frank Norwell's land. Hundreds of butterflies took flight from meadow flowers along the way, painting the sky with clouds of yellow. It was so exquisitely beautiful, Julia could have ridden for hours.

As soon as they entered the ranch yard, both Marcus and Flint stepped from the long, wooden porch to meet them. Unpretentious as always, Marcus gave them both a big, but gentle bear hug. Quickly he ushered Anna toward the house, under the soft strains of someone strumming a guitar.

Flint smiled a warm smile that melted the inside of her bones and took her hand. He was dressed in a dark suit that only made his hair appear more black.

"I'm so glad you're here, Julia. Come, I'd like you to meet the fifth member of our family."

He ushered her up the steps.

From the far end of the porch, a lanky man set his guitar aside and rose, closing the gap between them in a swaggering walk that was all too familiar. His faded blue eyes twinkled merrily, and he grinned at her like they had been caught in a childish prank.

Julia stopped, glued to the step. A sickening feeling wrapped itself around her heart as she fought to control any outward sign of astonishment. Her savior from her confrontation with Captain Bloomington had been Luke Ashmore! She stared at him, a dozen questions swirling in her mind. How much of her sorry past had he related to Flint and his brothers? Did they know about her engagement and subsequent broken engagement to Bloomington? She felt her face heat up when she thought back to their previous conversation. Gracious, she had even confessed to him that she loved Flint.

"Well, if that don't beat all," she heard Luke say. "She really is a red head, big brother, and a darlin' one at that." He moved to a spot directly in front of her. "And by gosh, that hair does outshine the color of a red fox."

From behind them, Betsy Ashmore's voice spoke, "Luke, for Pete's sake, stop that bloomin' blabbering and let Julia sit down."

Before Julia could utter a word, Luke had his arm encircled about her. He drew her toward Betsy. "You don't know how thankful we are that you were around when Bets was shot. Mighty fine job of stitching you did."

From a rocker bulging with soft pillows, Betsy Asmore's pale face smiled up at her. "The dinner is to thank you, Julia, but if you have to put up with this one all night, it may not be enough." She stared curiously at her. "You sure you're all right, you look a little pale?"

Pulling herself together, Julia smiled. "Why, I'm fine, just fine, perhaps a little famished. Sven and I were working all day on new designs for some greenware, and I've barely had time to eat."

"Then help me out of this blasted rocker. I'm tired of playing an invalid, and I'm a lot more than a little hungry."

Minutes later, Julia found herself seated around a rectangular oak table wedged between the broad shoulders of Flint and Luke. The table was simply, but tastefully set with plain china, surrounded by mountains of steamy food. It was obvious from the bantering that ensued the family was a close knit one. Had Julia's thoughts not strayed to the confrontation over and over again the dinner would have been enjoyable. Each brother amicably took his turn serving, despite Anna's earlier insistence that she and Julia were more than capable of doing it.

It was near the end, once Anna's apple pie had been devoured, when Marcus rose from his spot at the head of the table to fill everyone's glass with wine, and they grew silent. His bulky frame towered over them.

"Someone has to show some dang courage around here," he joked, blushing, "before we all end up old bachelors. Tonight I'd like to announce that Anna and I are getting married." He looked lovingly at the young Danish woman, who smiled radiantly up at him.

"Dear Lord, Anna, you didn't say yes, did you?" Luke piped up, clinking his glass against hers. "This one eats more than a grizzly. You'll never get out of the kitchen."

The bantering began again, with Marcus this time forced to take the brunt of the family jokes.

Only hours later, as the sun's rays faded, was Julia able to be alone with Flint. Together, they walked to the corrals below the house. The evening was still and serene. A few swallows sliced the sky overhead as they winged their way to the rafters of the barn to rest for the night.

Julia leaned against the rail, her eyes fastened to the horses. A white-faced sorrel trotted to the fence, looking for a hand-out or a bit of affection.

"Marcus is quite the joker," Flint said, as if he could sense her discomfort, "but you have to get used to Luke's humor. He's a little sassy, but he grows on you right fast." He reached out and stroked the some face.

...ed and looked at him. It was time to start shaking out the ...y linens. How was she ever going to make a home for herself, put down roots if she couldn't let go of the past? She remembered her father telling her a relationship was based on trust. There were never any secrets between her mother and him. He had loved her with an almost frightening loyalty, and had been faithful to even her memory.

"Has Luke ever mentioned he stopped at our ranch to water his horse the day he rode into Golden City?" she asked.

He shook his head. "Luke is a marshal first, brother second. Even though he has a tendency to babble like a brook, he's used to holding back a lot of information or storing it inside his head. I suppose he just forgot with all the hoopla centered on Betsy."

"No, he was being kind," she said. Slowly she related the incident with Charles Bloomington. When she finished, silence enveloped them. Overhead, stars began to struggle to show themselves. Finally, she looked up and searched his face. His eyes were unreadable.

"Say something," she said quietly.

He let out a long sigh before he spoke, "Julia, your past is none of my business. A man has a reason for doing the things he does. A woman has just as much right, I figure. What bothers me the most is you didn't tell me sooner. If Bloomington is as devious as you say, what will stop him from coming back? A man doesn't get his hide peeled and not hunger for revenge."

She shook her head. "This time I think he realizes he's met his match." Silently, she knew it was a lie, but maybe saying it might help to make it true. Hatred and scorn had carried him this far. She shivered and suddenly felt cold.

"Let me send Tye or Marcus to stay with you for a few weeks." He removed his coat and draped it over her shoulders, pulling her against his chest. She could hear his heart thudding beneath his shirt which smelled of bay rum and new mown hay.

"No, you need them here." The last thing she wanted was to cave in to her fears. She refused to allow herself to be helpless again. She refused to hide behind anyone, and especially someone she cared for.

"Marry me, Julia, just marry me," he whispered into her hair. "Forget about this hair-brained notion of having to make it on your own, having to run a ranch and turn a profit."

She pulled away and gazed up at him. "Flint, I just need a little more time. Time is a good thing. We can use it to get to know each other better." And give you time to tell me you truly love me, she thought, trying to ignore the passion his very presence stirred in her soul.

She felt him stiffen.

"Why?" he asked. "What difference will a few days, a few weeks or a month make? I'll not change my mind. There are no rules, Julia, that say two people have to wait a prescribed length of time before they marry. If you ask me, we're wasting time, and with Bloomington underfoot, all the better reason to hasten things a bit."

"Marry—to protect me?" she asked with a sinking heart.

"Why not?"

"No!" the word exploded from her. "Don't you see, just like the money, I'd be avoiding the issue? I'd be bringing my troubles straight to you and throwing them on your shoulders."

"I have strong shoulders. Why won't you let me help? Why are you so mule-brained?"

"Why are you so stubborn and insistent?" *If you're so concerned, then tell me you love me! Kiss me! Let me know you really care!* She wanted to scream the words at him.

"Pig-headed," he snarled. "That's what you are, pig-headed. You're out to prove you can do everything on your own, fool woman."

His anger and noble practicality grated on Julia's nerves. "Pig-headed? Flint Ashmore, you are the most stubborn, pragmatic man I've ever met in my life."

"Now just a second, that's just not true!"

"Careful, Flint, or your curly tail might grow longer," a deep voice teased from somewhere in the darkness. The smell of cigar reached them before they saw the glowing red of its tip.

"You stay out of this one, Marcus."

"Wish I could, but if you're both planning to draw blood, I'm obligated to get Luke out here." Like a giant bear, Marcus materialized from the darkness and leaned against the corral.

"Does Anna know you are inclined to puff on those disgusting things?" Flint asked irritably.

"Yeah, reckon so," Marcus said and clamped the cigar between his teeth. "I'll have you know this is not just a regular ol' disgusting cigar, Flint, this is a genuine, well-cured, Turkish cigar. Luke gave me a whole box of them as an engagement present."

"Tomorrow he dies," Flint muttered.

Marcus let out a low, coarse guffaw. "Come, both of you, put a lid on your tempers, just for tonight. Betsy just put on a fresh pot of coffee. Anna wants to dance, and Luke is agreeable to tune up the guitar and play a few songs. I made him promise he wouldn't sing." He left, heading toward the glowing light of the house.

"Marcus is right," Julia said, chastising herself for being so insensitive to Anna's and Marcus's happiness. It was a time for celebration, not warfare. Gently enfolding his hand in hers, she said apologetically, "I'm sorry, Flint, I didn't mean to anger you."

She felt him relax, and he slipped an arm around her shoulders, pulling her close. "Maybe a dance isn't a bad idea," he confessed., "at least I get to hold you in my arms."

She smiled, savoring his words as they strolled toward the laughter, light and music. "Your brother is a man of many talents. I didn't know he was a musician."

"He's not, I assure you. He can strum a few half-decent chords, but like Marcus said, don't ask him to sing or the racket of your pesky goats will seem like a heavenly melody to your ears."

Twenty-One

Flint Ashmore was in a foul mood.

So foul, all of his brothers had avoided him the following morning, going about their tasks as if he didn't exist.

Actually, ever since Julia Gast had confessed her confrontation with Charles Bloomington, Flint felt himself growing more and more irascible by the minute. He simply was unable to get it off his mind. Of equal concern were her naïve assumptions about the man. Bloomington was far from harmless. From what Luke had later told him, Charles Bloomington was mean-spirited and cruel. Luke had made it a point to keep track of his whereabouts, but after Bloomington had been spotted hanging around a saloon thirteen miles away in Denver, he disappeared.

Still harboring unsettling thoughts, Flint went in search of his brothers hiding out in the stables. The bunkhouse roof needed to be repaired, and it was a two-man chore.

"Take Marcus," Tye volunteered when Flint finally found them.

"Just a dad-burned minute! Why me?" Marcus demanded. "Why do I always have to work with him when he's in a wretched mood?"

Flint felt like he was invisible as his brothers verbally sparred back and forth.

"It only makes sense," Tye countered. "You're the handiest with tools, Marcus, and the only one who can stand him when he's like this." Tye headed to the door to make his escape from the barn.

He stopped and grinned. "If you leave him with us, Luke will shoot him or I'll end up skinning him with my knife."

"But he hates heights," Marcus called after Tye's retreating back. "You and I could do it and cut him some slack."

"Absolutely not!" Tye shouted back over his shoulder. "We're all praying you push him off the roof and give us hope for some peace around here."

Now, perched over the ground with a bundle of wooden shingles beside each of them, Flint watched Marcus merrily hammering away like an overstuffed woodpecker thumping on a hollow log. Every once in a while, he whistled a merry tune or belted out the lyrics of a song. The hammer he held never missed a nail, and already Flint had slammed this thumb three times.

Ironically, it was Marcus who suggested they take a break barely an hour later. Straddling the peak of the roof, he pulled out a cigar from his pocket and lit it. Cautiously, Flint crawled to the peak and sat opposite him. He avoided looking straight down to the ground. The thought alone made him feel nauseous. Once when he was a child, Marcus had coaxed him up to the top of a cherry tree. When he finally was able to shimmy down to go home, he had left the cherries he had just eaten behind.

"Why don't we just crawl down for a break?" he asked, hopefully.

"Nope," Marcus replied. "Waste of good time. This is the best seat in the house. Would you take a look at that beautiful view?"

"I would prefer not to," Flint replied grimly. "Tell me, Marcus, how do you always manage to be so cheerful?"

"You're looking at a man that just got himself betrothed to the most wonderful woman in the world and you ask such a silly question?" Marcus grinned. "How come you're always so miserable?"

"I work at it."

Marcus chuckled and ruined the smoke ring he was trying to make.

"What do you make of Norwell losing cattle just like us?" Flint asked, swatting a hole through the hazy screen drifting before his face.

Marcus rubbed his jaw. "I think we over-reacted a little with Betsy laid up. It was probably a one-time rustler sweeping the area, and then moving on. Look at it this way, if Norwell lost cattle, he's probably doubling his guard on the area. Tom Morton runs a pretty tight ship. We won't lose any more."

"What about Betsy getting shot?"

"Now, Flint, I've mulled that over a lot the past couple of days. I still don't think that bullet was meant for her."

"Who then?"

"Colin Norwell. The kid's got a right fine way of riling up people without even trying. Or maybe someone was trying to get to his old man, by getting to him."

"It's a possibility," Flint agreed. But somehow he wasn't convinced. "We still don't have a clue who tried to scare Julia off the ranch."

"That gal's really getting to you isn't she?" Marcus asked, smiling.

"I can't figure out how do you do it, Marcus."

"Do what?"

"Understand what women want."

Marcus let out a belly-laughing roar and had to grip the peak of the roof to keep from falling off. "If I had a surefire secret, I'd be a mighty rich man."

Flint looked at him sourly. "If she just weren't so hell-bent on making it on her own."

"Julia? She's got grit, all right," Marcus agreed. "You know, Flint, I'm no authority on women, but someone like Julia needs lots of room. She's got the temperament of a colt. Box her in and she's bound to get skittish."

"Lord, Marcus, if I give her anymore room, I'll be courting her from Texas."

"Now that we're on the subject," Marcus said, wedging the cigar between his teeth.

"About giving her room?"

"No, you nincompoop, about courting." They traded grins.

"You got to understand, Flint, that women are a little softer, a lot more sentimental, and have a short fuse when you fire them up. Shoot, you're treating Julia like she's your side-kick instead of someone special, and lately, you've been treating all of us like we're your enemies, instead of your brothers."

They stared at each other and let silence fall around them. Flint looked out over the land. It was striking all right, but was a whole lot better-looking from the ground. From where he was perched, the meadows undulated out in a checker board effect of greens and browns. Marcus was right, he decided, he needed to give Julia room. She had asked for time, and time was certainly something he had a lot of.

"I guess we'd better get this finished up before dark or I'll be playing rooster again tomorrow," Flint said, groaning as he uncurled himself to slither down the roof. "Feels like rain may be coming in. Are you going to see Anna tonight?"

"Naw, I promised the boys I'd play some cards. Anna and Sven left this morning for Denver. Anna wants some sort of fancy material for her wedding dress. They'll be back the day after tomorrow."

Flint blinked. "You mean Julia is alone at the ranch?" He felt his stomach turn over and suddenly wished solid ground was underneath his feet. The idea that she would be spending two days by herself sent a chill up his back.

"Maybe as soon as we finish, I'll wash-up and take a ride over, just to see if there's anything she needs," he suggested.

Marcus threw him a sly look. "I can finish this without you, you know. So far you've made a pancake of your thumb, ruined half my sack of nails, and dropped three bundles of shingles on the ground. To be perfectly honest, I really can't take much more of your help."

"Tell Betsy I'm going to miss supper, will you?" Flint said grinning. He felt his mood instantly lighten at the thought of seeing Julia Gast again. He started to crab-walk down the roof.

"Hey, wait a minute," Marcus called after him. "Why don't you take her something nice. A gift. Something from the heart. Women like those things, you know."

"Like what?" Flint asked, twisting around.

"I don't know," Marcus said with a shrug, "and if I did, then I'd be courting her instead, wouldn't I?"

Thunderheads were building on the horizon and a stiff breeze was blowing when Flint rode into the yard of the Gast ranch. Julia was nowhere in sight, so he dropped off a bundle on the front porch, tied his horse at the hitching rail and crossed to the shed.

She was inside, bent over the potter's wheel working on a pitcher recently air-dried. Carefully, she was etching something on its side with a knife-like object.

Flint leaned against the doorjamb and quietly watched her work. Unaware of his presence, she labored diligently, her eyes bright and excited, her flaming red hair tied back from her eager face. He could see that she was in love with her work, totally absorbed by the creativity of it all, like a child with a new toy. He was content to just stand there and watch her until the sun set.

Suddenly, like she had a sixth sense, she gazed up and smiled.

"I didn't hear you ride in," she said.

"I didn't mean to disturb you. Where is everyone?"

"When I saw it clouding up, I gave the hands time off and told them to be back once the sun shines. You can't break horses in the rain."

She motioned to him to join her. "I'm trying to fashion this for Anna and Marcus as a wedding present." She spun the wheel toward him and he could see she had etched an elaborate flowery pattern on the face of the pitcher, and below it had inscribed their names and the year 1868. "I'm going to try a new glaze as well. I want this to be special, very special. What do you think?"

"You're very talented," he said. "They'll be delighted." Beside him a stiff wind kicked up and blew a gust through the open window. He strode over and latched it shut. "We're going to get a dandy storm, Julia. It rode my heels all the way in. Do you have everything buttoned down?"

She jumped up quickly. "Oh, gracious, no! The goats and mule are still outside."

They rushed from the shed into a blast of wind which swirled around them, tearing at their clothes. Lightning streaked through the dismal sky, and in the distance thunder boomed.

"Get the goats," he shouted to her and raced toward the corral to gather the mule and untie his horse.

The sky split open and poured down buckets of rain. Minutes later, drenched, but with the animals in tow, they entered the barn. Flint stripped his saddle and blanket from his horse, then helped Julia rub down the dripping mule.

"It looks like it might be a long one," she said. "I was just about to warm up some stew for supper. You'll stay?" She shivered, grasping her thick tresses of red hair, set free by the strong wind. She deftly wrung the water from them as best she could. Water dripped from her long lashes.

"I can stay," he said simply, mesmerized by her flawless beauty. He felt a tightening in his loins.

"Well, come," she said gleefully and stepped out into the pouring rain again. "We're already wet, no sense in sitting in a smelly old barn all night."

Once inside the house she brought some soft cloths for him to dry off with and hurried to her room to change.

Unbuckling his gun belt, he shrugged out of his soaked shirt and built a small fire in the sitting room. He looked about. It was snug and pleasantly arranged with a vase of yellow and blue wildflowers on the mantle and hand-sewn pillows on the settee. He could see Julia's handiwork in the pottery that lined the windowsill and was scattered about the room. It smelled faintly of lemon and beeswax, but of earth and clay as well. It would be easy, he thought, to be part of these surroundings for the rest of his life.

Julia was mildly surprised to find Flint shirtless, squatting beside the windowsill with a small multi-colored vase in his callused hands when she returned.

"That's one of Anna's flukes," she said tearing her eyes from his well-muscled back. "Isn't it a beauty? We're toying with new glazes. Unfortunately, the thing about making a mistake is when it turns out to be worthwhile, we can't always figure out how to reproduce it. Not yet, anyhow."

She pointed to a crock at his feet. "That's yours. I just never got around to giving it to you. Spin it around."

He picked up the crock, rose and turned it slowly in his hands. The Circle A brand was etched on its side.

"This is a pleasant surprise, thank you," he said and smiled a smile that made her heart melt despite the chill from the rain. He had a way of turning her emotions upside down. His drawl, his solid chest, even the way he walked sent warm sensations through her body from her head to her toes.

"You're welcome. Betsy told me you liked buttermilk, so I thought you could keep it in the spring house." She stepped past him to go to the kitchen. "I'll make some coffee and warm up some stew. It looks like the rain is going to last a while. We can eat it here, near the warmth from the fireplace."

When she returned with a tray of food and coffee, she found him still bare-chested, but grinning from ear to ear. He swept his hand to the floor before the hearth. "You beat me to the draw, I was planning to give you this for a present. It's to cover the floor beside your bed. Anna told Marcus you hate cold winter floors."

Julia set the tray on a table and knelt beside a giant bear rug which was a good eight feet long. "This is exquisite," she murmured, touching the soft brown fur streaked with white. "Where did you get it?"

"It's a silvertip," he said. "A few years back, Marcus and I took a few weeks to explore the Rockies when we stumbled upon this big fellow. He didn't appreciate us barging into his territory.

"You shot this grizzly yourself?"

"Well, put it this way, we were both short-tempered that day, and this brute lost."

She laughed merrily and rose, gathering up the tray. "Oh, let's just eat here on the rug, before the fire. We can pretend it's a rained-out picnic."

They ate slowly, listening to the rain drum on the roof, and the snap and crackle of resin from the burning logs. When they were finished, Julia reached to take the tray. His hand came up and he stopped her. "Leave them be, we'll get them later." He stared at her and she felt like his eyes were burning holes inside her.

He reached up and cupped her face. "I love the fairy dust on your face," he whispered softly.

Julia felt her heart drumming in her chest. Without warning, he leaned closer and kissed her gently on the lips. The kiss deepened and suddenly she felt his arms envelope her, pushing her down into the softness of the rug.

A rain of kisses followed and Julia thought she was drowning as he traced a path down her throat and back to her mouth again. She felt his hand touch her breast and caress the fabric of her dress. She arched up and returned his kiss as his tongue tangled with her own.

He broke away, his lips traveling down her neck to her collar bone. "You're going to have to tell me to stop, tell me to leave," he groaned in her ear, and she heard her body and mind scream *no* together.

He stopped and looked into her eyes. "Tell me what you want, Julia," he insisted in a husky voice.

"Don't leave," she whispered.

"Are you sure?"

"Yes, don't leave," she whispered and reached up to pull his face back down to hers. The kiss was long and hard; and when it ended, he quickly removed his clothes. Slowly he disrobed her as well, gazing at her with a look of hunger and tenderness combined. She could feel the heat flowing from his body to hers.

He kissed her gently on her temple and threaded his fingers through her hair, holding her head while he spoke. "It will be good, I promise."

She nodded and felt his hands roam over her body, caressing her, as his mouth dipped to close over her breast. Suddenly she wanted him with a feeling so intense she could hardly bear it. She clawed at his shoulders, trying to get him to stop the want that was so close to exploding. She needed him, and every part of him.

He rolled on top of her and gently eased himself inside. She stiffened slightly, but his mouth came plunging down to cover hers, and the searing pain lasted but a brief moment before she felt a tension so strong again, so deep within, that she thought she'd die if it weren't fulfilled. They moved in rhythm together like the rain hammering on the roof above their heads, and with a fiery passion until she felt waves of euphoria wash over her like she was on a potter's wheel spinning, spinning, spinning and flying off into glorious space. He exploded inside her simultaneously, his lean, hard body going slack and satiated.

He rolled off her and smiled, kissing her on the ear and pulling her close. "You are the most beautiful woman I've even known," he whispered. He brushed a hand over her breast and pulled a handful of her hair toward him, fingering the silky strands. "You have beautiful eyes, an exquisite body and hair that drives a man wild."

She raised herself up on one elbow and traced the scar above his eye. "How'd you get that?" she asked and kissed it gently.

"This?" He rubbed the scar again. "Betsy threw a rock at me when she was younger. She and Tye pilfered my best shirt and cut it to shreds to use for sails on some stick boats they were playing with at the creek. I went after them. Would have had them both, if Tye hadn't decided to convince her to dig in and fight back—with rocks."

"And the one on your back?" She had felt it when they were making love.

"Scrapping with Luke. Betsy walloped me with a hoe trying to protect him."

"Did it hurt?"

Flint chuckled. "Not as much as our backsides when Pa was finished with us." He snuggled her close to him and drew an uneven breath. "Julia, we have to talk."

"I thought we were." She laughed lightly and swatted his chest.

"No, about us."

She laid a finger over his lips. "No, I won't let you," she said. "I won't let you ruin this perfect moment."

"What if you're pregn—"

"No, Flint, I refuse to have you spoil it with your practicality. I refuse to hear one word about marriage. You promised me that you'd give me time. Orders for pottery have just started flooding in. I can't keep up with the orders for ring flasks. A string of horses are supposed to be delivered to the Army next week, and the bakery is--"

"Confound it, Julia, I don't care about your money-making schemes. I care about us."

She heard the anger in his voice and she leaned down and kissed his shoulder. "If you care about us, then it's time to spend the next few weeks courting me." *And tell me you love me! Just say it once so I know.*

He rolled toward her and covered her mouth with a hungry kiss before speaking. "Three weeks, that's all you get. Then we talk marriage."

She grinned. "All right, three weeks."

"Does courting involve what we're doing now?" he asked and buried his face in her hair, nuzzling her ear.

"I suppose it could," she said, smiling, feeling a need building up inside her again.

He pushed her gently down into the soft fur, his hand roving sensually over her breast and stomach. "Then let the courting begin," he whispered softly.

Twenty-Two

"I dream of Julia with the bright red hair." The melody was Stephen Foster, but the words certainly were not.

Julia rolled over and snuggled deeper into the soft bear rug, savoring its warmth. Suddenly her eyes popped open. Someone was not only singing in her kitchen, but from the smell of bacon drifting through the door, he was also cooking.

She rolled over and discovered she was underneath a quilt taken from her bed. Beside her, the fire in the hearth burned merrily and outside the rain continued to patter softly on the roof. She smiled, remembering the night before.

Flint Ashmore. He was still here. Quickly she jumped up, realized she was naked and wound the quilt about her. She looked up to find him standing in the doorway with a mug in his hand.

"You don't have to wear that for my account," he said.

She ran her hand through her tangled hair. "I must look a sight," she said with a groan. She felt the heat rise to her face. She thought about how intimate he had been with her last night, and how utterly bold she had been.

"You look beautiful," he said, propping his hip against the jamb. He was dressed only in his denims, his shirt still draped over the back of a chair. "Coffee?"

She nodded and he handed her the mug.

"I'd better go wash up and get dressed," she stammered avoiding his eyes. She gathered up her discarded clothes and headed for her bedroom where she hurriedly scrubbed her face and dressed, then pulled a brush through her thick hair, tying it back from her face with a green ribbon.

When she returned, he had already fixed them a plate of bacon and eggs.

"Your call," he said smiling sensually. "We can eat here, or try the ol' rained-out picnic again."

"No, here," she blurted out and quickly pulled out a kitchen chair.

He leaned over, kissed her on the temple and whispered, "You're not helping me with this courting thing."

She felt herself blush again.

The sound of approaching riders brought them both to attention. "Your hands must be very loyal," he said, "to give up a second night on the town." He moved to the living room and pulled on his boots and shrugged into his shirt, jamming it behind his belt.

"Ashmore, if you're inside there, you'd better come out," someone yelled above the sound of horses thundering into the yard.

Julia watched Flint push back the curtains and peer out. He stepped quickly to the chair, buckled on his gun belt and pushed his hat on his head. "Get this out of here," he said stiffly, motioning to the tray of dried food left on the floor.

Julia sprung into action and gathered it up, so nervous she almost upset the bowls. Stoneware rattled and clinked against each other.

"Ashmore, no sense in hiding behind a woman's skirts," a familiar voice boomed.

Colin Norwell! Julia recognized the voice instantly. "What does Colin Norwell want?" she asked.

"I don't know, but I'm about to find out. You stay in here," he ordered.

"Flint, it's raining out there."

"I'll remind Norwell," he said sourly and tugged the brim of the hat lower. He pulled the door open, stepping out onto the porch.

Julia stood at the screen and tried to peer around Flint's broad back. The rain had lightened, but was still steady.

"You want something, Colin?" Flint asked.

From her vantage point Julia could see six riders in slickers, each with a gun drawn and pointed at Flint. Tom Morton was with them.

"Yeah, I want something," Colin sneered. "Last night or early this morning one of my men was killed between your property and mine. Shot in the back."

"What's that to do with me?" Flint asked.

"I talked with your sister, and she said you didn't come home last night," he said.

"That's right," Flint replied, "so what?"

"So where were you?"

"That's none of your business, Colin. I could be asking the same thing of any one of you. I do know I wasn't crazy enough to be checking

175

on our property line in the pouring rain."

Julia started to push the screen open.

"Get back inside," Flint hissed.

She eased the door shut, her heart pounding wildly in her chest. She knew he'd die before he'd drag her name through this to clear his own.

"Now unbuckle that gun belt," Colin ordered in a harsh voice. "You can't beat six rifles and guns."

"Only if you guarantee we go straight to the sheriff's office in Golden."

"Oh, we'll go, all right," Colin sneered. "I can't wait to see what kind of flimsy excuse you have to offer him."

Julia saw Flint's hands lower to his belt buckle.

"No!" she screamed, clawing at the door.

"Julia, I said to stay out of this," he warned harshly.

Stunned, she watched three riders dismount. Water tumbled from their slickers as they ambled up to the steps. Two surly-looking ones yanked him viciously by the arms and shoved him toward the horses. He tried to shrug off their hold, but the third man sent the butt of his rifle into his side. Flint groaned and doubled over, holding his waist.

"Let's just hang this crow bait on the spot!" Morton shouted, and a cry of agreement went up from the group of enraged men.

"Now just a second," Colin said. "I gave him my word we're headed for Golden."

"To hell with your promise," a slight-built man shouted angrily. "He killed Jess Williams, I'll bet my life on it."

Suddenly, frenzy broke out as mob rule took control. Someone tore a lariat from a saddle. The men dragged Flint, kicking and fighting, toward a large elm a few feet from the shed.

"String him up!" a voice yelled.

Fear coursed though Julia's veins as she stood transfixed, unable to move. Do something, she thought wildly and forced the screen open. Then she remembered her uncle's double barreled shot-gun just inside the door. She whirled and rushed to the dresser in her bedroom, rummaging around until she found a box of shells. She stuffed a handful into her pocket and raced back to the living room. Hands shaking, she jammed two shells into the barrels and pushed the screen door open so violently it crashed against the outside wall as she stumbled out.

Heart thudding, she raised the shotgun, firing into the air above the mob. Buckshot peppered the leaves on the elm and rained down upon their heads. Taken off-guard, the group ducked and scrambled for cover behind the gigantic tree trunk. The two men holding Flint flattened themselves to the ground and looked up with terror-filled eyes. Flint darted off to the side, but Colin Norwell blocked his path, gun drawn.

"I'm not real good with this," Julia screamed at them, "but someone told me you don't have to be very accurate."

"Take that away from her," Tom Morton shrieked to the men mulling around behind him. They stared warily at each other, but no one stepped forward.

Around her, Julia could smell the arid stench of gun powder, more keenly because of the rain still falling.

"Tell her, Ashmore, to put the shotgun down before someone gets hurt," Morton ordered.

"Why don't you come and get it, Tom?" she yelled. "I have one more shot and a handful in my pocket. I can load at least one more before the second man reaches me. Who's willing to volunteer? I understand this is powerful enough to leave only teeth and hair."

Before anyone had a chance to reply, a rider appeared, racing his blood bay up the rock-strewn road. Soon Frank Norwell's white-capped figure came into view. He spurred his lathered mount into the yard and drew up below the porch steps. "Now what the devil's going on here?" he asked tersely. He swept his dripping hat from his head.

A hollow-faced man with savage eyes spoke, "Flint Ashmore killed Jess Williams!"

"You got proof of that?" Frank Norwell asked.

The group fell silent.

He squinted through the drizzle at Julia, still holding the shotgun on the group. "Now, Miss Gast, you seem like the one in control at the moment, you want to start sorting this out for me."

"You don't have to tell him anything," Flint said, "and that includes the truth."

"See, see!" Morton yelled. "I knew he did it. I just knew it."

Eyebrows raised, Frank Norwell looked at Julia again.

"I'd like to talk in private," she admitted, "if you'll step inside the barn." She hesitated. "Only I don't trust your men."

"Don't do it, Julia," Flint said. "He's not the law, and you don't have to tell him anything."

Obviously confused, Frank Norwell asked, "Just what does he mean?"

"Don't pay him any mind," Julia ground out. She glared at Flint.

Frank Norwell addressed the group. "Miss Gast and I are going to take a little stroll together. Until we return, I'm warning everyone here, if you touch that man or get trigger happy, you'll answer to me. Understand?" He waited until he saw the men nod their heads. He motioned to Julia and she stepped off the porch. She carried the shotgun at her side.

Inside the barn, she spoke quickly, "Flint's horse is over there. Your men seem to have this foolish notion he was riding the line early this morning and shot Jess Williams. They decided to rough him up and string him up."

Frank Norwell ran his hand over the horse's back. "Why, this mount, Julia, hasn't been out in the rain." With a puzzled expression, he looked at the saddle and blanket. His eyes circled the barn coming to rest in the straw by the horse's hind hooves. It was evident the stable had not been mucked out since early yesterday. "Why, from the looks of things, this horse hasn't been out all night," he said.

Their gazes locked together for a long moment.

"Mr. Norwell," Julia said, collecting herself, "you're a very intelligent man. Do I have to spell it out for you?"

He pondered her revelation for barely a split second, and shook his head, sighing deeply. "No, Julia, that's not necessary." Rubbing his forehead thoughtfully, he muttered, "It's a right fine mess we have out there now, isn't it?"

"Yes," she agreed. If he was expecting her to be ashamed, she had no intentions of giving him that pleasure. Much to her surprise, he smiled the barest of smiles. His gray eyes brightened and danced on his weather-beaten face.

"Well, my dear, I guess we have our job cut out for us. Remember me saying half the fun of the battle is the fighting?"

She stared at him.

"The other half is laying down strategy. Stay close and let me do the talking," he suggested.

When they stepped from the barn, the rain had ended. Reluctantly, she followed him across the muddy yard to where his men were positioned.

"Looks like there's been a mistake," he said to Flint, "you have my apologies for this bunch of curs." He bent and picked up Flint's hat that had fallen in the ruckus and handed it to him.

"But Pa!" Colin blurted out. "We have no proof he wasn't there when Jess was killed."

"If you have proof he was, speak up," Norwell replied sharply, his eyes circling the group of men and coming to rest again on his son.

Colin shook his head.

Norwell's temper snapped like a twig in a wind storm, and Julia could see raw anger bubble up from deep inside him. "Then don't be a mule's hind end, son. You've messed this one up good. You can't go around accusing people of killing someone without proof."

He turned to Flint and asked gruffly, "Do I have your word you weren't near our property line last night?"

"I already told them I wasn't," Flint snarled in reply.

"His word's good enough for me," Norwell said in curt dismissal. "I think you boys all better cool off before you get your heads shot off. Egad, look at you. You've lowered yourselves to being vigilantes!"

"You're going to believe him?" Morton growled. "You're going to believe that snake? You must have a short memory. His father was your enemy."

"Of course I believe him. I have no reason, nor evidence not to." Norwell pinned his frosty eyes on Morton. "You," he barked, "should have had control of this situation. I expected much more of you than this!"

His eyes swept over his men. "Have you all gone completely mad? If it isn't bad enough you tried to hang a man without the law on your side, you tried to do it in front of a woman! You all ought to be soundly thrashed for such an indignity. Now get your sorry hides back to the ranch before I start docking your pay."

In a flurry of activity, the men scrambled to their mounts. Norwell waited until they were several yards out before he spoke to Flint. "Will you be all right?" he asked.

Flint's hand went to his side. "Yes, it's probably nothing more than a few bruised ribs. I've had worse. I guess I should be glad you showed up," he added begrudgingly.

Norwell barely acknowledged the compliment. He grunted. "It's Julia you should be thanking, man," he said. "The only thing I did was to keep some lead out of my men's wet carcasses." He smiled at Julia as she approached, leading her horse.

"Thank you, Mr. Norwell. It surely was a relief to see you," she admitted. She didn't care what anyone thought about Frank Norwell. If the truth were known, she wanted to hug the old man.

Norwell slipped up into the saddle with catlike grace. "You'd better see to his ribs." His gaze fell on Flint. "We still have to sort out this Jess Williams thing, Flint. I don't like this at all. Jess was a good man. I relied on him as much as I do Morton."

"I'll put Luke on it right quick."

"I'd be obliged," he said.

Julia waited until he disappeared from view, hugging her arms at her waist. She had little doubt trouble was brewing. "Why would a man be out riding the line in the pouring rain?" she asked and searched Flint's face.

"I don't know. It doesn't make sense unless he was meeting someone." He set his hat on his soggy head and winced.

"Let's take a look at that side," she suggested. "You need to dry off." Above them the sun was struggling to peer through the drab sky.

"What did you tell him?" Flint asked.

"Frank Norwell?" she asked, walking toward the house. "Nothing, he figured it out without any help."

"Next time I tell you to do something, I mean it," he said. There was fury building in his voice. "You could have been killed pulling a fool stunt like that. You don't even have the foggiest notion how to handle that shotgun."

After all that had happened, the remark was the final straw. Desperately, all Julia wanted was to sit down. Her heart had only stilled itself to normal, and her legs still felt like soft clay. She turned on him, "If I hadn't tried to do something, your neck might have been six inches longer, you fool."

He opened his mouth to speak, but she cut him off with a sharp voice. "Now get inside the house, Flint Ashmore, and let me take a look at those battered ribs. And if you say one thing, just one more thing, I swear I'll bind your mouth instead!"

Twenty-Three

The morning was gray and dim, like so many mornings before daylight blossoms when Julia awoke with a start, and lay still listening, barely daring to breathe. Something was wrong. At first she thought someone was moving in the house, but then she realized it was outside. Near the corrals.

Dressing quietly and quickly, she crept down the stairs and opened the back door, taking great care to be sure the hinges glided open and shut without their usual creaky whine. Gun in hand, she skimmed the back of the house, her back scraping against the coarse log sides. Thick dark shadows still lay close to the buildings and offered her some much-needed protection. She edged around the corner and stood motionless, listening to the sifting wind before she silently glided toward the barn disappearing into deeper shadows on the western side.

"Something's out there."

She jumped at the voice.

"Mercy, Toby," she whispered. "You almost scared me to death."

"Sorry, ma'am," he said lowly, coming to stand beside her. "Reckon you heard it, too."

"Shhh," she whispered.

The wind shifted again and the mares in the corral laid back their ears, picked up a scent and snorted to each other. Julia heard Sugar let out a husky whinny and trot to the far side of the corral. Suddenly, the rest of the bunch grew alert and followed suit.

"Ha! Looks like it's more four-legged, than two," Toby said and stepped bravely out into the open yard.

"How can you be sure?" she hissed at his back.

"Ma'am, those fillies are acting a might too fussy and frisky. Somehow women can always tell when a stud's around." He looked sheepishly at Julia. "Uh, sorry ma'am, no offense."

Warily, Julia followed him into the yard.

"Look-ee here," Toby said quietly, whistling under his breath. "Have you ever seen anything so pretty?"

A brilliant white stallion, wearing a fresh Flying N brand, sashayed up to the mares' corral and snorted as he pawed the ground. He was well-groomed, sleek and strong, at least seventeen hands high.

"Wonder what he's doing here?" Julia asked.

"Probably got randy and jumped the fence."

"Think we can catch him?"

It was a silly statement, she realized instantly. Toby was already shaking loose a lariat draped over a post near them.

"Miss Julia," he said, "this critter ain't about to go away, if you know what I mean." His face reddened. "In fact, if we don't catch him, you may have a slew of white colts you weren't counting on come spring."

Julia laughed. "That would certainly make Frank Norwell one delighted man."

She watched Toby expertly throw the lasso around the stallion and calmly approach it. He waited until the snorting beast settled before he stroked its huge neck, speaking tenderly, talking soft words of nonsense to it. Sometimes Julia almost felt overwhelmed by his natural ability to work with the stock. Never once had he raised a hand in anger to any of the animals on the ranch, including the finicky mule and bothersome goats. The other ranch hands had often joked that the horses were not really broken, just talked into submission.

"Keep him tied, away from the mares," Julia said. "I'm meeting Flint Ashmore in an hour to go fishing. I can take him over to the Flying N, drop him off and double back to the creek."

Toby nodded. "I'll saddle that brown gelding for you. As jumpy as this ol' boy is, it's might be best if you stay off a stallion or mare."

Julia frowned. She had been hoping to ride the sorrel. He needed the edginess run off him, but Toby's concern was justified. It could cause her more problems, and problems were something she didn't need at the moment.

Gun in hand, she picked up her skirts and headed for the house.

The air tasted of dust and shimmered in the summer heat when Julia rode into the deserted yard of the Flying N spread.

Frank Norwell was known to be a shrewd cattle baron, and his ranch was said to be a well-guarded fortress. Julia had no doubt the moment she reached the first corral where a spotted stallion circled the fence and pawed the ground restlessly that Norwell had been alerted to her arrival. Three men, Tom Morton among them, emerged from the barn almost instantly and headed her way.

"Well, Miss Gast, what have we here?" Tom Morton asked, coming to stand beside her.

"Your stallion. Guess he jumped the fence last night." She dismounted and handed him the lead rope. "My mares must have lured him over."

The stallion, docile since he had left the scent of her horses, stepped sideways with ears laid back.

"This wild thing will be the death of us yet," Morton said sourly. He yanked viciously on the rope, and the stallion reared back and shrieked shrilly.

Morton's eyes grew black. With another sharp tug, he tried bringing the stallion back to its front feet and failing, grabbed the end of the lariat and began whipping the horse about its shoulders. The horse screamed again, the whites of its eyes gleaming.

"Don't!" Julia shouted. "He's only nervous." Her hand shot out to grab the rope, but Morton shook her off.

"Get away," he ordered. "This miserable bag of bones has been asking for a thrashing for weeks now."

Fright and anger seeping into her bones, Julia lunged again for the rope, just as a shot a split the air.

Everyone stopped, eyes transfixed at the huge sprawling porch that encircled the gigantic two-story house of Frank Norwell.

"You whip that horse one more time, Tom," Norwell said, crossing the yard toward them with forceful strides, "and I'll cut your pay in half for every lash I count."

Julia could see that although his face was masked calmness, his gray eyes were angry enough to set kindling on fire. He holstered his gun.

"Joe," he ordered, gesturing to a man in a plaid shirt standing nearby, "take this stallion and put him in the farthest corral, and take it easy on him. Most males who've been out all night need a little pampering, not a beating."

He turned on Tom Morton. "We'll discuss this later," he said in harsh dismissal.

"That horse has been a pile of troubles since it arrived," Morton shot back.

"He only reacts to what he receives," Norwell said. "I said we'd talk about this later."

"But—"

"Egad, Tom, are you deaf? Later, man!"

Sullenly, Morton spun and walked to the barn.

A moment later, Julia would have never known the soft-spoken man before her was the same angered one who had dressed down Tom Morton. He looked at her with genuine warmth in his eyes. "Come up to the house for some lemonade, my dear," he said. "The least I can do is offer you some refreshments for returning my stallion."

His gaze skidded to the corral where the penned stallion had trotted to the water trough and was drinking greedily. "I just had him shipped in from Kentucky a few weeks ago. He's not used to this type of climate and gets a mite restless."

"If your men keep trying to beat the restlessness out of him, he won't be worth a plumb nickel," Julia countered.

"I assure you, they won't." He gestured to the house. "Come," he urged. "Maybe a bite to eat, too? I know you won't believe this, but we can be civilized at times."

"No, I can't, thank you." Julia squinted in the bright light and raised her hand to shade her eyes. "I'm meeting Flint Ashmore in an hour. He's going to teach me to fish."

"Ah," he said, smiling, looking at the clear sky. "You couldn't have chosen a finer day."

"You've fished?" she asked.

"Yes, many times, but not since my wife died."

Julia was sure she heard sadness in his voice.

"You might try below that small pool that collects just before it spills off onto my land," he suggested. "There was a time when trout would gather in scores to hide among those rocks."

She nodded. "I never really had a chance to thank you for helping the other day or for buying those newspapers."

"Actually, my dear, the papers were a cleansing experience. I felt like a kid playing a prank on the entire town of Golden. I'm only sorry it didn't work out. I heard Luke Ashmore had to run this Bloomington fellow off."

"Charles was never one to give up easily," she replied through a sigh.

"One of my men spotted him near the Army encampment, but that was over a week ago. Perhaps he truly has grown tired of our coarse manners and has headed out."

Graciously, he held her horse while she mounted.

"Betsy Ashmore," he said, "I'm told she's feeling better?"

It had been over three weeks since the mishap.

"Much better. She's up and about now. Doc still insists the arm should be trussed up, so we don't know how much damage is done."

"Tell Flint my offer still holds. There are some mighty good doctors on the East coast. After the other day, I don't think he'd appreciate a social call from me."

"I'll tell him," Julia said, smiling. She nudged the gelding and cantered off, riding past the barn where Tom Morton stood, glaring at her like she was little more than a nuisance, a cockroach to be squashed beneath his boot heels.

Julia pulled her line out of the water for the tenth time in an hour and came up with an empty hook. She was glad that Flint was agreeable to bait it each time. The thought of threading the slimy worms onto the hook sent shivers up her neck.

She frowned and swung the line toward herself. Deftly, she caught it, the hook dangling from the last foot of line. Overhead, the sun was bright. Hawks made lazy circles in the sky. Frogs croaked among the cattails along the river's edge beyond.

"I thought you said this was easy." She glanced at Flint who was stretched out on the knoll beside her, dozing with his hat shading his face. He rose up on elbows and squinted at the wormless hook.

"When you feel a fish take hold, jerk the pole, set the hook and yank it out," he said for what seemed the tenth time.

She watched him take another worm from a small wooden box and bait the hook. He rose, walked to the pool and washed his hands, wiping them on his worn denims. His gun and holster were lying beside them on the blanket. It was rare to see them off his hips.

He tossed the line into the sparkling cold water, sat down next to her, and handed it to her, resuming his catnap position. Five minutes ticked by. It seemed like an eternity to her. She was not used to having her hands idle. She had no idea in heavens name why she even agreed to this. He was carrying this courting thing a bit too far.

"How you doing?" he finally asked.

"I think I'd better stick with the pottery."

He laughed, sat upright and took the pole from her. It was a rich, deep vibrant laugh. "You have as much patience as my sister."

"When will Doc let her move her arm?"

"Dunno, but he says she's doing well, thanks to you. She's also giving poor Luke a run for his money. Every time he turns around, someone's at the ranch to deliver gifts or check on her. Jamie Banes, Colin Norwell, Charlie from the stage line, Syrus from the feed mill, even dear old man Finley, and the list goes on and on."

"They probably feel guilty."

"As some of them should. The only good thing that came of it is that I won't have to talk her out of riding in that fool race at the end of the week."

"Toby has a half Indian pony, he's hoping to ride if he can get it calmed down enough." Out of the corner of her eye, Julia watched him shoot her a narrow, sideways glance. Nervously, she removed the straw hat Anna had insisted she wear and let the cool breeze fan her face before she reset it again.

"I suppose it's a dandy. Never knew Two Bears to scare up anything but good horseflesh."

A cold, sinking feeling came over her. "How do you know—"

"Two Bears is involved?" he asked tonelessly. "Who else would be supplying your horses?"

"I have a letter from a man in Pueblo who sells stock," she lied.

"Julia, Julia, Julia," Flint said smiling wryly, "do I look daft?"

She caught the playful gleam in his eyes.

"You'd better warn that toothless redskin that no matter how hard he conceals his tracks, Tye can still tell every time he delivers a string." He pulled out a stalk of grass, propping it between his lips and chewing on it.

"Does Frank Norwell know?"

Flint shrugged. "I don't think so, Two Bears has been mighty careful to move them across my land or yours, and steer clear of the Flying N. I don't need to tell you--"

"That my crocks have a few cracks in them?"

"No, that it's a very dangerous game you're playing," he said gruffly. "Confound it, Julia, I wish you'd give up this notion of trying to get rich overnight. There are a lot of people who have lost kin to the Indians, and they don't take kindly to people consorting with them. Even Tom Morton lost a brother."

"And Finley lost a granddaughter."

"Well, that's a little different. Finley plays the game because he has to."

"You mean he sells to the renegades?" Julia asked. Suddenly, everything fell into place. She remembered Two Bears saying that supplies were not difficult to come by.

"I thought you knew," he said and threw the grass away. "He hangs on to the slim chance that someday one of the renegades will hear about his granddaughter and send word to him."

The line on the end of the fishing pole twitched and Flint jerked on it. He handed it back to Julia. "Here, haul it out."

Excitedly, Julia stood and tugged at the fishing pole. A large glistening trout shot out of the water and flip-flopped on the grassy bank.

"Do we keep it and try for a meal, or let it go and fish for fun?" he asked.

She looked doubtfully at the fluttering fish. It returned her gaze with big, sad eyes and she felt pangs of remorse. Even if they decided to keep it, she doubted she could bring herself to eat it.

"Aw, I knew it," Flint said, even before she could reply, "just like Betsy, you get all sorrowful about killing things." Carefully, he removed the hook and carried the trout to the stream. The fish jumped as soon as he released it in the water and its silver sides sparkled like glass in the sunlight.

"Well, at least that's one I won't have to clean." He turned back toward her.

She stared at him, then glanced toward the sunlit sky. Not a cloud skidded across its brilliant blue surface.

"Now what's wrong?" he asked impatiently.

"Thunder," she said. "It doesn't feel like rain, does it?"

"Thunder?" He cocked his head and listened, then moved like a blur, grabbing her by the wrist. "It's a stampede, and it's headed our way!"

He looked wildly about. Instinctively, Julia knew he was searching for cover. Out in the open and just below a knoll, they were too far away to reach the safety of a line of willows farther upstream.

"Can you swim?" he asked, glancing at the other side of the riverbank where a pile of boulders jutted up, dark and foreboding.

"No."

"You can't swim?" he asked in a near shriek, whirling to face her. "And you spend most of your time around water, gathering clay? Are you plumb loco?"

"I don't have to get into the water to gather clay from the river banks," she answered defensively, and followed it with a frantic gesture of helplessness. Her lips quivered. "I never saw the need to learn."

"Well, let's hope you don't now." He snatched up his abandoned gun and holster and stopped for a brief second. They stared at each other. Suddenly, he gathered her in his arms and kissed her soundly, but quickly.

In the next instant, she felt herself being dragged toward the river where the water swirled wide and fast before dumping into the quiet pool.

"The horses!" she shouted.

"They're ground tied. They're smart enough to get out of the way or run with the stampede until the cattle calm themselves."

A breeze caught under the brim of her hat and it flew off, skipping backwards over the grassy bank. "Flint, my hat!"

"Forget it." He plunged into the frigid river, sending up a cascade of water drenching them both. Gun held high above him, he gripped her hand and pulled her along. At one point they were waist high in water. Julia could feel the vicious tug of the current and was glad she was wearing a split riding skirt, instead of a clumsy dress with petticoats to weight her down. The wind swirled and shifted above them, tearing her hair from the loop of ribbons at the back of her neck and sending it flying into her face.

On the opposite side, Flint headed for the rocky incline, scrambling up it, pulling her with him. Once, both their boots slipped on the slick mossy surface and Julia fell, slamming her elbow on the rock. They reached the top and ducked around a large boulder just as the first wave of cattle hit the water on the opposite bank. Julia could hear the bawling and squealing of the steers as they plunged into the creek below, forced onward by a wide surging wave of others behind them.

Crouched behind the boulder, she watched the rolling-eyed animals thunder up the bank and rush past them. The brands that flew by were a mixture of Flying N and Circle A, but there were others, including a Double H from farther down river. She wondered whether Flint noticed as well. She wanted to speak, but the noise was deafening.

It was over within minutes.

As soon as the last calf stumbled out of the water, Julia started to rise from her spot behind the boulder, but Flint's hand reached out, grabbed her by the back of her hair and yanked her down.

"Just hold up a minute or so," he ordered. "I want to be sure there's no one around. I don't enjoy being trampled, but I don't cotton to being picked off with a rifle either."

They waited. Julia sank down on a flat rock, feeling her inadequacy. She realized there was still so much she didn't know about living in a land like this. Across the river, she could see that the cattle had destroyed everything in their path. The blanket, picnic basket, her straw hat, even the poor worms and fishing pole were lost. The day was one she'd never forget.

She removed her boots, emptied the water, then stretched out her legs and pulled at the soggy skirt sticking to them. She watched him unbutton his shirt, the kiss obviously forgotten.

"I wonder what startled them," she asked and rubbed her elbow where it still hurt.

He shed his shirt and proceeded to wring it out. He frowned. "I don't know. I'd almost be inclined to think something or someone spooked them and started them, but no one knows we're here."

Julia went still for a second, staring at his broad back and scarred shoulder. How to tell him the truth? He was so angry, she hardly dared to speak. He needed to calm down first.

Silent seconds ticked by. She bit her lower lip.

"Toby does," she finally admitted, "and Frank Norwell."

"Frank Norwell?" he asked curtly, turning. "How does he know?"

She took a deep breath then grimaced. "I told him when I delivered his runaway stallion this morning."

"Oh, did you now?" he asked and gave her a heated look more than ample to dry their clothes without help from the sun.

Twenty-Four

It was a perfect day for a race.

Flint stood under a gigantic sprawling oak tree at the far end of town and searched the crowds for Julia Gast. A warm breeze rustled the leaves overhead. Just a few feet away, Marcus, Anna and Betsy stood in the bed of a wagon, their eyes pinned far up the dusty road where riders were beginning to gather for the three-mile race. Miners, ranchers, and townsfolk lounged against the hitching rail, joking and placing private wagers among themselves. Even the saloon stood empty, its double doors hanging like buck teeth in a gaping black mouth.

Flint's gaze strayed to his sister. A hint of color had returned to her cheeks and her voice was light and animated again, even though the doctor had insisted she keep her arm in a sling for a while longer. Despite troublesome and recurring pain, it appeared she would recoup total use of it.

He could tell by the eager look on her face as her eyes sifted the riders, she was searching for Luke. He was going to ride the Appaloosa, the same one she had been forbidden to buy weeks ago. Of course, since the accident, Luke had been acting like his head was stuffed with cotton. He refused to deny her anything, especially a horse, and especially with Jamie Banes hovering around her, vying for her affection like a drooling pup.

He moved to the wagon bed and leapt aboard.

"It's not like Julia to be late," he said.

"Yes, it is," Anna replied. She always had a warm smile for him. "Julia always tries to squeeze in one more task in her long list of chores."

Reluctantly, her eyes met his, but they were anything but reassuring. He wondered whether the one more thing Anna was referring to could be the movement of another herd of horses onto the ranch with the help of Two Bears. It would be the ideal time with the entire countryside gathered in one spot. He hoped she would soon come to her senses and give up her crazy idea of trying to amass a fortune.

He heard Marcus laugh. "If she has an ounce of common sense, she's probably steering clear of you."

"Why's that?"

"Well now, figure it out. Most women who have their heart set on a romantic picnic usually don't end up being dragged across a bone chilling stream and soaked to the skin."

"Or stomped to death by a herd of restless cattle," Betsy added with a teasing glint in her eyes.

Flint let out a low grunt. "What amazes me, Betsy, is that someone with a vented shoulder and who forgot to duck has room to spout off."

He motioned Marcus to a corner of the wagon. Earlier he had sent Tye out to check the area near the river where the stampede had occurred.

"What did Tye find?" he asked.

The big man shook his head. "Well, he's certain someone started that stampede, it was no accident. There were tracks from at least three shod horses just before the herd were bunched together and set off with their tails a flyin'."

"Strange thing," Marcus continued, squinting up the road. "The cattle were then rounded up and chased upstream and back across the creek."

"Upstream?" Flint's brow furrowed. The best of Norwell's grazing was downstream.

"Yeah, but he couldn't follow them because he ran across Colin Norwell looking for strays. Tye couldn't just go waltzin' over on Norwell's land without causing suspicion."

Cheers and whistles from the anxious crowd brought both their heads up.

"What did Luke find out about Jess Williams?"

"Not much, the rains pretty well destroyed any tracks or evidence of struggle. It doesn't make sense why the man would be so far north of the ranch in the pouring rain."

Flint felt Betsy tug on his sleeve.

"Oh, look! They're about to start, and Tye and Luke are both there."

"Toby and Colin Norwell, too," Anna said excitedly.

Marcus spoke, "Good thing we were able to get a place here at the finish line. This is going to be one exciting race."

Flint peered up the road where the riders were huddling to take their mark. An uneasy feeling settled over him. Yes, it would be an exciting race, but he'd feel a lot better if Julia Gast were standing beside him to see it. Especially since someone wanted one of them dead.

In working clothes, with her hair tucked up into an old battered hat, Julia Gast pulled her sorrel up under a gnarled pine tree, just beyond the circle of riders. She had registered herself as J. Bonnie, using her mother's maiden name, given to her at birth as her middle one. Her only concern was that Luke, Tye or Colin Norwell might recognize her. But even if they did, it would be too late for them to do anything about it.

The stallion beneath her was bigger than most of the others and restless. She knew he was powerful and sure-footed, but she also knew he was uncomfortable when caged in by other mounts. Two Bears had watched them practice. Hold back in the beginning, he had cautioned her, let the others go first. The sorrel's hunger to catch up will be so great, he'll run like lightning across the sky.

Julia retied the strings on her hat snugly under her chin, checked to see that her whip was well-hidden under her oversized canvas coat, and moved her mount to the farthest position away from what seemed like two dozen contestants. She had taken the time to ride the course two days earlier and had memorized any peculiarities along the way.

She had also mapped out the exact place in the last mile where she would take the lead. Mouth dry, heart thumping, she waited for the signal to begin.

The crack of a pistol sent them flying down the road.

Dust and clods of earth flew up as the pack, still wedged tight, surged forward.

Slung low in the saddle, Julia let the riders string out before she urged the stout, big-boned stallion ahead, slipping past the first dozen riders easily. He was born to run, and Julia could feel it in his powerful muscles that strained beneath her. A miner on a dirty brown mount tried to nudge them off the road, but the sorrel shouldered the other horse over with little difficulty.

Far ahead, Toby and Tye were already vying for first position. Colin Norwell, Luke and two others trailed, just a few yards behind.

They raced onward, moving past the two-mile marker, tension high as riders and lathered mounts sensed the eagerness to win.

Suddenly a flash of silver from one of the riders in front of her brought Julia to attention. She saw him clumsily remove a gun and point it at Luke Ashmore's back. Heedless to the poor horse beneath him, the gunman viciously kicked it again and again, crouching low in the saddle in an attempt to draw near for a better aim.

It took only a moment for Julia to realize the gunman was riding a stallion. A spotted one. The same one she had seen at the Flying N.

With cool precision, she urged her sorrel ahead.

Now more than ever, every second counted. If she could tighten the gap between them, she had a chance to thwart him before he could draw a steady bead on Luke.

Tearing at the buttons on her coat, she withdrew her whip from underneath where it was tied to the side of her saddle. Around her the ground flew by in a blur. Dust billowed, clinging to her sweaty face, filling her nostrils and stinging her eyes. Her hat flew off, and her hair tumbled out like a red flag flapping in the wind. The drumroll of hooves pounded in her ears.

The man fired and missed.

Luke, alerted by the noise, turned abruptly in his saddle. Julia couldn't tell whether his look of astonishment was for the gunman or for herself.

Forcing her mount onward until she was barely a few yards behind the armed man, she flicked the whip. It snaked out so fast the rider was completely taken off-guard when its thin tongue curled itself around his wrist. His gun plummeted onto the road.

Unarmed now, the rider jerked his arm, wrenching the whip from Julia's grasp and freeing himself. The whip sailed into the tall grass beside the road. Then, without warning, the man spurred his mount and leapt the stallion off the course and onto a small path fringed with ferns and popular.

Julia was about to rein in and follow when she heard Luke's low guttural yell. He had wheeled the Appaloosa about and was racing back toward her

"Go, go! Ride! Ride!" He waved her onward as he swept past at a dead run in the opposite direction.

She let the sorrel have his head. He rushed on, eating up the ground beneath her, and minutes later, brushed past two riders and Colin

Norwell.

Ahead, the finish line loomed up.

Tye Ashmore, followed by Toby nosed across it. The sorrel, biting on Toby's heels, took third in a screen of gritty dust.

But it wasn't the race that Julia was thinking about when she dismounted, shaking with a combination of fear and rage. Rage ran so great, she hardly heard the cheering of the crowd, the shouts from the wagon bed nearby.

She waited as Colin Norwell reined his horse and turned back toward the finish line.

"Norwell," she screamed, "if I was a man I'd shoot you through your ugly black heart!"

"What?" He dismounted from his lathered horse and removed his dusty hat, smacking it on his thigh.

"No," she said, stalking up and poking a finger at his dust-covered chest. "That's too good for you. You should be dragged the entire three-mile course on the seat of your britches."

"Tell me, who did you hire?" She jabbed at his chest again, and he jumped backwards like a jack rabbit.

A crowd quickly gathered.

"For what?"

"Don't act like a simpleton! Who did you hire to kill Luke Ashmore?"

The shock on Norwell's face was as clear as his luminous light eyes.

"I—I don't know what you're talking about."

"Horsefeathers!"

"I really don't know—"

"Liar," she shouted, then suddenly raised a fist and with a quick firm stroke punched Colin Norwell square in his bulging right eye.

He went reeling backwards, howling.

Her hand lashed out again, but was caught in a firm grip. She looked up to see Flint Ashmore's fingers clamped around her wrist.

"Enough, Julia, before you kill the kid." Behind him, Luke Ashmore appeared. In his hands, he held Julia's whip.

"The gunman," she frantically hissed to Luke, "was on a horse I saw at the Flying N ranch."

Luke's eyes darkened and grew deadly serious. "Julia, are you sure?"

The crowd parted and Frank Norwell shouldered through, behind him the portly sheriff lumbered along.

"Just what is this all about?" Norwell demanded above the curses and wails of his son. He glanced over at him. "Could we have a little silence, son? It's not like you've never taken a few hits, or given some, for that matter."

Luke briefly explained, while Julia sent murderous looks toward Colin Norwell. He had stepped out of the way and was still holding his eye, glaring silently at her from the other.

"I lost him," Luke said as he finished, referring to the gunman. "He had too much of a start on me."

"Ah, I know what you're all thinking," Frank Norwell said. His entire demeanor was that of a man in absolute control. He pulled a piece of paper from his coat pocket and handed it to Luke. "My son's been known to do foolish things, but he's not childish enough to think he could kill a U.S. Marshall and get away with it."

"What is it?" Julia asked. Her knuckles had begun to sting from the blow and she rubbed them gently. She felt Flint's hand on her shoulder and knew, for her sake, he was there to restrain her from any further outburst.

"It's a signed bill of acceptance from the Army," Luke replied, "for twenty horses sold to them six days ago."

"That doesn't mean a thing," Julia muttered.

"Among them was the spotted stallion," Frank Norwell said. "This officer here will vouch for it." He nodded to a man in military uniform a few feet away.

"Yes, sir, Marshal," the soldier agreed. "A spotted stallion was in that bunch."

For a moment Julia just stared in disbelief. A tomblike silence settled over the group.

She felt her face flame and hung her head, feeling foolish.

Colin Norwell had already moved away. His hat was pulled low to shade his face, and she suspected he was feeling just as angry and just as embarrassed.

Finally, she looked at Frank Norwell. "I guess I owe your son an apology."

Frank Norwell spoke, "It might be best if I convey the message this time." He leveled a gaze at her and realized her embarrassment. "Now, my dear, don't trouble yourself. Colin's got a pretty hard head, he will recover."

"Most men do," Flint said.

"Yes, most men do," Norwell agreed, shooting a covert look at his injured son. "But then most men are smart enough to know when to shy clear of an angered woman." He glanced at Julia. A smile lifted the corner of his mouth. "That's a wicked right swing you have, my dear."

Julia felt her face flame again and was relieved when the crowd around them parted and Betsy Ashmore squirmed her way through, waving a fistful of money high above her head with her uninjured arm.

"Julia, Julia, we've done it this time," she said breathlessly. She glanced first at Norwell, then at Flint and smiled a slow, easy smile that put Julia in mind of a wolf fleecing innocent lambs. "I told you those miners would lay out a pretty penny."

Julia looked at her dismayed. She was flashing enough money to tie the ranch over until Christmas, with spare to buy themselves the fanciest dresses around.

"I'm surprised anyone would give you good odds," Frank Norwell said. "Everyone knows Tye rides like a demon."

"Tye? Heavens no, I didn't bet on him."

"Luke?"

"No, no, no." She did a little jig, eyes twinkling. "I bet on Julia."

"You bet against your brothers?" Norwell asked incredulously.

"Uh-huh, and then I confessed to everyone the rider on the sorrel was a woman. You ought to have seen them. The fools started laying down their cash like it was water. I had twenty to one odds she'd even place."

Frank Norwell shook his head sadly. "Egad, if a man is that stupid, I can't feel sorry for him. He deserves to have his pockets stripped clean. Congratulations, Betsy."

When he left, Julia spoke, "For a man whose son I just publicly humiliated, he sure took it graciously." Maybe she was naive, but she wasn't convinced Frank Norwell was the root of anyone's problems. The man had more character than anyone was willing to give him credit for.

"Maybe he's just biding his time," Flint offered.

Betsy laughed. "Oh, he's a reasonable enough man. Give him an hour or so, and we'll see the old Frank Norwell again." She rattled the bills in her hand and added, "Once word is out that over half the pay-outs on these bets are from Flying N hands."

 Twenty-Five

Flint Ashmore paced the office of John Greenfeld, stopping once to look out the window at the busy street where freight teams plodded along beside riders on high-stepping mounts eager to be at their destinations. Despite the early morning hour, the day was destined to be miserably hot and muggy. Already thunderheads had begun to build in the west.

Across the room, his sister sat quietly in a leather chair, all color drained from her face. A chilling silence surrounded her. Both had received word the old lawyer wanted to meet with them immediately.

Like a panther, Flint crossed the room again, turned and stalked back to the window.

"Stop it, will you?" Betsy said in an edgy voice.

"Stop what?"

"That infernal pacing!"

Flint glanced at her, removing his hat to jam his fingers through his hair. He remembered a day not so long ago when he sat in the same seat next to Julia Gast. Nothing good had come of that meeting, and he doubted that anything good would happen again. The old man had been almost secretive when he sent his clerk to get them.

"What do you think he wants?" Betsy asked.

Flint shrugged. "I have the feeling there's something wrong with the deed for the Gast ranch. What else? We've no other legal business hanging in the fire."

John Greenfeld entered his office by the back door and took his seat behind his massive cherry desk.

"I appreciate your promptness," he said. "Anyone follow you?"

Flint's head snapped up. "Is someone supposed to be?"

The old lawyer shook his head. "No, no, I hope not, it's just that—. Sit down, will you? You're making me dizzy."

Flint buckled down into a chair beside his sister.

"For some reason, someone has been closely screening and culling all Ashmore mail and wires. I didn't think it was possible until I received this hand-delivered letter yesterday. A lawyer back East has been trying to get in touch with you for over a month now, but all his wires and letters have been unanswered."

"They sold Pa's land?" Flint asked.

"No, not that I'm aware of," Greenfeld replied. "This is a lawyer from Georgia who needs to locate Betsy."

"Me?" Betsy sat up straighter. "Why me?"

"As you well know now, Gretchen Warner was your real mother. Before she died, she instructed her lawyer to turn her estate, a quite large one, I understand, over to her only living heir. That would be you. Well, I needn't tell you how difficult it must have been for her poor lawyer to find you. The only lead he had was Rusty Gast who was also deceased."

Greenfeld removed his spectacles and rubbed the bridge of his nose. "Luckily, Luke showed up in Virginia, asking too many questions, and that put Gretchen's lawyer onto your Aunt Mildred."

"Ah, yes," Flint said. "Dear finicky old Aunt Mildred."

"Is there something wrong with being old?" Greenfeld asked in a crisp voice and stared at him.

Flint smiled ruefully. "No, it's just that Aunt Millie is a fortress of family secrets."

"So Gretchen's lawyer found out," Greenfeld admitted. "But with a little persuasion, a little persistence, he was able to find out Betsy was still very much alive and still living here in Golden City. However, all his communications sent to you both seemed to be ignored, so he had a friend heading for Utah drop off the correspondence to me."

"Ignored? How could that be?" Betsy asked, coming to full attention.

Greenfeld shook his head. "Someone's been intercepting everything coming in from Georgia or Virginia."

"It's not possible."

Greenfeld waved a hand, palm up. "Someone is. . .someone who has authority to do it, Betsy. Someone linked to the government, the Army, perhaps."

Betsy looked at Flint. "Jamie Banes," she whispered, stunned.

"Yeah," Flint agreed.

"But why?"

"Figure it out," Flint said sourly. "Greenfeld just told you." He was sorry he said it when he saw the anguished look on her face. Her eyes bleached from blue to gray.

"The money." Her voice was barely audible. "He's interested in the money. He knows about the inheritance. That's why he agreed to take a position out here with the Army."

"Looks that way. He certainly had all the right connections back East."

Greenfeld cleared his throat. "I sent a rider down to Colorado Springs to wire Gretchen's lawyer, telling him of your injury. To date, I've heard no word back. At some point, you're going to have to go East and clean up some paperwork when you're feeling well enough to travel."

"How much money are we talking about?" she asked.

Greenfeld nervously glanced at Flint, and asked, "Ah, Betsy, are you sure you want to discuss this now?"

She nodded. "Yes, there are no secrets between my brothers and me."

"Very rich, extremely rich. To the tune of six rather hefty digits. I should also tell you, there was a little clause which now seems to bear more weight than I first imagined."

"Go on," she urged.

"If you were not found in a reasonable length of time or were dead, then Rusty Gast--or his heirs--would receive the money."

"Oh, Lord," Flint said as the statement registered. She looked at Betsy who was staring wide-eyed back at him. Her hands shook. He knew she was thinking the bullet she took might very well have been meant for her.

"Now Betsy, take it easy, we're jumping to conclusions," he said, reaching to touch her hand gently. "We know for certain Julia would never harm you, nor do anything heinous."

"No," she agreed. "But we have no idea how many people know about this. . .this inheritance. Someone may want Julia to have the money for any number of reasons. I can be shot in the back walking down the street!"

Flint's eyes found Greenfeld's. "How soon can you execute the papers?"

Betsy shook her head. "No, Flint, I need to think about this. I need to decide if I even want it." She looked at him with bewildered eyes, confused by all that had transpired."

"Betsy, there *is* no time," Flint scolded.

With a glum face Greenfeld toyed with a silver letter opener on his desk. "Unfortunately, you're at risk if you take it or you don't. What a sorry mess if I ever saw one." He looked thoughtfully at them both and sighed. "Flint's right, it's better to have the will legally executed and the money in your name. You can always decide what you want to do with it later. I can draw up some preliminary papers today to make it legal."

For a moment, all three sat quietly, listening to the noise of wagons and the jingle of harnesses as town folk moved in the street. Finally Greenfeld asked, "Can you get someone to ride to Colorado Springs to send a message to Gretchen's lawyer? Lord knows we can't wire him from here or Denver."

"But how does that protect me?" Betsy asked, her voice rose and cracked, almost hysterically. "Someone who is gunning for me, hoping the money will go to Julia, isn't going to know that it has been legally turned over."

Flint nodded. "That's true, unless we send the wire from here *and* Colorado Springs, stating you've accepted the estate. It's bound to fall into the right hands and maybe buy us a little time to find out who's behind all this."

"How?" she asked.

"They'll probably try to dispose of anyone you name as your beneficiary, maybe try to approach you with some deal, or maybe even try to woo you. Or God forbid, hold you or someone close to you for ransom."

Greenfeld leaned back in his chair and scowled. "It does put everyone in a tight place. Perhaps, if Luke were willing to be the beneficiary."

"No, I forbid it!" Betsy said and sprang from her chair. "I will not make Luke a target for some mad man's bullet. Bloomington and that horrid man in the race already want him dead." She stared at Flint with worried eyes. "And come to think of it, you as well."

"It's probably Banes," Flint replied bluntly. "I knew I should have sent that little weasel packing the night you were shot."

She stared at him dumbstruck, then crumpled down into the chair, clutching the locket in her hand as his words registered.

She shook her head. "No, Flint, Jamie Banes may be seeking an easy fortune, but I don't believe he'd resort to murder."

"Why wouldn't he?"

Greenfeld, hands steepled as he listened to the discussion, leaned forward and spoke, "Anyone could be gunning for Flint, and God knows

U.S. Marshals aren't very popular around these parts. My concern is for you, Betsy. As you pointed out, others might very well know. It's possible Banes isn't operating alone, or maybe it's not Banes at all. He may just be the necessary link for intercepting the communications." He stared off into space, pondering the situation a moment.

"That's it!" he said suddenly, his face lighting up. He lightly slammed his hand face down on his desk.

"What is?" Betsy asked.

"We name all your brothers as beneficiaries, then the money will be as safe as if it's in vault. Only a complete lunatic would try to kill all five of you."

Flint nodded and heaved a sigh. "You know, it just might work, Bets. You'll be as cozy as a kitten in a basket, I promise. All we have to do is keep you out of sight for a few hours, sign the papers and let the cat out of the bag that you're an heiress."

"I still want that second wire sent from Colorado Springs to be certain Gretchen's lawyer is informed," Greenfeld said.

Flint nodded. "I'll send Tye."

Betsy rose. "All right, get the papers ready. I'll be back this afternoon." She felt as exhausted and hollow as her voice sounded. Her eyes were troubled as she turned to her brother. "We need to let the others know. We need to stick together until this is resolved."

"We will, Betsy, I promise." He playfully winked at her to try to lighten the moment. "We'll stick like burrs on woolly sheep as Marcus would say."

"Don't let her out of your sight," Greenfeld warned as they started for the door, "and be back here at three o'clock sharp, you hear?"

Outside, they took the most direct route to the blacksmith shop where they found Luke, trying to sweet talk the Appaloosa while the smithy labored to fix a loose shoe. Briefly Flint explained what had occurred on their walk back to the General Store.

He noticed Betsy's face was growing pale, and she barely spoke one word the entire time. He knew the discovery of Jamie Banes's treachery was wearing hard on her, not to mention the overwhelming sadness she felt for a mother she never knew, a mother who could never risk seeing her only living child for fear of losing the very inheritance she wanted to give her.

Once inside her room at the back of the store, Betsy glanced at them with watery eyes. "I need to lie down, this has been too much. Give me an hour, and then we'll sort this through together. Flint, you'd better ride over to Julia's, she ought to know."

"You sure you'll be all right?" Flint asked.

She rose on tiptoe and lightly kissed each brother on the cheek. "Just tired. I have nothing to worry about with Luke close by, right?"

"Absolutely," Luke agreed. "I promise I won't move from this spot." He slumped into a nearby chair.

She closed the bedroom door quietly.

"Don't take your eyes off that door," Flint warned, "and don't let anyone near it. Whoever Banes is working with may be someone we least suspect." He pulled out his gun and checked the chambers.

Luke chewed on the inside of his lower lip, a worried look on face. "Be careful, Flint," he said. "I know a lot of brave men who are dead."

Betsy Ashmore lay on the squeaky mattress, rolling around on the old springs only long enough to make her brother believe she was restless before falling asleep. Easing herself off the bed, she discarded her sling, quietly changed her clothes into a riding skirt, and slipped out the open window. Lowering herself gently to the ground, she winced as a sharp pain shot through her shoulder.

It was easier to get her horse. The livery stable was empty, except for an old farmer working out back on a harness. He never looked up when she saddled her black, led him out, and walked him around the side behind the blacksmith shop.

She mounted before she rode past the feed mill. Syrus Bentley was in his usual spot, deep in the shade against the front of the building.

"Nice to see you're up and around," he said, grinning. "We were sure worried about you."

She forced a smile. "I thought I could use a little fresh air and sunshine." She had hoped to get out of town without being seen. Yet, she reasoned, the old man was harmless. Rarely did he move from his spot.

"Yep, that's what I'm doing, too," he said, sucking on a cold pipe. "Getting some air and sunshine."

She touched her heels to the horse and rode west toward the Army encampment. She thought about Jamie Banes. How could she have been such a fool? How could she have misjudged him? Yet, all the signs were there. He had never spoken enthusiastically about the Colorado territory. In fact, he had never talked about his job with the Army and rarely mentioned anything about horses. She was angered his attentiveness toward her was simply out of fear that she might die and end his hopes for a wealthy, comfortable life.

Fifteen minutes later, she found the encampment near a grove of cottonwoods and willows which fringed a quick running stream. It seemed deserted, except for a few men who lounged around playing cards and cleaning weapons. Jamie Banes was standing in front of the officer's tent when she rode up.

"Betsy, should you be here?" He hurried to where she dismounted and held her horse's head until she slipped easily out of the saddle.

"Should I?"

"What's that supposed to mean?"

"Find us a private spot to talk, Jamie."

She noticed the curious concern in his eyes as he tied her mount to a nearby bush and led her to a secluded area up stream beneath a stately cottonwood.

"If it's about the spotted stallion, I assure you we're still trying to find out who's responsible," he said and nervously toyed with the tip of his mustache.

Betsy laughed, but she was angered. "Sometimes, Jamie, I think I'm more of a fool than you are."

"What?" He squinted at her with baffled eyes.

"I'm silly enough to believe that your concern for me over the past few weeks was a reflection of your honest, caring nature, maybe because we were old friends. Childhood sweethearts."

"I don't understand."

"Oh, for heaven's sake, Jamie, forget the charade. You know I'm rich, and I know you arranged to try to kill Luke."

"Listen, Betsy, you don't understand—" He reached for her, but she shrugged him off.

"I love you," he said.

"Love?" she asked. "Love, is it? Anyone who loves me doesn't try to kill one of my brothers."

"They're not even your real brothers," he said with disgust. "I wasn't trying to kill Luke, just scare him off."

"With a bullet in his back?

"I had no idea Bloomington had his dander up enough to attempt murder!"

"Bloomington? You know Charles Bloomington? How does he fit into this whole sordid mess?"

"Captain Bloomington stopped by several weeks ago trying to locate Julia Gast." Banes puffed out his chest. "It was refreshing to meet the man. The good Captain and I have a lot in common. He fought for a great cause. He fought for our Union, our nation."

"Your Union, your precious Union, is that all you think about?" She stamped her booted foot. "What about me, Jamie?"

"Listen, I can explain it all, that was an unfortunate accident. Come to my quarters and hear me out."

"Hog wash! Who tried to kill me, Jamie?"

"I don't know," he said sullenly. "Someone Tom Morton hired."

"Tom Morton?" Her mouth dropped open. "So you planned to kill me and use Julia as your pawn?"

"No, of course not. You have this all wrong!"

"Talk, Jamie, and make it quick," she said through gritted teeth. She pulled a gun from her coat pocket, aimed it at him and cocked the hammer. "Only. . the truth. . . this time."

"You wouldn't kill me," he said softly.

"No, I wouldn't," she admitted, "but I wouldn't think twice about putting a bullet hole in your shoulder, just like you did to me. Now I know how my mother, the mother I consider my real mother, must have felt when she stepped in front of my father the day she died."

"It wasn't meant for you," Banes blurted out. "It was meant for Finley standing behind you."

"Finley? Why old man Finley?"

"He's been double crossing the whites and trading with the Indians for years. He even trades with that renegade Two Bears. The same one that killed Tom Morton's brother." Jamie Banes laughed a crazed laugh. "It doesn't matter. At this very moment Tom is luring both Two Bears and that Confederate-loving Julia Gast into an ambush. Once they're both taken care of, this will be a safe place for settlers."

"And what about Bloomington?"

"I told him to lay low for a while. He's much too an important a man to waste his time on Julia Gast. Once she's dead, he'll realize how foolish he's being and come to his senses. All three of us can head East again where it's civilized and refined, or West where we can start over in California. Why, you and I can get married."

Betsy lowered the gun. She sighed. "Jamie, you've been in the sun way too long. The only place you're headed for is jail."

"You can't leave, Betsy," he said. "You'll ruin the plan!"

She brushed past him in angry strides. The man's mind was so twisted it would be a waste of time to argue further. She needed to find Julia Gast before Tom Morton got to her.

It was the soft sound of metal sliding from leather that caught her attention as she stormed away. She whirled just in time, taking a step sideways, and fired at the same instant a knife whizzed past her shoulder and clattered on the rocks at her feet.

Jamie Banes howled, clutching his bloody wrist. "Over here!" he bellowed to the men in camp. "Someone grab this woman. She just shot me!"

Betsy Ashmore stared at him, seeing him for the first time as the spineless, worthless creature he was. He would allow death and destruction in order to put wealth at his fingertips.

"You can't stop him," Banes said through a groan. "Even if Two Bears gets Morton, I've sent out a hand-picked patrol and ordered them to kill everyone in the area and make it look like it was an Indian attack. I have it planned, Betsy."

An old, bow-legged soldier ambled up. Betsy knew him from his trips into town to get supplies at Finley's store. He picked up the knife and looked at it curiously, then just as curiously squinted at both of them.

"What's going on here, young-uns?" he asked as he spit a wad of brown tobacco juice into the dirt.

"Ask Banes, I don't have time. And make sure he doesn't leave camp. He's going to be wanted for attempted murder." She turned and sprinted for her horse. She hoped he wasn't too late. She had to reach Julia Gast. Morton was an unforgiving, heartless man, capable of harming anyone who tried to obstruct his path of vengeance.

"Get her!" she heard Jamie Banes shouting. "I order you to apprehend her. She tried to kill me. Get her, I say. Owoooo, my wrist! Look, she shot me."

"Lieutenant," the old soldier ordered tersely, "quit that infernal bleating, will you? It's barely a nick."

"But she tried to kill me!" Banes insisted.

The old soldier spit another stream of tobacco juice before he spoke,

"Lieutenant Banes, I'd count my blessings if I were you. I know Betsy Ashmore. I also know if Betsy Ashmore had meant to kill you, she would have."

Twenty-Six

Flint stepped out onto the wooden walk in front of the General Store and paused, squinting under the brassy haze of the sun. Up the street a barrel-chested man closed the door of the telegraph office and hurried toward a dust-covered horse which looked like he had seen little rest and food. The man's hat was pulled low to shade his eyes and face. Even from a distance, Flint was certain there was something vaguely familiar about him.

Swinging atop the tired beast, the man spurred him toward the edge of town where he halted only long enough to briefly chat with a soldier slouched against the trunk of tree. Seconds later, the two men parted. The soldier reined his mount toward the Army encampment while the man turned his horse south, toward the hills and a remote back trail that cut across Frank Norwell's property.

Flint moved quickly toward the livery stable, a multitude of thoughts needling him. If his hunch was correct, the barrel-chested man was working under the direction of Jamie Banes, and already the message about Betsy's inheritance, sent from town, had been intercepted and would be passed to the proper hands. But why hadn't the man personally delivered the message? And why was he now riding into sheer wilderness, using an old back trail, once beaten smooth by the hard hooves of wild mustangs, but now so overgrown and abandoned a man would have to fight shoulder-high brush to reach his destination?

Saddling his bay, he rode in the same direction the barrel-chested man had taken. As far as Flint was concerned, there would be little time wasted reaching the Gast ranch if he veered from the main road, and later angled east, then southward again.

The land was quiet and lonely as he rode along, pushing his way through scrub oak and brush, carefully avoiding rocks where the sound of a metal shoe might alert someone to his whereabouts. Occasionally, a bird flitted in the trees overhead and sang out a warning to its mate. A red fox, flushed from the brush, crossed the trail ahead of him, and trotted down into a gully in search of a careless rabbit. The animal's russet coat glistened in the sunlight, and Flint smiled, thinking how accurately Two Bears had described Julia Gast.

Fifteen miles onward, he turned off the rutted trail into a clump of aspen that rimmed a small clearing.

It was the bay that picked up the smell of smoke first, laying back his ears and sniffing the air. Carefully, Flint threaded his way through the stand, until he reached the edge. He discovered he was now situated on a low knoll above a narrow rocky draw which meandered back to a box canyon beyond. In the draw, two men lounged in the shade, one of them whittling. Soft tendrils of smoke curled up from a small fire beside him, and a skillet lay on a glowing bed of coals. A few feet away, the barrel-chested man was stripping the saddle from the tired horse.

Flint eased his mount back into the security of the trees and sighed. There was no way he could approach, unless he circled the area, crossed the draw far below and descended from the hills on the other side. He removed his hat and disgustedly swiped the sweat from his brow before he turned around to double back.

A half hour later, he picked his way up the last hilly incline which led him to the side of the canyon where a winding footpath snaked down into the camp. He had barely topped out over the rise when he heard the cattle before he saw them. Onward, under the cover of the brush, he maneuvered himself to a vantage point when he could gaze into the long canyon. At least five hundred cattle of various brands milled about, hemmed in by an intricate brush fence which sealed the canyon's mouth. Even without a spyglass, Flint's keen eyes could pick out Circle A and Flying N brands on their thick, dull hides.

He slipped off the bay with his rifle and started cautiously down the brush-strewn path toward the camp. It was the restless snort of the bay that saved his life. Shifting sideways, he whirled to check the area behind him at the same instant the barrel-chested man stepped out from behind a tree, squeezing off a quick shot that flew past his shoulder.

Flint dove behind a dead fall and crawled toward a gray boulder, weathered round and smooth by the wind and rain. Behind him, a wall of sandstone rose steeply upward trapping him solidly in a rock cage. He cursed softly under his breath, realizing his mistake, realizing, too, the entire camp would now be alerted.

"Come on out!" the barrel-chested man shouted. "There ain't no way you can get out or get away. You're as good as in a coffin."

When Flint failed to respond, the man taunted, "Ah common on, man, you some kind of coward?"

Despite the heat and his cramped muscles, Flint smiled grimly. He had spent too many of his childhood days playing hide and seek with his brothers to be foolish enough to advertise his position. Yards down the trail he heard the crunch of boots on gravel and muttered conversation.

"Come on, mister," the voice called again. "Throw out your guns, and we'll let you be on your way."

Flint's eyes darted up and down the trail. One man above him and two below were odds he didn't relish. Suddenly, the shadow of a man on the downhill side appeared, and Flint swung and fired from his crouched position. The man went reeling backwards from sight. Simultaneously, a bullet slammed against the rocks above him, sending bits of sandstone showering down over his hat and shoulders.

Then, without warning, the second man sprung from his cover behind an outcropping of rock. Flint knew instantly he meant to cross the trail and corner him, and he coiled upward, firing again and flattening him, but not before a bullet from the barrel-chested man behind him whistled out and blazed a fiery path across his ribs under his left arm.

He dropped to the ground, clutching his side, and felt warm drops of blood start to slide down his waist. Sweat trickled into his face and over his back. He waited, listening intently. In the stillness, there was no sound, no movement from the lower end of the path.

"LeBeau, Bannon," the barrel-chested man, now finally growing restless, shouted, "you still there?"

After another lengthy pause, Flint yelled, "Looks like your friends won't be doing too much cattle rustling anymore. They either lit out and left you high and dry or they're greeting St. Peter as we speak."

A rain of bullets answered, slamming the rocks and air in front of him.

Flint could feel his side burning fiery hot now. "Listen," he said, "you have only one way out, my friend, and that's up, and I've got you covered. I'm game to sit here all day, but both of us will be getting mighty hungry and thirsty before the sun sets."

The voice behind the tree spoke, "Why don't you and me just call it a draw? We can divvy up the cattle and be on our way."

"Sounds good to me, but half the cattle are already mine."

"You an Ashmore?"

"Last time I checked."

"Which one?" The voice sounded worried now.

"Toss your guns my way and find out."

There was another long stretch of time.

"I'm coming out, mister," the man finally said sourly. "I ain't gettin' myself kilt to make Tom Morton a rich man."

A pistol and rifle flew through the air and clattered on the rocky path. The barrel-chested man stood, hands raised and emerged from behind the tree. Little piggy eyes glaring, he walked down the trail toward Flint.

Flint stepped onto the path, pistol drawn, and looked at him in disgust. He was the same man he and Julia had tangled with over the stolen horses. "Mister, you seem to have a need--."

Without warning the man's hand dropped to his waistband. Flint dove to the left, falling on his injured side, his hand a blur as he fired two shots into man's chest just as the barrel of the man's hidden gun came level and exploded, missing him. The man tumbled to the ground. His gun landed close by his side.

"--to learn the hard way," Flint finished and stumbled up.

Gripping his bloody side, he limped painfully up the path, pausing once to turn back. Such a waste, he thought, as he looked grimly at the fallen body. He knew the man needed to be identified and his next of kin notified. He needed a proper burial. But not now, not when the living needed his attention first.

Minutes later, he pulled himself onto the awaiting bay and turned southward toward the Gast ranch. Every step of the horse brought a sharp searing pain, and he felt light-headed, so he let the bay choose his own trail, knowing he had to reach Julia Gast. Above his head, the sun beat down its relentless burning rays.

An hour later, Flint reined into the yard of the ranch. Toby was in the corral, breaking a horse when he rode up and tumbled from his saddle into the dirt to land on his knees.

The boy leaped the corral in a single bound and shouted for Anna as he crossed the yard. Together, they helped him to the shade of the porch.

"Get Julia," Flint said through a groan. "I need to talk to her now!"

He watched Anna stare at his blood-stained shirt.

"Call Julia," he insisted with a hiss. He slumped into a caned back rocking chair and held his sticky, burning side.

"She's gone," Anna said. "She rode out earlier with Tom Morton. He said he found some stray horses he thought were hers."

"On Norwell's property?" he asked.

"No, on yours," Toby said.

Flint stared at him, puzzled. Suddenly the boy's words chilled him to the marrow of his bones. Everything fell into place. Tom Morton had lured Julia away to trap Two Bears. The only time Julia ever crossed Cherry Creek onto his land was to meet with the renegade in a secluded spot where she wouldn't be discovered. Tye had picked out the tracks weeks ago and even figured out the covert signals they left as messages to each other.

Flint struggled up, swaying on his feet. "He means to kill Two Bears."

"You can't go anywhere in the condition you're in," Anna said.

"He doesn't mean for Julia to walk away either. Toby, ride into Golden and get Luke."

"It would be easier to get Frank Norwell."

"No, Luke! Or Marcus."

Anna pushed him down into the rocker. He toppled under her strong hand like a broken twig. "Toby, hurry! Ride fast. Drop Flint's weary horse at the watering trough on the way out," she ordered.

She looked at Flint's face and frowned. "You," she said, shaking a finger under his nose, "will not leave until I bind those ribs and you drink something, ja? You have lost a lot of blood and look like a walking sheet. This will only take a moment. What good are you to Julia, if you are lying unconscious somewhere?"

Flint heaved a sigh and leaned his spinning head back against the solid back of the rocker. He heard her skirts rustle as she left him. The front door slammed.

A split second later, he heard nothing. Everything went black.

Twenty-Seven

Whistling, Marcus sat atop the wagon while he plodded down the road with the team, returning to the ranch with grain and supplies from the feed store. His horse, tied behind, snickered irritably at the dust the wagon threw in its face. Earlier, he had stopped to talk with Luke, who related the events of Flint's and Betsy's meeting with Attorney Greenfeld. He grinned as he thought about his little sister. Soon to be rich little sister, he corrected himself silently. If anyone deserved a fair shake in life, Betsy was at the top of his list.

The road he followed was lined with dense cottonwoods and brush, and hugged the banks of Cherry Creek as it meandered southward. Marcus heard the rider opposite him long before he saw him. The sharp sound of ringing hooves against rock meant he was holding tight to the riverbed and moving fast.

He slowed the team and stopped just seconds before a sleek black horse and rider splashed through the water, plowed through the laurel, and raced up the grassy bank in front of him.

"Hold up," he shouted when he saw the small figure, obviously female, rein her horse effortlessly onto the roadway, avoiding any rutted areas.

Betsy Ashmore whirled in her saddle. "Marcus!"

She turned her horse toward him. "Oh, Marcus," she repeated breathlessly, "you are a sight for sore eyes."

Somehow her appearance was not very satisfying to him. He spoke, "Tell me I'm seeing double, Bets, 'cause I just left town and Luke was supposed to be guarding you."

"No, he's guarding an empty room," she said, and hurriedly recounted her meeting with Jamie Banes. When she finished, she looked at him with desperate eyes. "Julia Gast—"

"Flint rode out to tell her, but he sure didn't know Tom Morton was involved."

"He may be too late," she wailed.

Marcus fished in his pocket for his watch. "How long you reckon you've been gone?"

"Couple hours."

Frowning, he snapped it shut, pulled the wagon beside the road and jumped down, untying his horse.

"I'll go to the ranch," she offered.

"No," he replied sharply. He stepped into the saddle. "You ride back to town and round up Luke. No sense in riding there now. If Flint didn't make it in time, I know exactly where Tom Morton is headed. Flint will know, too. Two Bears always meets Julia under those steep ledges on our property, right smack across Cherry Creek in that stone-walled gulch."

Betsy's face showed signs of strain. "He'll kill her and Two Bears."

Marcus felt a chill run up his spine at her words, and his eyes leaped miles ahead. "Not if I can help it," he said in a voice he hoped sounded reassuring. He squinted at her. "Betsy, we're losing time chewing up words, instead of distance. Now ride!"

He kicked his horse and flew down the hard-packed road.

Flint awoke and thought he was in heaven. He stared into big blue eyes as tender, efficient hands wiped his face and forehead with a cold refreshing cloth. His side had been tightly bound and the searing pain had abated, leaving a dull throbbing ache instead.

"Easy does it, ja?" Anna's voice above him said. "Here drink." She lifted his head and touched a glass to his lips. Delightfully tasting lemonade, laced with extra sugar, slid down his parched throat. A fly buzzed around them, and he realized he was lying flat on his back on Julia Gast's porch. He made a feeble attempt to raise his head, and for a moment thought he would pass out again. Everything inside seemed to be rolling about.

"How long have I been like this?" he asked, lowering it for moment.

"Ten minutes, the most," Anna said and steadied him as he tried again and managed to come to a sitting position.

He touched his ribs. "You are efficient, Anna Holberg, I'll say that."

She laughed nervously and helped him to his feet. He swayed a moment and grabbed the porch railing, then managed to jam his shirt tails into his denims.

"Drink more," she said with worried eyes, handing him the glass, "you have lost much blood. The sugar is good for you, ja? I have loaded your gun and your horse is watered and ready."

He drained it and smiled weakly. "I take that back." He walked down the steps and turned. She stood, wringing her hands in her crisp, but now bloodied apron. "You are *very* efficient. Marcus has chosen well."

"God speed," she only replied in a hushed, worried voice.

Hands tied behind her back, Julia Gast sat under the overhang of a ragged cliff and felt the chill of the rough stone penetrate straight through the back of her canvas coat. Several feet in front of her, Tom Morton squatted, peering out into an area which was nature's poor replica of an impenetrable alcove. Cliffs protected the back and right side melting into a dangerously steep rock slide which circled the small ravine until it met the river on the left, the only possible way to enter.

"He won't come," Julia said aloud.

Tom Morton turned and sneered at her. "Oh, he'll come all right, and I hope he brings a slew of redskins with him."

"Two Bears is too smart to walk into a trap."

"Maybe, but he's not about to let honor and revenge slip from his grasp. He killed my brother, you know."

"So now you want to kill him?"

"Something like that. You see, this has been boiling for a long time, ever since we wiped out his family in a raid a few years back."

"You killed his wife *and* children?" Julia asked, unable to hide her astonishment.

"Squaw, you mean, and his two little brats. The red devils were out hunting when we hit the village. I saw no sense in letting them go free to breed more traitorous heathens."

Julia let his words sink in. She thought about the pain Two Bears must have felt when he found his family and friends riddled with bullets.

Innocent women and children. She squeezed her eyes shut trying to block the tears that were threatening to start.

After a moment she asked, "Your brother was killed afterwards?"

"Yeah," Morton said sourly. "That heathen dogged us for three days. He knifed my brother and killed two other men in our party before we were able to join up with an Army detachment in the area and scare him off."

Julia sighed. "And that's not enough bloodshed for you? Will there never be peace?"

"Enough?" Morton shouted and heaved himself erect. His eyes were savage. "We'll only have peace when Two Bears is dead and all the Indians in the territory are wiped out or forced to leave!"

"Then what?" she asked coldly as the chilling thought struck her that she was trying to reason with a maniac.

Morton glowered at her. "Then we chase all the redskin lovers like you and Finley out, too." He paced the area under the ledge. "We'll build homes, towns, and ranches all over the area."

"It sounds so simple," Julia said, "but homes, towns and ranches take money and time. Stock is expensive, too."

"Not if you're clever enough to know how." Morton laughed lowly. "I got me a pretty good size herd already, and I didn't have to put down one red cent."

"Stolen?"

He only stared at her, and she knew the answer.

"There's no place around here where you're going to be able to run a spread with stolen cattle," she said flatly.

"Once we clean up the Indians from the land to the south, there'll be lots of room where a man can change his name and start his own place without interference from the law."

"Tell me," Julia said. "Were you responsible for stealing my horses?"

He snickered. "And the stampede, too."

"Why?"

"Why?" His voice had a menacing edge to it. "Why, you ask? I thought I could scare you off, get you to pull up and move into town, or go back East. With you living on Rusty's ranch, it made it ten times harder to steal the cattle I wanted."

"You stole from your own boss?" Her tone was a mixture of incredible disbelief and disgust.

Morton sank to his knees on the ledge and scanned the clearing, his back to her. "Norwell has more than enough, he'll never miss them."

"It's still stealing!"

"You and me, girl, see it different. I gave most of my life to that tight-fisted, ruthless old man who saw fit to toss me little more than a measly paycheck each month for my loyalty and long hours of hard work. I even had to take orders from that wet-behind-the-ears kid of his."

"What about Jess Williams?"

"What about him? The man was a fool." Morton gave a weak chuckle. "He suspected what I was doing and was stupid enough to confront me. He got what he deserved."

A silence passed between them and Julia's thoughts strayed to all the things he had told her. Somehow, she had to get free. After his confession, there was no way she would be allowed to live. She worked frantically at the knots that were binding her wrists. Still, there was something more nagging at her. Her uncle had somehow played a part in this whole scheme.

"My uncle, Rusty Gast," she said. "You knew him, didn't you?"

Morton snorted. "Knew him? Sure, knew him for the Indian lover he was. Must run in the family." He turned and offered her an ugly smile. "Stupid man, too."

Julia sat up straighter, her wrists burning from the bite of the rope. "What do you mean?"

Morton waved a hand wildly in the air. "Thanks to him, I'm a lot richer. It wasn't hard to blackmail him once I found out he was in cahoots with Two Bears. Paid me a nice chunk of change, he did, on a regular basis, until he foolishly decided he'd had enough."

"Foolishly?" Julia asked, startled.

"Yeah, when I went back to his ranch the last time to try to squeeze him a little more, he refused. Guess he was fed up trying to round up more cash." Morton laughed. "So I clipped him on the side of the head, and his miserable heart just caved in from the excitement. Lucky for me, he had that heart condition. It saved me from having to kill him."

Julia shivered and licked her dry lips nervously. She was as good as dead if she couldn't get the ropes untied and find a way to escape.

"I'm hungry," she said. She tilted her head toward a sack of food thrown beside her booted foot. "I could fry us up some bacon to eat."

Morton stared at her, and she could see he was mulling it around in his head.

"It's silly for us to go hungry while we wait," she urged. "What if he doesn't show until sundown?"

Morton was all attention now, taking in her every word.

"You have the gun," she persisted softly.

He walked toward her and withdrew his knife. For one horrible moment, she thought she saw hatred in his savage eyes, so great the possibility of him slitting her throat crossed her mind. Instead, he yanked her to her feet and to her relief, sliced the ropes at her wrists.

"I'm warning you," he growled. "Don't try anything. It really doesn't matter whether I kill you now or later."

She nodded, hands trembling, and moved to get the bacon from the sack. Inside her head, a voice kept screaming, *free, free, finally free.. well, almost.*

The heat of day still hung heavy over the land when Flint arrived on the opposite side of the Cherry Creek where Tom Morton held Julia Gast hostage. Marcus was sitting under the leafy shade of an oak, his back slumped against its trunk. A worried expression wrinkled his brow.

He stood and spat at the ground. "Took you long enough to get here."

Flint winced at the pain still throbbing in his side. "Had a little argument with some of Morton's hired help over some of our cattle."

"Hope they're worse off than you look," Marcus replied, his eyes taking in the bloodied shirt.

"One of them is feeling no pain, for sure," Flint said brusquely. "Where's Two Bears?"

"Here." The Indian glided silently out of the forest beside them.

"Julia with Morton?" Flint asked.

Marcus nodded. "It looks like they're fixing to have a bite to eat. You think they'll invite us?"

"Want to ask?"

Their eyes met, and for a split second a smile tugged at corners of the burly man's lips.

"The way I see it," Marcus said, "we got ourselves a real problem.

Morton's locked in there tight as a bear in a winter's den, with no way for us to enter unless we use the river."

Flint grunted. "He'll pick us off like ducks over a blind."

"I'll go," Two Bears offered. He thumped his chest. "It's me, he wants."

Flint frowned. "He won't let Julia out alive either. By now, he's probably filled her ears with his every transgression."

"Banes wants her dead, too," Marcus added. "In his twisted mind, he thinks she's a Confederate lover. He's got a hand-picked group tearing up the ground to reach us and make sure no one breathes another breath of Colorado air. We can't wait until dark. We need one of your highfalutin' plans, and we need it right quick."

Flint watched Two Bears keen eyes circle the area, pausing to stare at the high steep rock slide.

"I know what you're thinking, Two Bears, but it's ludicrous to take a horse down that slide. You'll break your neck."

The Indian smiled. "I go in and talk, stall for time. One man comes down the rock slide, other man covers him from above."

"Whoa, just wait a dadburned minute here," Marcus piped up. "No way will that work. I said we needed a plan, not a death ride."

"Who is better rider?" Two Bears asked. His eyes darted from Flint to Marcus and back again.

"Next to Tye, Flint has it hands down." Visibly relieved, Marcus patted his rifle. "Now, Mr. Winchester here, well, he and I have become good friends over the last couple of weeks."

"My horse can't take that slide," Flint said, suddenly feeling nauseous just at the thought of the height of the enbankment, "and I doubt my ribs can either."

"No, not your horse," Two Bears agreed. "My horse."

"What in blue blazes makes you think he'll even let me climb on his back?"

"I thought Marcus said you were a good rider."

"With a saddle, yes, but even without, that critter of yours will balk as soon as he smells me."

The Indian nodded. "This is so, you smell bad."

"I smell bad?" Flint's eyes widened. "Now just a minute—"

"To him, you smell like white man," Two Bears elaborated and wrinkled his nose. He removed his grease-stained vest. The leather reeked of smoke and horse manure. "Here, take my vest."

"*My* vest," Flint reminded him.

Two Bears grinned his toothless grin. "Ah, yes, it was once yours, Flint Ashmore. But you got fair trade, Red Fox Woman is worth many vests." The Indian removed a knife from his moccasin and slid it behind his back inside the waist of his buckskins.

"If we get her out alive, I'll get you a half-dozen of these," Flint said. Grimacing, he slipped his arms into the holes of the grimy garment. Two Bears's horse snorted, and he walked to where it was tied and patted him affectionately on his stout neck. "We only have one chance to make this work. There can be no mistakes."

Minutes later, Flint found himself seated on Two Bears's stallion above the rock slide, several yards back from its rim. Marcus lay belly down in front of him, peering over the edge. Beneath him, Two Bears's horse stamped and pawed the ground impatiently.

"As soon as Two Bears is in position," he instructed Marcus, "I want you to signal me. Let's not have this stallion see what's coming until it's too late."

He watched Marcus's head bob in agreement and swivel toward him. "Actually, Flint, it's best if you don't see it either."

"It's steep and high, isn't it?"

"Well, let's just say the bunk house roof looks mighty fine right now."

Flint sighed and slipped his gun from his holster. "One more thing, Marcus," he whispered.

"Now what?" Marcus rolled to his side and looked at him.

"Just in case I break my neck, you make darn sure Morton is never able to raise his head either."

"Count on that," Marcus agreed in a solemn voice.

"And tell Julia I love her."

Through a disgruntled groan, Marcus rolled back to his stomach. "Ah, cripes, Flint," he said. "Now you've gone too far. Best you plan on doing that yourself."

Twenty-Eight

Julia squatted by the small fire she had thrown together and glanced surreptitiously out into the gulch where tall thin buffalo grass, rippled in the breeze, baked brown from the sun. She was certain someone was out there, beyond the river. Around her, the air had grown silent except for the bacon which sizzled and popped in the skillet. Not even a bird cried out or winged its way in the clear blue sky overhead.

Carefully, she searched the area for a plausible weapon. Only her ring flask lay within reach, and she picked it up, uncorked it, and pretended to drink, then laid it beside her. Behind her, Tom Morton, his mouth pulled into a frown, was slouched on the ground as he played a game of solitaire with a dog-eared deck of cards. His pistol lay beside him.

Julia stared at the fire. How had she gotten herself embroiled in all this? She had been crazy to think she could amass a fortune overnight. And what would she do once she had it? There was little reward in leading a solitary life, and she already knew the horrors of a lonely childhood. Flint Ashmore had offered her everything he owned, including his heart, and she had let her pride get in the way. She had been a fool! Why couldn't she just admit she was in love with him? If she made it out alive, she promised herself she was going to make some changes.

"Tom Morton!"

The voice that called out came from Two Bears, and Julia froze.

Morton stumbled up, the cards fluttering to the ground as he grabbed his gun.

"Git up," he said and crossed the distance to stand beside her. His eyes were wild and bloodthirsty.

She rose, the ring flask in her hand. He waved the barrel of the gun towards the river. "Now you go first, and remember this is loaded and pointed at your back."

Julia walked out from the ledges, coming to stand in the grassy clearing. Fifty yards away, Two Bears had crossed the creek and stood at the water's edge. His lean ramrod straight figure blended with the cottonwoods along it.

"Let the woman go," Two Bears said. "She is not part of this fight."

"I'll decide who's part of the fight," Tom Morton said. He shoved Julia in the spine with his gun. "Move up closer," he ordered.

She dug in her heels. "I'll not be part of killing anyone in cold blood." She felt the cold steel of the barrel prod her none too gently again.

"Come, Red Fox Woman," Two Bears urged. The tone of his voice was reassuring, almost mesmerizing. "The snake cannot strike when there is much distance between him and his prey. Is that not so, Morton?"

Morton's laugh was shrill. "Yeah, that's right, and there's no sense in having bullets flying off these stone walls. Waste of good lead, and a ricochet could hit the wrong person."

Julia hesitated for a moment, then proceeded forward until she was only several yards from Two Bears. She noticed he was weaponless. No gun. No knife in his moccasin. His face was solemn, his coal black eyes, expressionless.

So this was how it was going to end? Both of them gunned down by a madman? She knew she should feel desperately frightened, but instead a strange calmness enveloped her.

Two Bears spoke. "Remember the first time we met, Red Fox Woman?"

She nodded. "You almost ripped the hair from my scalp and you were rewarded for it. I see you lost your vest."

"Yes," he replied, "I gave it back to the owner. Remember when you scampered like the red squirrel instead of the sly red fox?" He smiled the barest of smiles. "Then it was my turn to be scared like a rabbit when Flint Ashmore pulled a gun on me."

Julia stared at him curiously as time stretched between them. What was he trying to tell her? Was Flint somewhere around? He wanted her to move out of the way, but how?"

"If you two are gonna reminisce about every meeting you've ever had, we're gonna be here until sundown," she heard Morton grumble. "Let's get this over with. I've got a long ride ahead of me."

Julia felt a chill at his words. Suddenly, the pieces fell into place, and she knew what she had to do. She straightened, the ring flask still in her hand, her eyes trained on Two Bears. He would give her a signal. She would have to act quickly.

Morton nudged the barrel of the gun against her back again. "Now why don't you just walk forward nice and slow and find a place next to your Indian friend over there."

Julia saw Two Bears barely nod. She took three steps forward, hesitating.

"Git, I say," Tom Morton urged impatiently.

She looked with desperate eyes at Two Bear, unsure of what to do next.

"Now!" he said in a low voice, and she feigned a step to the left, ducked and rolled to the right instead, pitching the ring flask at Morton's arm before she hit the ground, tumbling head over heels. Behind her, a series of shots rang out from the rim of the rock slide, and she heard a horse crashing down the steep embankment.

She looked up to see Flint, firing from his mount as he held fast, the horse sliding on his haunches as it scrambled downward, gravel spewing from beneath its hooves. Tom Morton's body jerked like a puppet and his gun, pointed at Two Bears, exploded. Julia saw Two Bears crumple onto his side, but not before a knife flashed from his hands and whizzed through the air.

It ended as quickly as it began. The gunfire ceased and Tom Morton lay in the grass, riddled with bullets, a knife protruding from his chest.

Julia scrambled up and rushed to where Two Bears lay. Painfully he pushed himself erect. A red stream of blood raced down his arm to his elbow.

Flint rode to where they stood and slid off the horse. Quickly he untied his bandanna. "Bind that wound, Julia," he ordered and walked to the limp body. He extracted the knife from Morton's chest and wiped the blade on the grass to remove any traces of blood, then strode to where they stood.

"Can you ride?" he asked Two Bears.

The Indian nodded. "It is just a flesh wound."

From the rim, Marcus frantically waved his arms and shouted before starting on foot down the steep embankment.

Julia watched the bear-like figure barrel through the rocks. She had never seen him move so fast. Something was wrong. Terribly wrong.

"The Army is breathing down our necks," Flint explained grimly and handed Two Bears his knife. "You have to get out of here. Now."

The Indian grimaced as Julia tied the knot on the bandanna tight.

"Not without my vest, Flint Ashmore," he said through gritted teeth.

Chuckling, Flint shed the grimy vest, and Two Bears slipped it on and threw himself onto his mount.

Julia picked up her ring flask. It was unbroken. "I don't know how to thank you," she said and held it up for him to take.

The Indian reached out and touched her flaming hair. "You are strong and brave, Red Fox Woman."

He smiled and took the ring flask. "I would ask for many ponies tied to my door before I accepted a marriage proposal." He glanced at Flint, grinning. "Many, many ponies."

Flint squinted up at him. "You keep yammering and the Army will have all your damn ponies. Ride north," he suggested. "They'll expect you to head south."

Wordlessly the Indian galloped away, turning only once to raise a hand in farewell before slipping into the leafy growth of the forest to disappear as silently as he had arrived.

Flint, Marcus and Julia were gathering the horses and supplies from under the ledge when the Army rode in a few minutes later. Much to Julia's surprise, they were accompanied by Frank and Colin Norwell. She was not surprised to see Charles Bloomington. The horses they rode splashed through the frigid waters of Cherry Creek and drew up directly in front of them.

A surly, pot-bellied Army sergeant dismounted first. It was obvious he was uncomfortable with Norwell's presence.

Frank Norwell stepped from his saddle. "I thought maybe these boys would need a little help. I bumped into Betsy on my way out of town."

"Just a second here, I'll do the talking," the sergeant interrupted and gestured at the prone body of Tom Morton. "Who's responsible for this man's death?"

"I am," Marcus and Flint said in unison.

"Apprehend them," the sergeant ordered.

"No," Julia said. "Tom Morton tried to kill me and was stealing every piece of young stock in the area he could lay his hands on."

"I'm in charge," the sergeant snapped. "I said to apprehend them."

"You're not the law in these parts," Frank Norwell spoke up.

"I'm acting on behalf of it."

"Not without your captain, you're not. Who gave you orders to come here in the first place?"

Julia could see that the surly man was taken by surprise. He nervously pulled on his beard and beads of sweat began to pop out around his forehead. His little weasel eyes flitted to the other men in uniform. They fell silent, staring red-faced at the ground. If they were planning to back him, they had now given it more thought.

"Lieutenant Banes," he said.

"That gutless coward rode out of town over an hour ago and he wasn't in uniform," Norwell said sharply. "It looked to me like he was giving up on Army life. You telling me you're taking orders from that varmint?"

As they spoke, Sheriff Anderson rode up. His face was flushed as he plodded his weary horse to the back of the group and hefted his ample frame off.

"Step aside, step aside," he ordered, pushing his way through the tightly packed men. The chink of spurs sounded with each step. "I'll handle this. I'm the law in these parts, you know."

"It's about time," Marcus said. He crossed his arms at his chest, spit in the dust and smiled. "I was afraid you'd miss all the excitement, Anderson. Sure wish you'd been here a little sooner when Tom Morton was waving a gun at us."

"This woman is consorting with that renegade Two Bears to get horses," the sergeant said sourly to Anderson. "Tom Morton tried to stop her and these men killed him."

"Now hold up a moment." The sheriff scratched behind his ear. "Why would a renegade want to round up horses and supply the very same Army that's hunting him? Makes no sense. Nope, no sense, whatsoever."

"I'm telling you, he was doing it!"

"You boys been hitting the bottle?" The sheriff peered at the circle of uniformed men.

Charles Bloomington stepped forward. Ramrod straight, he spoke in a pompous tone, "I'm Captain Charles Bloomington. I think you should be aware, Sheriff, that this woman's character is questionable, to say the least. During the war she was a Southern sympathizer. Why, she even went as far as helping wounded Confederates caught on the wrong side of the line."

The sheriff scratched his balding head again. "Listen, Bloomin'-field, or whatever your name is, I don't know what you're getting at, but out here we don't get excited what the Rebs and Union soldiers did back East. We sure do appreciate a woman who has a knack for patching up the wounded, 'tho."

"Why don't you just ask her for proof of where she's getting her stock?" the surly sergeant challenged with a dark gaze.

The group of men fell silent, waiting expectantly for her to reply.

Under her coat, Julia could feel her heart thudding in her chest. If her charade was discovered, she could be facing a lifetime of peering out from behind iron bars. Why hadn't she listened to Betsy and Flint? She glanced briefly at Flint. His face was poker straight, revealing nothing.

"I've been dealing with a man from Pueblo, Sheriff," she said. "Will Parker has been supplying me with horses for the last month." She had overheard a conversation between her hands and Toby, shortly after he arrived at the ranch. She glanced at Flint again who nervously sucked in a breath through clamped teeth.

"Will Parker?" Colin Norwell sputtered and stepped forward. "Will Parker, you say? Why everyone knows, Will Parker is dead—"

"—darned near eighty and still the best horse wrangler in the territory," Frank Norwell interrupted, shooting an icy glare at his son. "Know him well, Sheriff, rode with him in Texas when I was younger."

He steered the sheriff by his elbow out of earshot and motioned for Julia to join him. "Listen, Sheriff," he said in a low voice, "to be honest, Julia and I have been in the stock business together, but it's best if the Army doesn't know our little secret. They think competition drives the price down, and they get a better deal if we're working separately. Know what I mean?" He winked at Anderson.

"Oh, sure, sure," Anderson said, as if he was part of the conspiracy himself. He returned to the group, a sly smirk on his face.

Norwell's eyes were gentle and fatherly when they met Julia's, and a warm glint simmered in their gray depths.

"Why," she whispered. "Why are you doing this?" She thought about the many times he had come to her rescue since she arrived in Colorado: the newspapers, the day she socked his son in the eye, and the time he helped her save Flint's life.

He smiled. "Actually, Julia, we share a mutual friend. Before you arrived, I received word from Lancaster asking me to keep an eye on you."

"From whom?" she asked, curiously.

"Father McMillen."

"Father McMillen?" She was completely bewildered. She had never remembered the old priest mentioning anyone in the Colorado territory.

"You see, a long time ago when I was a carefree, and somewhat careless, young man living back East, I was beaten and robbed, and left to die along a stinking, rat-infested wharf in Philadelphia. A good priest stumbled upon me on his way home from making his rounds to the sick. He took me to his rectory, treated my wounds and scraped up enough money to send me along my way. We corresponded frequently from then on, even after he was assigned to a parish in Lancaster. I told him if I could ever return the favor to contact me. Just before your arrival, Father McMillen sent a wire asking for my help. He had great respect for your ability to heal the wounded."

He nudged her gently by her shoulder. "Come, we can discuss this over dinner some day. Best we get back to the group before it looks like we really have formed an alliance."

Julia rewarded him with a grateful smile as a surge of relief coursed through her. Together they rejoined the group of men.

"A man is dead here," the surly sergeant reminded the sheriff. "Shot full of bullet holes. Someone is responsible."

The sheriff rubbed his fat forehead, confused. "I guess I need a statement. . .from someone."

Marcus clapped him on the back. "I'll ride in with you, Anderson, and spell out the entire story. It's really quite simple once I put it in order. Betsy will also be able to fill you in and straighten out a few twists." He looked casually around the group of soldiers. "Once Banes is apprehended, it might be interesting to see how all your stories shake out."

The sergeant stared at him. "Well, I can see we're not needed here," he announced brusquely. He strode to his horse and looked back at them with an uncomfortable gaze. "Which way did you say that redskin was headed?"

"Didn't say," Marcus replied.

"North," Flint offered.

Julia's mouth dropped open in horror, and she started to speak. She saw Marcus shake his head in warning.

"Aw, come on," the sergeant said. "I know you're lying through your teeth to protect that cowardly renegade." He turned to his men and ordered, "Saddle up, we're heading south."

Minutes later, when everyone had moved away, only Julia and Flint, and Frank Norwell and Charles Bloomington remained.

Bloomington took a step toward Julia, a menacing scowl darkening his features. "Julia, I insist you accompany me to California this very minute. It was your father's last wish that I care for you. Do not disrespect the dead."

Flint Ashmore advanced toward him. "With all respect to the dead, maybe Julia doesn't want to go to California. It seems to me like the living should have equal weight in deciding the direction of their lives."

"Sir, this is none of your business!"

"I'd be mighty careful, Bloomington," Frank Norwell interrupted. "This is Luke Ashmore's brother you're talking to."

Bloomington stiffened. "I've no intention of being humiliated by some meaningless drifter or his brother, for that matter."

"Egad, man, is that what Banes told you? Luke Ashmore is a U.S. Marshal."

Bloomington eyes widened and his face deepened to scarlet. Worry began to chase the arrogance away.

Julia, unable to restrain herself a minute more, spoke, "There's nothing for you here, Charles. Absolutely nothing. I think it's best for you to be on your way."

"Julia, I beg you to come with me," he sputtered. "We can go to California and start fresh. Put away those silly dreams. Do you enjoy being penniless?"

"The poorest of all men, Charles, is not the man without a cent, but the man without a dream," Julia said. "No," she said. "I already have a home here. . .and a dream." She watched him with guarded concern. The man was like a gun with a hair trigger, ready to explode at the slightest provocation.

"Here?" He waved his hand. Disgust colored his tone. "There's nothing here. A pile of shabby rocks and a sun so hot it scorches your feet through your boots."

Julia turned to Flint and gave him a meaningful stare. "Yes, here, Charles. Everything I want is here."

"Ah, I thought so," Bloomington said, sneering, an evil grin forming. "And tell me, my dear, just what special favors have you been forced to hand out for such undying protection and attention?"

Julia's eyes shot bullets, but before she was able to utter a stinging retort, Flint's fist shot out and connected with Bloomington's chin. She heard the sickening crack of a jaw breaking as he reeled backwards. He barely regained his balance when Flint grabbed him by the shirt and fired another punch at his stomach which doubled him over.

"Stop it, Flint!" she screamed, rushing to him. She tried unsuccessfully to yank him away from Bloomington. "I don't want his death on our heads. There's been enough already. Mr. Norwell, please help me."

Flint paused and glanced at her, then dragged Bloomington upright, jerking him toward his horse. "You're lucky Julia has such compassion," he spat. "Don't bother to stop to pack anything, Bloomington, just keep riding. West, hear me?"

Pulling himself painfully into the saddle, Bloomington kicked his horse into a trot and rode away.

When he left, Frank Norwell mounted his powerful bay and paused, hands clasped over the pommel. "I'm sorry about Tom Morton. He was a good foreman for many years."

"Sometimes temptation, greed and stupidity are so great that a man allows himself to become a fool and take the wrong trail, Frank. Morton wanted to take the easy route to riches."

Frank Norwell grunted disgustedly. "I would have given him anything he asked for."

Flint shook his head, rubbing his bruised knuckles. "It wouldn't have worked. Some men never seem to stop wanting, always seem to have a hunger for more. And always have a hunger for what other men have worked long and hard to get." He paused. "Our cattle are in that brush-strewn box canyon in that desolate property of yours, north of the ranch."

"I'll send some men to round them up."

"There is at least one body, too."

"We'll clean up." Frank Norwell started to leave, but swung his mount around to face them again. "You know, I could use a couple of favors myself, Ashmore."

Startled, both Julia and Flint looked up at the white-haired man.

"What kind?" Flint asked. "I guess I owe you a few. I sorely misjudged you."

ANTH

"Those ring flasks, everyone in town is toting one except me, and I'm told they're all sold out at the bakery and Finley's store. Maybe you can lay your hands on one?"

Flint grinned. "I think so. What else?"

Norwell reined his horse northward, heading toward town at a brisk trot. He called out above the drum of hooves, "Send me an invitation to the wedding when you set the date. I've always enjoyed a good Virginia reel."

Together, Julia and Flint watched him urge the bay into the creek, kicking up a spray of water.

"I've been thinking," Flint said as soon as Norwell disappeared.

Julia watched him turn toward her, a playful smile on his lips.

"Horsefeathers, no, I know what you're thinking, Flint Ashmore," she said. "I'm not about to marry you, don't even ask."

"Confound it, Julia, why in tarnation not?"

She noticed his face redden beneath his tan. He stood, feet apart, looking dumfounded at her. This time, she decided, she was going to speak her mind.

She huffed, "Why is it that you've never once uttered you love me?"

There, she had said it, as foolish as it seemed. She stared at him, and for a long moment their eyes held. Around them, the land had come alive again with the song of birds, the lazy hum of insects and the rustle of a warm breeze in the aspen along the creek.

"Is that all that's bothering you?" he asked, thumbing back his hat.

She nodded and felt her face grow hot. Her gaze slipped to the ground.

"Well, that can be rectified," he said in his deep, no-nonsense voice she would never tire of hearing if she lived to be a hundred years old. "I love you. I guess I have from the very first moment you pointed that blasted shotgun at my nose."

He scratched behind his ear and looked up. "I suppose you want me to shout it from the mountain tops?"

She shook her head and searched his lean face. "No, I want you to kiss me, really kiss me. Like you mean it."

He smiled and bent his head toward her, his eyes sparkling with devilry. Slowly, his lips moved closer and closer until they were barely an inch away from hers.

"Obliged," he whispered, "but I'm warning you. This can be a *very* dangerous activity."

LaVergne, TN USA
23 September 2010
198158LV00005B/166/P